D1384012

FIELDS OF GOLD

A STEAMPUNK ADVENTURE NOVEL

SHELLEY ADINA

Moonshell
Books

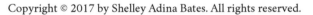

Cover art by Claudia McKinney at Phat Puppy Studios, with images from DepositPhotos.com, used under license, and Mike Jimenez of Vanity Force Images. Cover design by Kalen O'Donnell. Author font by Anthony Piraino at OneButtonMouse.com.

Fields of Gold / Shelley Adina—1st ed April 2017

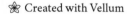 Created with Vellum

PRAISE FOR SHELLEY ADINA

"I love how we can have several capable, intelligent, skilled women who are happy to work together without competing, without hating each other, without unnecessary dislike or conflict, without jealousy, without rivalry but with genuine friendship and respect. ... All of this comes with some excellent writing." —on *Fields of Gold*

— FANGS FOR THE FANTASY

"This is the first in a series of well-reviewed books set in the steampunk world. For those who like the melding of Victorian culture with the fantastic fantasy of reality-bending science fiction, this one will be right up their alley." —on *Lady of Devices*

— READERS' REALM

"It's another excellent chapter in this ongoing epic adventure of this series. I love this world and the story of these excellent women and the saga will never end. No. It will not." —on *Fields of Iron*

— FANGS FOR THE FANTASY

For the flock
With thanks for joining me on the journey

And with gratitude to
Elly Catmull, Carol Douglas, and Timons Esaias

FIELDS OF GOLD

CHAPTER 1

Somewhere in the Wild West
March 1895

It was one thing to be afraid for yourself—that cold, paralyzing fear that paradoxically made your innards turn to liquid instead of a solid block of ice. It was quite another to be afraid for someone you loved—in a massive, towering cloud of fear that blotted out even the memory of sunshine.

Alice, Lady Hollys, crouched in the dirt next to the prone form of her husband, beneath the ironwood trees in an arroyo that fed runoff into the mighty Rio de Sangre Colorado de Christo. "Ian," she whispered through dry lips. "Ian, hang on. I'm going for help, but you have to wake up, and press this handkerchief against the wound."

His eyelids fluttered open and tears of relief sprang into her eyes.

"What ... happened?"

"That dadblamed Prussian she-wolf shot you." And if it was the last thing she did on this earth, Alice was going to return the favor. In spades. The kind you dug a grave with, and that was a promise.

Ian turned his head weakly, and frowned. "Where ... are they?"

"Back on the steamboat and already a mile upriver, no doubt. There's a Texican Ranger airship in a mooring pattern overhead, and the witches vanished like water on a hot griddle."

"What's a griddle?"

Alice's grim face contorted in pain that radiated from deep inside. "Oh, my darling," she said brokenly. "This is no time for jokes. She might have been aiming for the heart, but you moved at the last second and she got you right below the collarbone. Heaven only knows where the bullet is, but I have to get you to a doctor, and our only hope is that ship."

"Santa Fe." His dear gray eyes searched hers. "You'll be ... recognized."

"I don't care," she told him gently. "If I'm lucky, it'll happen after I get you into the hospital, and not before. Dearest, I hate to ask this of you, but you must stand and try to walk. We need to signal them, and then find some open ground so they can lower a basket."

"I'll try."

That was her man. Not a word of complaint, not a moan. Simply determination—and a harshly indrawn breath that told her just what it cost him to do as she asked.

A quarter of an hour ago, they had been intent on ways to destroy the dam the Californios were building across the river. A dam that threatened the lives and homes of everyone along its banks as the water rose. And while Alice didn't give a plug nickel about many of the witches who had come unwillingly to their aid, others were good, compassionate people who did not deserve to drown or be displaced simply because of the greed of others. But the arroyo that had made such a superb hiding place for the reconnaissance party had become a disaster for two people needing help. Alice searched frantically from side to side, looking for a place clear enough for the airship's crew to see them, and large enough for them to let its basket down and get Ian into it safely. But these canyons had long been used for concealment, not rescue. Half a mile from the river, it became obvious that Ian's strength was at an end, and she was going to have to leave him and widen her search alone.

She made him as comfortable as possible with his back against a red boulder. "I'll be back as soon as I can. You'll see the ship lose altitude, and then you'll see me, I promise."

"Be ... careful."

She kissed him and rose. But before she could choose a path to higher ground, a voice hailed them from the direction of the river. In a moment, two of the witches came pelting into sight, with something that looked suspiciously like a door suspended between them.

"Alice!" Betsy Trelawney called when she was within earshot. "Where is he? Is he all right?"

Alice's grip tightened on her lightning pistol, and in a moment, when she recognized Gretchen the she-wolf in the rear, she pulled it off her belt and thumbed on the ignition switch. The pistol began to hum in a cheerful treble.

"Don't shoot!" Gretchen shouted, skidding to a halt. This jerked the door out of Betsy's hands, and before it even crashed to the ground, Gretchen had flipped it up to crouch behind it. "We mean you no harm. We went back to the steamboat to get something to carry him with."

Alice lost her tenuous grip on her temper. A bolt of lightning sizzled past Betsy, who threw herself to the dirt with a scream, and fried the top off a pinon pine where Gretchen's head had just been.

"Alice!" Betsy shrieked as smoke curled up and the air filled with the scent of hot resin. "We're trying to help you!"

"The only thing that will help me is the sight of her dead body," Alice snapped. "Get out from behind that door, you yellow-bellied sapsucker." She cast a glance upward, but the Ranger ship was nowhere to be seen. Were they circling around for another pass? Or had this ridiculous delay cost her Ian's only chance at getting to a doctor?

"Forgive me," came from behind the door. "I lost my temper. I intended to shoot wide, but he moved."

"Liar!" Alice's voice was hoarse with fear and dust and tears. "You aimed at his heart, you filthy toad. Now, stand up and take what's coming to you."

Betsy scrambled to her feet and leaped into Alice's line of fire, her hands extended in a plea. "Alice—Alice—this is no time for revenge if we hope to get your husband to Sister Clara."

"What is a cook going to do for him?" Tears of fear and frustration leaked from Alice's eyes, which did nothing for her temper. "I need to get him to Santa Fe, and now the Ranger ship is gone!"

"The others are causing a distraction," came from behind the door.

"What?" Alice's trigger finger jerked, and the top left corner

4

of the door blew off. Blue tendrils of light explored each panel, dancing and sizzling. With a shriek, Gretchen shoved it over and leaped away from it.

Finding nothing to ease its appetite in the wood, which bore only knob and hinges, the lightning attacked a rock. It exploded, and a chunk of it struck the other woman, knocking her to the ground.

Alice smiled the smile with which air pirates from Santa Fe to the Canadas had become all too familiar. She buffed the flared barrel of the pistol with her sleeve and deactivated it.

"Dadgummit, Alice," Betsy said furiously, "Sister Clara and May Lin between them do our doctoring. They've pulled out plenty of bullets. Now stop this nonsense and take us to your husband."

"I'll take you." Alice jerked her chin at the moaning Gretchen. "She stays out of range or I'll shoot a bigger boulder."

Gretchen was no fool. She pulled herself out of the way as Alice and Betsy picked up the door and jogged back to where Ian lay. Her heart ached at the fresh blood that oozed from the wound as they laid him on the door. He was heavy, but the strength of desperation and love seemed to fill her muscles, enabling her to cover the distance to the river at something approaching a fast shamble.

The boat and crew were waiting on watch, as though every witch aboard was anxious to rectify the mistake their sister had committed.

"You get him home," Gretchen told the man at the wheel. "I'll join the distraction party and make sure you aren't followed."

Which suited Alice right down to the ground. Maybe the Rangers would get a good shot at her.

The witch had barely leaped to the rocks when a crewman dragged the gangplank in and they were under way. The walls of the canyons slid past faster than anyone could walk, echoing the chug of the steam engines and the splash of the great paddles in the stern back to them, but still it was not fast enough for Alice. She crouched next to Ian on the deck—for the door was too wide to carry him into the main saloon from which it had come—and held his hand in both of hers, trying to smile reassuringly when all she wanted to do was weep.

Or shoot something.

A cloud passed over the sun, and instinctively she looked up.

"There they are!"

"So much for a distraction," Betsy said anxiously. "What happened?"

But there was no answer to this. Then Alice realized something else. "Are they—? Yes, they are. They're following us."

Betsy scrambled to her feet. "They'll discover the village. I must tell Jack. He cannot take us home yet."

"He better dadblamed well take us or I'll shoot him myself!"

Betsy squeezed her shoulder, no doubt feeling the tremors that Alice couldn't control, as though she'd been soaked and now huddled in the cold. "We must protect the village. Jack knows a thing or two about the river. It will be all right."

"But there's no *time*. And what if they can help—"

But Betsy had already released her and gone forward, and in a moment, the pitch of the engine changed, the great brass wheels in the stern digging into the water and increasing their speed against the powerful current. Now even a steam landau running wide open could not match them as the rocks and water churned by at a hectic pace.

Alice sagged onto the deck. She should have stuck to her guns, and flagged the Rangers down when she had the chance. What had she been thinking—trusting the witches when other than Betsy, she had no reason to? Ian's beloved face blurred in her vision.

And then a shadow passed over them again, and the sun went out. With a gasp, she wiped her eyes with the heel of her hand and looked up.

Her mouth fell open.

They slid under an arch of red rock so massive that the steamboat was dwarfed to the size of a child's toy. Below openings in the rock, light played on the water, and as they chugged into the middle of the vast natural chamber, she felt the engines slow and the sounds echo as from a great distance.

Betsy jumped down the steps from the wheelhouse. "Jack is going to bide here until they get tired of looking for us."

"What is this place?" Her fear backed off just a fraction as she stared up ... and up ... to the arched ceiling, where ripples of light seemed to dance and play.

"One of our little secrets." Betsy's lips, painted black with flowers at the corners, tilted up. "One of the very few we let the boatmen in on."

An eternity passed in which Ian's breathing became increasingly labored, and Alice's fear stampeded back in to seize up her lungs and burn the edges of her temper. Finally she could bear it no longer.

She stomped up the iron stairs, thumbing on the lightning pistol as the filigree treads rang under her boots.

"Get this boat back to the village now," she rasped, "or I'll put a hole through you and do it myself."

The man who must be Jack turned from the wheel to face her. His eyes widened at the sight of the pistol. "What does that do?"

"You won't survive the answer," she snapped. "Get this tub moving."

"But the Rangers—"

"I don't care about the village, or the Rangers. All I care about is getting that bullet out of my husband before it's too late. Now *move!*"

Watching her as though she were a she-bear and he stood between her and her cub, Jack found the acceleration levers by feel alone. In a moment the pitch of the engines changed again and they began to make way across the lake, heading for the bright daylight glow of the arch on the far side.

When they emerged, the skies were empty.

But Alice did not leave the wheelhouse. Instead, she kept the humming pistol aimed at the captain's left ear, her face grim. Her hand did not shake. But her heart was pounding in her chest, her legs shaking from more than the vibrating deck. She hoped beyond hope he could not see that pride and fierce love were the only things holding her upright.

CHAPTER 2

*S*omething was gravely amiss in the world when a woman could not accomplish what she set out to do without having to *marry* someone.

The shock and frustration presently rolling beneath Gloria Meriwether-Astor Fremont's well-worn corset was making her feel positively ill. Whether king or scientist, peasant or witch, boat captain or ... oh, dear. Why could people not simply do the right thing and forsake all these machinations? How had her friend Lady Claire Trevelyan managed to change the world all on her own, without resorting to the authority and power of a husband, however high or low he might be placed? For that matter, how had Claire managed to choose the one she wanted when Gloria couldn't seem able to manage it at all despite any number of willing prospects?

But never mind all that. She must speak.

For still he knelt at her feet, this slender boy of nineteen with the hollow eyes, curling hair, and tanned skin. This boy gazing up at her as though he had not just tipped her entire world off its axis and set all her hopes at naught with one sentence.

One sentence that she must answer. Immediately.

She clasped his hand in both of hers and tugged. "Please, sir, do get up. This is a—a most extraordinary situation."

The Viceroy of the Royal Kingdom of Spain and the Californias, Defender of the Faith, and General of the Armies of Heaven obligingly got to his feet, though he did not release her hand. "Please, you must call me Felipe," he said. "Will you allow me to call you Gloria?"

Good heavens. The rules of polite society dictated that only family or gentlemen in a very close relationship might call one by one's Christian name. But the rules of polite society did not cover what one was supposed to do when one was married and had just been most illegally proposed to by a prince.

"Our situation may be extraordinary," he went on, "but it is one with which you are not unfamiliar."

"That is only partly true," she retorted, shock having burned away the polite civilities this situation might warrant under normal circumstances, "since I was unattached at the time. You cannot seriously mean this, sir—er, Felipe. You would have my marriage annulled and marry me yourself in exchange for what I ask? Why not simply issue a command as —as the General of the Armies of Heaven, and stop this dreadful war? I'm afraid I do not understand why I must be part of the bargain."

"Because then you would not marry me," he said simply.

"I cannot say I am inclined to marry you now," she blurted. No, no, that would not do. "Felipe, please, what conditions are these in which two people could be expected to find happiness? It is impossible."

He gazed at her, and his thoughts seemed to withdraw, as though he were looking into the past. "I have never expected to find happiness," he admitted at last.

Her panic subsided just a little, and compassion trickled in. "Why should you not?" Her voice softened, for he did look so painfully young. "Why should any man or woman not expect to find love, and companionship, and the refuge of a home?"

"Because such is not the lot of princes." His hand, so warm a moment ago, began to chill. "The most we may expect is companionship. But with you, I know I may expect more than that. You are a woman of business, of determination, of resources. And you are so beautiful I could gaze upon your face from dawn until sunset and never tire of it. I have it on good authority that you contracted your marriage with Captain Fremont in order to journey here safely to meet me, and put your case before me. Not one woman in ten thousand would have done so, and succeeded."

"If I may be so bold, sir, ten thousand women in this country would not have needed me to, if women were given the respect they deserve and were allowed to manage their own business and travel about as they see fit, without the oversight and authority of a man."

He squeezed her hand and released it, then indicated they should sit upon the sofa. Their tea had gone cold, so Gloria put the cups upon the tray and pushed it to the end of the low table.

"You speak of changing an entire culture," he said with some amusement.

"I speak simply of what other cultures have realized is a sensible manner of proceeding. In my opinion, the Royal Kingdom must make its way out of the age of medievalism and join the ranks of modern governments."

"Precisely," he said eagerly. "With you at my side, I will be able to do so. You will open doors of transportation and commerce that have been closed until now. My father, rest his soul, was a man who looked backward, to the past and the way things have always been done. But I am not that sort of man. I—" His breath shortened, and he stopped, drawing air into his lungs with difficulty. "Excuse me. Your Evan Douglas suggested last night that I stop taking my evening tonic, but I have seen no real change—unless it is for the worse."

Had the Viceroy had a dream last night, and called Evan in to interpret it? Had that somehow triggered this mad situation in which she was now embroiled? "Sir—Felipe—give it a little time to improve. Perhaps you ought to let Evan examine you properly."

"My doctors would rise up as one like a hissing cobra, I am afraid."

"But he is trained in the latest methods—"

"He specializes in the sleeping mind, not the waking body. And he is very good at it. He has made me face the truth, much as I did not like it." He sat beside her on the sofa and took her hand again. "I cannot do what must be done without your strength and goodness by my side, Gloria." He gazed earnestly into her eyes. "And I promise you, I will be a good and faithful husband. I will not take mistresses—for frankly, I have not seen a woman in the kingdom who may hold a candle to you."

Thank you very much. "I'm sure that cannot be so," she

managed. This was not going well. "Why, the young ladies of the de la Carrera y Borreaga household here seem a lively, pretty lot."

"Do they? I had not noticed. The point is, you will help me lead the Royal Kingdom into a new age, like Isabela and Ferdinand of old. You will establish schools for children who are not so fortunate as to be born into rancho families. You will extend the resources of the Meriwether-Astor Manufacturing Works across the entire country. Once the dam is built across the Rio de Sangre Colorado de Christo, our riverboats will be able to penetrate into the very heart of the continent, where trains and goods from the Fifteen Colonies will meet them to buy our fine cattle and grain."

"Sir, about the dam—"

But in his eagerness, he overrode her. "You have a fleet of undersea dirigibles. Think how we might use them to trade on both coasts, not just the eastern."

"I have airships, too. But the dam—"

"Airships!" he repeated, a smile brightening his somber face. "That is the first thing we will change. Oh, I know the monks and missions will object, but when they see how these marvelous vessels improve shipping and travel, how quickly and comfortably one may go from one end of the country to the other, they will change their minds. They must. For I will have my way, regardless of what they or anyone else thinks."

Never mind the dam just now, there was something she must say before this marvelous castle he was building in the air grew any higher.

"Felipe, this is all wonderful. Truly, you are a visionary. What is to stop you from making these changes on your own? You are a prince, and I ... I must point out once again that despite the unusual circumstances of our marriage, I am not inclined to abandon my husband."

His gaze fell, and the animation faded a little from his features. She was struck by the line of his hawklike nose, and the firmness of his chin. Goodness, where had she seen features like this before? And recently, too.

"I have already granted your friend Evan Douglas his freedom," the Viceroy said, "and this morning before you came, I signed the fiat of citizenship for his translator, José San Gregorio."

"Have you?" Gloria said. Well, at least there was some good news to be celebrated.

"With the stroke of a pen, I gave two men their freedom. With another, I can take a man's freedom from him." His lashes lifted.

Their gazes locked.

After a long moment in which understanding spread like a stain, Gloria said very gently, "You know, blackmail is not the most effective method with which to convince a lady of the sincerity of your suit."

"Can you think of another?"

All she could think of at the moment was how she might get a message to her husband to leave the country immediately. The thought of him in gaol, perhaps forever, his humor and capability drained, his body withering under hard labor while she fled to safety in Philadelphia, was completely impossible.

"I can think of many. With such a beginning, you hope for companionship and affection?" It took quite an effort to keep her voice low and gentle, and not fling the teapot at his head. For truly, how could he know any better, brought up in this country? Especially if Ambassador de Aragon—whose mania for other people's land and gold was the source of the war—had been one of his models of gentlemanly behavior.

His gaze held naked honesty now. "Can you suggest a better way in which to convince you to accept me?"

Her outrage and fear drained away and she gripped his hand. "Oh, Felipe, my dear, you would make a wonderful husband for any woman. Why do you not choose a young lady from one of your noble houses, and be happy?"

"Because they are not like you," he said miserably. "They are silly, and have no conversation, and if you asked them to double a recipe they would have no idea how to do it."

She felt some surprise at his even knowing such a thing as a recipe existed, never mind how to double it. "Then establishing proper schools might be a good solution," she suggested. "Girls have every bit the brain capacity and ability of boys, you know."

"I am learning that," he admitted. "You could certainly rule on your own without me."

"But this is your kingdom, not mine."

"It could be." Oh, his eyes! Full of desperate emotion, like a prisoner who sees the open door and cannot run fast enough toward it before it closes. "Please, Gloria. Say yes and become my Vicereine, to change the world at my side—and to change me."

How much he needed to learn of women—and of himself! For one did not marry to change another. One married because one wanted to change *with* the other—to create something new that had not been there before, that was only possible in a particular combination of two unique lives.

As she was just beginning to discover with the captain.

She pressed the prince's cold hand to her hot cheek. It curved around her jaw, and in its uncertainty she realized that he had never touched a woman in this manner before. "Will you allow me some time?" she asked softly. "Your offer deserves consideration and great care."

"Then you are not saying no?" He straightened, his eyes wide. His hand fell away with reluctance.

"He may not be my husband for much longer, but I do value the captain's life," she said dryly. "All I ask is a day and a night to ... to talk with him. And to make the wisest decision."

"If you will only consider it, I rescind what I said about taking away his freedom. I did not mean it. I want you to make up your mind free of such considerations."

"Thank you." She could not keep the dryness from her tone, but he did not seem to notice. Hope had infused him with an energy he had not possessed before.

"May I escort you to your conveyance?" he asked eagerly. "We might walk through the gardens."

"I am afraid that the captain is waiting out in the courtyard to escort me, but thank you. It was kind of you."

"Ah. Of course." His face fell. "Let me call a carriage for you, at least."

"Truly, sir. The walk will do us good. And perhaps ... when I tell him ... it would be better if there were trees and air and birds about us. He is that kind of man."

It was clear he did not understand, but he nodded. "Thank you for coming. And for ... considering a future that I hold most dear."

She sank into a curtsey, and rose before he could raise her. "I am honored by it. Believe me," she said, "in my wildest dreams, I could never have imagined such a thing."

He took her hand one last time and kissed it. "You have been in my dreams since last night. But I am tired of dreams. I want to wake to reality. The reality of *you*, Gloria."

She blushed, and dipped her knees, and somehow got herself out of the room. The guards at the door bowed as she passed, and the majordomo bowed practically in half as he opened the door for her.

"*Gracias*," she said a little breathlessly, and walked slowly across the flagstones and between the pots of flowers.

Her husband waited for her by the fountain. "Well?" he said when she was within earshot. "What did he say?"

How on earth did one even begin to reply? "Come," she said, to gain a little time. "Let us walk down the avenue, where we cannot be heard."

Obligingly, he offered her his arm and they left the plaza, then the gardens, at a companionable stroll. At least, she hoped it looked so to the observers at door and window. Inside, her nerves were wound to screaming pitch.

"You are to be given your freedom, at least," she said in an attempt to work up to it.

An eyebrow lifted. "I was not aware that I had lost it."

"Evan has his as well, and his translator is to be given his citizenship."

"I am delighted, though I have no idea what this has to do with your audience with him to stop the war."

They passed through the great wrought-iron gates, nodding to the Viceroy's guard, and when they were clear she gasped out a sound that was supposed to be a laugh, but instead held both relief at her escape and a little hysteria at what she must tell him.

"In actual fact it has everything to do with stopping the war. You see, he told me he would indeed command it—"

"Gloria!" Her husband took her shoulders in his warm hands and gazed into her face in frank delight. "You did it! You did what no one thought you could do. I do not know whether to be proud of you—or frightened that I am married to a woman of such influence." And now the tears welled up, causing the delight to fade from his face. "What is it, dear?"

"That is just it." Her voice shook. "The price is too high. I do not know if I can pay it—and yet it seems I must if I am to accomplish what I have sacrificed so much for already."

"What ... price?"

She tucked herself more closely against his side, and they walked on, otherwise her knees would have been tempted to fold. "The price is the annulment of our marriage and the subsequent announcement of my engagement to the prince."

The captain stopped dead in the middle of the gravel avenue to stare at her. "I beg your pardon?"

With the brilliant sun in her eyes making her tear up, she repeated it. And still he stared, as though she were speaking Italian and he was trying to parse the words.

At last his jaw tightened, and he put his hand over the one tucked into the crook of his elbow, as if she might try to pull away, and walked on. "Why, that lily-livered, no-good, jumped-up boy masquerading as a man ... I ought to go back there and turn him over my knee. He needs nothing more than a good walloping. How dared he speak that way to you? Is this some kind of joke? It's in the worst possible taste if it is. Tell me at once, dear—did he make advances to you?"

"Not in the way you mean. I am afraid he was every bit as sincere as one could wish on such an occasion. He even went down upon one knee. The only thing missing was a vulgar diamond of impeccable vintage belonging to some long-dead queen."

It took a moment for him to get his breath back. "You mean he ... is quite serious?"

"Deadly serious. When I asked him what the consequences would be if I refused him, the subject of your freedom came up immediately."

"Blackmail!" Her husband seemed to be having difficulty catching his breath.

"That was the very word I used. Then he came to his senses and rescinded his threat, but there will be no such charity when it comes to the war. If I do not accept him, it will go ahead and all that we fear most will come to pass. Particularly the dam. In fact, even if the war comes to a grinding halt, the dam will not. He has great plans for shipping and commerce, and the river is a key part of it."

"The witches may have something to say about that."

"Not if they are a hundred feet below the surface—or displaced into another territory altogether." She clutched his arm as though they stood in a high wind. "Stanford, what on earth am I to do?"

"I am still feeling a little stunned over what he said to you. How in heaven's name—annulled! There is only one circumstance under which that may be accomplished. I realize that one does not speak of such things, but—"

"But somehow he knew that we have not—" She took a breath. She had promised him honesty, and she would keep that smallest and most vital of promises, though a lady certainly did not speak of such things, especially out in the open air. "We have not consummated our marriage."

A fact that she was coming to regret with all the gathering force of an avalanche.

He said a word that he had never spoken in front of her before, but that she, unbeknownst to him, had used on several occasions of high emotion. "This is impossible." He gazed heavenward, but there was no help forthcoming. Only gulls, and a pelican heading out to sea. "Surely you are not thinking of going through with it."

"I do not see that I have a choice, if thousands of lives are to be saved."

"And what of *your* life?"

They had reached the mission at the end of the avenue, where no more could be said. Instead, he allowed the question to hang unanswered between them until they had passed through the great gates and reached the bottom of the hill, where the bustle of the town embraced them.

"I cannot go back to the inn," she said suddenly. "I cannot face them and tell them this. Not yet."

"Very well."

A few minutes later she found herself at the far end of the harbor wall, where they had spoken two nights ago. The tide was again low, exposing the rocks and glistening weed and the sea creatures clinging for dear life, waiting until their proper environment should return.

She envied them. At least they had the assurance that it would.

Her husband folded himself down upon the sea wall and invited her to sit beside him on the warm stone. She leaned into his side, wondering a little hysterically how many opportunities she might have left in which to do this simple, homely thing.

"What of your life, Gloria?" he asked again, softly. "Are you prepared to live here for fifty years, isolated behind those mountains? In a culture that—forgive my saying so—does not agree with your temperament?"

She huffed what passed for a laugh. "He intends that I should change all that. To open schools for girls, to open the skies to airships, to invite all manner of commerce here. Why, he even has plans for my undersea dirigibles. He was rather frighteningly well informed about the assets of Father's company for a boy who has been away at school in Holy Mother Spain for several years."

"He is no boy, if he can come up with a plan like this. But plans are just that. Plans. Why has he not put them into action himself? He has been on the throne a year at least."

"I asked him that, too. He says he needs me before he can do it. Though I hardly see why. He is an absolute monarch, and if he wishes his council to agree with him, he has only to make it plain it is in their best interests to do so."

"What are the odds that, even if you were to agree to this mad proposal, the council and the Ambassador would allow what the Viceroy wants? For you and I both know who really seems to rule the roost in these parts."

And therein lay the rub. What would be the point of sacrificing her life for the sake of thousands of other people if all that the Viceroy promised were prevented by powerful and determined men?

"Allowing airships over the border seems a very simple thing to begin with, doesn't it?" she mused aloud. "And yet he has not had the courage to attempt even that. Though he did hint that the missions would object rather strongly."

"Perhaps his dreams have become so real that he cannot

tell the difference between them and reality. But Gloria, you cannot sacrifice your life for dreams."

"I have not even had the chance to sacrifice it for my *own* dreams, let alone his," she agreed wryly.

He passed an arm about her. "And what do you dream of?"

Laying her head upon his shoulder, she watched an orange starfish begin its infinitely slow journey toward a purple one some inches away. "I have given up on castles in the air, I can assure you of that."

He chuckled. "Don't be so quick to do so. I enjoy a nice castle now and again. But mostly I prefer a less exalted view."

"From the wheelhouse of your steamboat?"

"Yes. And perhaps from the window of a cottage somewhere, with a river rushing past and a decent pier."

"The Rio de Sangre Colorado?"

"That is the only one available at present, though I hear there are nice ones in the Canadas and back in the Fifteen Colonies, too."

"I have a nice house in Philadelphia, though sadly it does not possess a river. It has an airfield and an orchard, however."

"I am partial to apples. What kind?"

"Spartan, and one Golden Delicious. And a couple of small ones that I believe will be Pippins in time."

"Can you make pie?"

"I can." She smiled, the cotton of his shirt soft and warm beneath her cheek. "Do you know, the Viceroy said the oddest thing. He said that he didn't want a wife from the rancho families because none of the girls had any conversation, and they knew so little of arithmetic that they could not double a recipe—which I find hard to believe, since most of them will be running ranchos of their own some day, and a fiesta must involve tremendous amounts of arithmetic. But why would a prince know anything of recipes, I wonder?"

"Perhaps, with a father like that, and a mother who had passed away, he spent some time in the kitchens with women who knew their way around a bag of flour."

"Perhaps. Women who were kind to him." She sighed. "Stanford, I must give him my answer in the morning."

He laid his cheek upon her hair, and she could have wept at the sweetness of it. "I suppose now is not the time to suggest taking up our original plan for this evening?"

Her eyes welled up again as the avalanche of understanding crashed in and told her exactly what price she would be required to pay if she agreed to the Viceroy's mad plan. She had had every intention of becoming a wife to her husband in every way, beginning this very evening. But now …

"Now that I am about to lose it, I realize how very much I wanted it," she whispered.

"You need not lose it," he said tenderly. "We could leave on the dawn train and return to Philadelphia. Everyone here can simply fend for themselves as they have done for centuries."

"But I cannot leave the witches—my sisters, to whom I owe my very life." How comforting his arm was about her shoulders. How little she wanted to leave his side. "I cannot let them be drowned or flooded out of their homes knowing that I might have been able to prevent it."

"They have resources of which outsiders know nothing," he reminded her. "They will survive."

But there was a difference between merely surviving … and living a life full of purpose, and joy, and productive work. All of which the witches enjoyed now.

"And what of you?" she asked him. "If I were to agree, what would you do?"

"I have hardly had time to wonder, to be honest. I suppose I could hang about the palace gardens, waiting for him to lose interest so that you could take me as your lover."

"Ah, but he has already promised me he will not take a mistress. I can do no less than promise the same, can I?"

"Dear me. These principles of yours are more troublesome than even I suspected."

"They are, aren't they?" She sighed. "It is at times like this that I wish I were a different woman."

He laughed. "If you were a different woman, you would never have come out to the Wild West, and we would never have met. And somehow, troublesome as you are, I could never wish that."

Gloria could not speak. Instead, she turned her face into his shoulder and to her horror, left his shirt wet with her tears.

CHAPTER 3

$\mathcal{E}$van and Joe were walking in the garden after breakfast, enjoying the sunshine and keeping an eye on the windows of the guest wing into which Gloria had gone. Joe nudged him. "Ain't we going to have a word with Captain Stan?"

"You may. I have nothing to say to him—he is a stranger to me." But not to Gloria. And therein lay the rub.

For it was the captain's privilege to escort Gloria here, to protect her, to enjoy her company at any time. She might waltz with prince or peasant, but she would leave the ball with her husband, and the thought of it irritated Evan beyond endurance. But endure he must. She had made her choice, no matter the reasons behind it, and he must respect her enough to let her go, and live with it.

With a shrug, Joe ambled over into the central quadrangle, where it was clear the good captain was having a difficult time concentrating on his conversation. His gaze kept turning toward the house. Finally Joe took pity on him and left him in solitude, pacing circles around the generous circumference of the fountain.

"Take a walk down the avenue?" he suggested when he rejoined Evan. "Put our freedom to the test?"

"Certainly."

Evan couldn't help a little uneasiness as they strolled away from the hacienda, the gravel crunching under their feet and the sun warming their shoulders. The air was scented with oranges and lavender, and the soft hum of bees provided a gentle counterpoint to the chirrup of small birds in the box hedges. He expected to be hailed at any moment by soldiers jogging in pursuit, but heard only the cries of gulls wheeling over the harbor, and the occasional conversation in the Californio tongue as parties and couples passed them on their way from mission to rancho.

"Maybe it's really true," he mused aloud as they entered the mission grounds. "The Viceroy has commanded it, and so it must be."

"Until we attempt to go to the harbor," Joe pointed out. "Want to try it?"

"Why not? Though I am anxious to hear whether Gloria's goal is accomplished. Perhaps we should wait and meet them in the avenue."

"Whichever way it goes, I have no doubt everyone within a mile will hear about it within seconds."

"That is not the same as hearing it from her own lips."

"Her lips, my friend, are no longer any of your business—if they ever were."

"Thank you for that reminder," Evan said sourly.

"Just trying to be helpful."

The trouble was, he was perfectly right. Which didn't improve Evan's temper.

They were just progressing down the mission's colonnade toward the great set of gates that would set them on the public road, when a door opened and Commander de Sola emerged carrying a leather folder.

"Senor Douglas—Senor San Gregorio. I was just coming to the hacienda to look for you. This was just put into my hands moments ago." With a bow just a shade more shallow than it would have been had Joe's parentage been without fault, de Sola presented the leather folder to him. "The document of citizenship. Blessings upon you, sir."

Evan could see Joe struggle to keep the amused astonishment from his expression. Apparently he had as little faith in the promises of military commanders as Evan had in the promises of kings. And so far, they had both been wrong.

With a murmur of thanks and an absent bow, Joe took the folder, unfastened its leather strings, and opened it up. A heavily embossed, creamy document lay inside, with a blue-and-gold seal from which a gold ribbon depended.

"What does it say?" he asked, looking over Joe's shoulder.

After a moment, Joe began to translate.

"Know all men in the sight of God that our right loyal subject and liege man, José San Gregorio, does on this seventh day of the month of March in the year 1895, receive all the rights and benefits accruing to a citizen of the Royal Kingdom of Spain and the Californias. Let it be known that no man shall detail, imprison, or otherwise hinder him save if he shall break the laws of the kingdom. Let it be known in addition that he enjoys my personal regard;

therefore hinder him at your peril. Signed, Carlos Felipe, Viceroy et cetera."

Evan was quite impressed. "His personal regard, is it? That and a piece of eight will buy you a night at the inn. Congratulations, my friend."

De Sola looked mildly affronted. "Indeed not, sir. The personal regard of the Viceroy attached to one's citizenship entitles a man to certain privileges. For instance, in a court of law, he may call upon the attorney of his choosing, and that individual must defend him. Should he wish to open a business, the state bank may not turn him away. I would say that Senor San Gregorio is a very fortunate man, considering his situation as little as a week ago."

"So I may not be returned to that situation?" Joe asked.

"Certainly not. I told you so, on our journey here."

"Then I am free to leave as soon as I please?"

"I hope you will stay to assist your friend, should you be needed." The commander nodded in Evan's direction. "But yes, you are free to return to San Gregorio ... or not. For that is the third benefit of the sovereign's regard. Though you are *mestizo*, you are no longer tied to the rancho of your birth. You may travel within the kingdom as though you enjoyed the full rights of birth. Sadly, however, if you were to marry, your children would not bear the same benefits. Not unless you married a woman of the *gente de razón.*"

"Not likely," Joe said.

"Still, the benefits are not to be scoffed at. You are for all intents and purposes a citizen just as I."

Joe regarded him for a moment. "I hope I may be as fair and compassionate as you, sir. You have treated us with nothing but consideration and goodness, and I for one appreciate it."

This was one of the longest speeches Evan had ever heard out of Joe's mouth. "As do I," he hastened to add. "My own circumstances are not as clear-cut, but I wish to assure you that I will be returning with you to the dam."

"You will?" De Sola's eyebrows rose. "Despite His Serene Highness's having given you your freedom?" From within his jacket, he withdrew a second, much smaller packet. "Your traveling papers, sir, freshly signed."

Evan took the thick paper and unfolded it slowly. Joe translated in a swift murmur. "Thank you, Commander. I must at least train one of your men to operate *el Gigante*," Evan said, hoping his face was not flushing and giving him away as he tucked the paper into the inside pocket of his short jacket. "And a fair wage would not go amiss, either, for I am afraid I am quite penniless, and freedom is a costly thing."

Under his military moustache, the commander's lips softened into a smile. "You speak the truth, Senor Douglas. Very well. I will give you a wage of one piece of eight per day for your assistance. That is the same wage one of my corporals is paid—which I think is more than fair."

Evan nodded, and offered his hand. "Agreed, sir."

His fingers were cold, but they did not shake. The commander took his leave and went about his business, leaving Joe and Evan to pass through the mission gates in something of a daze.

"Free men," Evan breathed, gazing out to the sea, heaving and glittering below. "At least, as free as one can be on this side of the mountains."

"And north of the dam," Joe added in his practical way. "So you're going back, for true?"

"I must. Barnaby is still there, and Dutch, and our plans."

"Whether or not Gloria succeeds, it's the dam, then? Good." Joe's mouth settled into a grim line. "No one takes the witches into account, except—" He stopped. "Thank you. You are risking your life again, and without hope of an attorney who is obliged to represent you at your trial."

"If I am alive to undergo a trial. This will be, of course, an act of war."

"You must simply use your ingenuity to make it look like an accident." He clapped Evan on the back, and steered him toward the road down the hill into the town. "Come. I want to tell Ella the good news."

Though he made himself smile, Evan's heart seemed to contract in his chest with loneliness. Joe had inexplicably found Ella, with whom he had a history and apparently enjoyed the kind of relationship that Evan could only wish for.

Would there ever be such happiness for him?

But the gulls only cried, and wheeled, and offered him no comfort.

AT THE INN, Joe found Ella pacing in the taproom, waiting for Gloria and the captain to return, and suggested that they walk back up to the mission in hopes of meeting them. Evan considered staying and ordering a drink rather than being a third to their happy pair, but the danger in his faculties being addled even a little in this strange and unpredictable country made his stomach plunge with unease. Traveling papers could be stolen, and he would not risk being imprisoned again.

But they had barely emerged from the inn door when Joe's gaze sharpened and he pointed down the waterfront. "There they are. They must have passed the inn altogether. Why, I wonder?"

Gloria waved as they approached, but under her outdated bonnet her face was pale and bore the tracks of tears.

Ella drew in a soft breath. "What has happened? Come up to our rooms, quickly. It is plain that we must have privacy."

Evan did his best not to look about him once the door to the Fremonts' room closed and they could no longer be heard. It was not that the small room was untidy, for it was not—a trunk sat near the window, no discarded clothes lay about, and the bed was neatly made. But he had never been in a lady's room before, and that this one was Gloria's, and shared with her husband ...

Miserably, Evan sat on the sill in the deeply recessed window. Joe leaned on the wall along with the captain, while Ella took Gloria's hands and drew her down next to her on the counterpane. "Tell us, sister. I cannot bear the suspense."

Gloria glanced at her husband, who nodded encouragingly. "I do not know if I can say it. Stanford, you must help me if I—"

"Of course, dear."

Evan's lips thinned. Did he realize the privilege he enjoyed, calling her by such an endearment? Did he take it for granted?

"He will not command that the war be stopped, then?" Joe asked, his voice clearly showing his tension. "Our journey has been fruitless?"

"Oh, he will give the command," Gloria said dully. "For a price."

"And what is that?" Ella asked, her hands tightening.

The captain removed his bowler hat with its driving goggles and scrubbed his fingers through his hair. "The price is the annulment of our marriage and the subsequent nuptials of my wife and the Viceroy."

Three mouths dropped open. All the breath seemed to rush from Ella's lungs in a sharp hiss as she released Gloria's hands and gripped the edge of the bed, as though the world were rocking and she might fall off.

Evan could not have heard him correctly. He struggled to speak, and could not.

Joe got out a single word. "Impossible."

"So one might have thought," the captain said, "had not His Serene Highness been in possession of intimate knowledge that made the entire preposterous proposal quite straight-forward."

"I don't understand," Ella said. "He does not know you well enough for intimacy."

"Someone does," Gloria said bluntly. "For how else could he know that the captain and I have not— That is, we—"

"Our marriage has not yet been consummated," Fremont finished as though his wife were not in a paroxysm of embarrassment. "And this leaves the door open for an annulment. Which, I am told, can be in his hands in no more than three days."

Slowly, cold horror poured through his veins. Evan's gaze found that of Ella. The blood was draining from her face in exactly the same manner as they silently acknowledged their mutual guilt.

"What I would like to know is, what spies does he have about the place that he could know such a thing?" the captain asked no one in particular.

He must tell the truth.

I cannot. Gloria will never forgive me.

This was all his fault. He must make amends.

There are no amends for a betrayal of this magnitude. For consequences so appalling.

He could give her nothing, for she had asked nothing of him. But she deserved to know the truth, though that meant never seeing her again, never hearing her soft voice or her delighted laughter.

"I told him," Evan said, his voice leached of all sound into a hoarse whisper. He swallowed. "I interpreted his dream, and he spoke of you and the captain, and—and somehow it came out."

"You?" Gloria stared at him in confusion. "But we only met last night for the first time in weeks. You have known nothing of me since we were parted in Resolution."

Again, he found Ella's stricken gaze, and Gloria pressed a hand to her own pale cheek. "Oh, Ella. Not you."

Ella seized her hand and covered it with kisses. "I am so sorry, sister! I meant no harm. He is your friend, and cares for you, and I thought—"

"You thought you would share intimate details that only you would know with someone who is a stranger to you?" Gloria rose abruptly from where she had been seated on the bed. "I see I shall have to keep more secrets from now on. If I have any left, that is."

Ella's eyes welled with tears, and Evan felt rather like

breaking down, too. Perhaps he ought to try flinging himself to his knees and begging her forgiveness.

Joe's hands had bunched into fists, and he relaxed them with an effort. "Seems to me the question is no longer how the Viceroy came by this knowledge, but how you are going to answer his proposal, Senora Fremont."

She gazed at him as though she had only just realized he was in the room. "Ah. Another witness to my difficulties."

"Witness. Friend. Help." Joe crossed the room and sat next to Ella, drawing her sobbing form against his side with one arm. "The thing is done, and we're in no position to turn each other into enemies. If there's one thing me and Evan have learned, it's that our friends are the only thing of value either of us possesses, whether they make mistakes or not."

"Well said," the captain said. "To the main point—she has asked for a night to consider his proposal."

"Do you believe him to be serious?" If Joe was going to take a practical tack, then Evan would postpone flinging himself to his knees—or out of the window—and do the same. "I must say it sounds ludicrous—proposing to a woman he knows to be married already. Rumors of his madness may not be exaggerated after all."

If her marriage is annulled, then perhaps you have a chance.

But he pushed away the shameful thought. Princes aside, there was no mistaking the affection and respect that had begun to grow between Gloria and her husband. It was obvious to anyone with eyes—and Evan's powers of observation were his stock in trade.

"We do think he is serious," Fremont said, his arms around his wife, when it was clear she could not yet speak. "I have already suggested the dawn train and a fast escape, but Gloria, being a woman of principle, has not taken me up on it."

"But surely you will not allow her to—"

The captain held up a hand. "I do not think the word *allow* comes into this situation at all, Mr. Douglas."

Balderdash! This simply could not be allowed to happen. He spread his hands in appeal. "Gloria, you must see sense. Only a madman would force a woman to marry him in exchange for an order he could give perfectly well as a single man—a prince."

She took a ragged breath. "He is not mad. He is young, and idealistic, and perhaps he has lived too long in the shadow of powerful men. He wishes to kick off the traces with an unsuitable marriage, as many a young man before him has done. I am perfectly capable of seeing sense on my own, Evan. I do not need you to inform me of it."

She was in an impossible position. He knew that. She spoke the truth. He knew that, too. And still the words burrowed deep into his heart, hurting him as surely as his own betrayal had hurt her. "What—what answer will you give him?" he croaked, his throat thickening.

"That is what we must decide," the captain said, his arms tightening about her once more.

If Evan had not been convinced before that Gloria was learning to care for her husband, his powers of observation clinched the matter. For she laid her head upon his shoulder and clung to him as though he were her last refuge on this earth.

Ella and Joe leaned into one another on the bed. Evan looked from one couple to the other and wished he had never come down here with Joe. He ought to have sought out

Isabela for a walk in the gardens. To request her assistance in locating an apothecary to discover the ingredients in the Viceroy's evening tincture. To do anything but stand here like a homeless stork incapable of finding a mate.

He forced himself to speak over the pain of a loneliness he had always been able to keep in check with work and study. "We have three options, then. In the first, Gloria accepts the Viceroy's hand, becomes the Vicereine of this kingdom, and—"

"And ushers in a new era of transportation, commerce, and prosperity that does not involve imaginary caches of gold." Gloria straightened, but did not leave the circle of her husband's arm.

"Very commendable. Anything else?"

"Education for girls and the children of the poor."

"A difficult prospect to pass up."

"Quite," the captain said dryly. "Fame, fortune, and philanthropy in one fell swoop."

"How is the army going to feel about that?" Joe asked. "To say nothing of the man who commands it. We still have not heard anything of Ambassador de Aragon's whereabouts, and I'm sure that can't be good."

"I have asked myself that same question," Gloria agreed. "The moment he hears of this scheme, he will stoop upon us breathing fire and will no doubt promptly have me assassinated."

"On the contrary ... I understand that *you* are the one breathing fire and raining destruction," Evan offered. "That is, if Commander de Sola's dreams are to be taken into account."

Gloria stared at him. "What on earth do you mean?"

"He dreamed you were walking in the desert, looking for

something the Viceroy had lost. We believe it to be his power. In any case, you went from being a witch dressed in a most unladylike manner in a layered skirt and a man's waistcoat, to a fire-breathing iron dragon that burned him up with one blast."

"Dear me." Gloria looked quite taken aback. "My mother would have been appalled were she still living."

Ella slid from the bed and crossed to the trunk. After a moment of rummaging through its contents, she drew out a ruffled, multilayered cotton skirt and a brown herringbone waistcoat similar to one Evan himself had once owned. "Like this?"

A chill tiptoed across Evan's shoulders that had nothing to do with the window at his back, or with his previous feelings of guilt and horror.

It was the chill of premonition. Of certainty. Of the realization that de Sola dreamed true.

Somehow, some way, Gloria was to be instrumental in bringing down this kingdom. *But please ... please ... let it not be as the Viceroy's wife.*

CHAPTER 4

"**Y**es. Exactly like that," Evan said after a moment.

But of all today's revelations, Gloria could not help but feel this was the least of them. Who could think of dragons when weddings were much more imminent, dangerous, and terrifying?

"You said three choices," she reminded him. She must put aside the fact that Evan and Ella had got her into this pickle and force them to think their way out of it. "Of course the second would be to flee—which the captain will endorse wholeheartedly."

"It solves my most pressing concerns, though not the long-term ones," he agreed.

"So the third is …?"

Evan hesitated, and a flush colored the thin cheeks that had been so pale. "I do not believe it is your destiny to flee. Your third choice, then, is to—er—put the lie to what the Viceroy believes about your marriage."

Gloria froze for a moment before the hysterical urge to

laugh overcame her completely. "Evan!" she gasped. "I cannot believe you just said what I think you said."

"What did he say?" Ella wanted to know, folding the clothes back into the trunk. Joe whispered something in her ear, and understanding gave way to delight. "Of course! That would solve everything, wouldn't it? Once the examination is completed and the proof discovered, there is nothing anyone can do, and you are free."

"Proof?" the captain said sharply.

"Examination?" Gloria said at the same time.

"Why, yes. All the noblewomen have to have it, to prove they are virgins before marriage. Though," Ella amended, "you would be proving the opposite, in this case."

"Ella Maria Balboa, how on earth do you know such things?" Gloria demanded. The entire subject made her feel ill —to say nothing of speaking in such intimate detail in front of gentlemen.

"From talking with the women, of course. There are no secrets at fiesta, and with Esperanza dancing so openly with the heir to Carmel, of course it came up. Some of the most old-fashioned ladies believe that vigorous dancing or riding or anything but sitting and serving chocolate can affect the results of the examination and put a marriage in jeopardy. Of all the silliness I ever heard."

These things never came up at balls in Philadelphia.

"Never mind." Gloria's cheeks burned. "I will not be subjecting myself to such an examination. If the Viceroy does not accept my word, he can—can—" She bit back an epithet at the last moment.

"So this is the path you choose?" her husband asked. "I have no objections, of course, unless it is to the fact that our relationship is being bandied about this room in a most unsettling manner."

At least *he* was being a gentleman about it.

"What will be the Viceroy's reaction to not getting what he wants?" Joe wanted to know. "If he flies into a rage, he can have the lot of us thrown in gaol—or off a cliff into the sea."

"He could," the captain acknowledged, "though that is hardly the way to garner support for his plans with the nobles."

Try as she might to see another option, Gloria could not. And though it mortified her to speak of her wedding night in terms of a political gambit, physical defiance seemed their only course. "I think we must take the risk," she said slowly. "If nothing else, we will have lost nothing we would have otherwise lost on the dawn train, and we will be together, and not fugitives."

"We?" Stanford looked down at her. "The five of us?"

"Yes ... you and I in particular. We will simply do what we can from behind the mountains. We will be disgraced and probably banished there, but I shall not count *that* as a loss."

"Not by a long shot," her husband agreed. His tone was light, but in his eyes she saw the dawning realization that she did not mean for them to be separated. If she had to face public humiliation in order to remain at his side—beginning with this blunt and unladylike speech in front of Evan and Joe —then she would do it.

The Viceroy might deprive her and her friends of many things, but she would not be deprived of her wedding night, delayed as it was.

"We may depart together, disgraced or not, but not for long," Evan said. "I must return to the dam, and see to its destruction. Commander de Sola has kept his word and issued traveling papers, as well as the offer of a wage. I have one other thing to regret in this venture, and that is that I must betray him, too, to achieve the greater good."

"He will pay you to destroy the dam?" Ella's eyebrows rose in astonishment.

"He does not know we plan to do that," he told her, clearly mustering a smile with difficulty. "He is paying me to operate *el Gigante,* which is a step up from being marched across the yard under pain of a whipping to do the same."

"How do you plan to do it?" Captain Stan asked. "We've had a look round the fort since the construction began, and you've got a job ahead of you."

"Between Barnaby and Dutch and I, we'll see to it," Evan said. "I don't want to say too much in case—" His eyes held misery. "My tongue has been loose enough, and has endangered those I care about. I can only make amends and protect you all by saying less and doing more."

"Hear, hear," the captain said with what Gloria thought was admirable civility. "I suppose if my wife is not to be Vicereine, it will not matter that this will be viewed as an act of war, will it?"

When no one spoke, Gloria said quietly, "It seems that events will move forward in spite of our best efforts to prevent them. I hope you do destroy the dam, Evan," she said with sudden ferocity. "It is our best hope of all the hopes I came here with. The witches' lives and homes will be saved, and this wretched country can go to the—er, can manage its own future without our help."

"But what of the Texicans—the invasion?" the captain reminded her.

"I don't know," she was forced to admit. "Perhaps I shall return to Resolution and see if the mechanicals are still there. If so, I shall sell them to the Rangers immediately, tell them what to do with them, dust off my hands, and go home."

"And if they are not there?" Evan asked.

"Then the last two actions still apply."

Joe got up and held out a hand to Ella. "I'm for the dam, too, but not before I escort Ella here back to her family and mine." He glanced at Evan. "That should give you time to get the plan back under way."

"Escort me—what?" Ella said. "I'm staying with Gloria."

"There is no need to separate. We will travel back to the river as a party," the captain said. "I'll give Riley the word to make ready to leave on the noon train. If Gloria gives the Viceroy her regrets early in the morning, we can be on our way immediately afterward. Mr. Douglas, you are welcome to accompany us as well, at least as far as the crossing point at Nuestra Senora de los Angeles."

"I would appreciate that. Safety in numbers, you know. I will say my good-byes in the morning to Commander de Sola. And to Senor de la Carrera. And his family."

To Gloria's amusement, he blushed, but she forbore to make the same kind of remarks to him as they had all been making about her own relationship. They must remain united. To do that, she must forgive and forget.

Though at the moment, the former seemed much more possible than the latter.

WHEN EVAN HAD TAKEN his leave and returned to the hacienda, and Joe and Ella had gone for a walk on the grassy slopes above the mission, Gloria found herself alone with her husband at last.

He drew her down upon the bed, which was the only place the tiny room boasted where one could sit aside from the whitewashed windowsill. "I hope that was not too painful for you," he said. "I confess that even I was shocked at Mr. Douglas's third solution to our difficulties—mostly because I wish I had thought of it myself."

"I am sure you would have come around to it in time," she assured him, leaning in such a way that it seemed natural he should slide one arm about her shoulders. "Though I am very glad I had already decided upon the same course."

"Had you?" Mischief glinted in his eyes—and something deeper. Warmer. Something that made the blood beat through her veins in anticipation. "And when were you going to inform me of this?"

"About now, in fact."

To her immense satisfaction, he did not waste another moment on words. And when Ella and Joe returned at sunset, they found the door locked and received no reply from within.

"OH, he's going to be so angry." Ella handed Gloria her bonnet, and tied its ribbons under her chin in a jaunty bow. "I do not envy you this interview."

Gloria felt almost giddy from lack of sleep and from the unfamiliarity of her own body. She had been made anew last night—made a woman, a wife, and a lover, and no amount of princely anger or boyish blustering was about to put a dent in her happiness.

"You mean *us*," she said, "for the captain believes that I ought not to see the Viceroy alone. Our whole party is to go. Riley took the message to Evan and Joe before breakfast, and will wait for us at the station with our trunks."

"I am to attend the Viceroy as well?" Ella frowned down at her secondhand dress. "I had best change, then, and quickly. Can you do my hair? Oh Gloria, how I wish we could be painted!"

"As do I." She helped her friend out of her cotton and into the black beribboned dress in which she'd gone to the fiesta, similar to Gloria's own. "I should feel much more brave and competent. Isn't it strange?"

Ella touched her cheek a moment before turning her attention to buttoning the tight bodice. "Not so strange. It is who we are. We hold the power of death. At least let us wear our roses, so we do not forget, and to give us courage."

Ella had been forgiven, and in her exaltation this morning Gloria was willing to forget. They were sisters under the paint, after all, and sisters protected one another. Gloria pinned her roses to her bonnet, while Ella slid two of the silk blooms into the side of her own chignon and secured them. The two of them looked feminine and demure and betrayed their own capabilities to no one, not even those closest to them.

Perhaps, when they finally reached the *Colorado Queen* again, Gloria mused, she would allow Stanford to remove the roses from her hair, one at a time.

The three of them made a silent party as they walked up the hill in the early morning light. The gulls circled and mewed around the fishing boats in the harbor, and the night chill still hung in the air though the sun had risen a little way above the horizon. Evan and Joe were waiting in the court-yard, and while Joe fell back to take Ella's hand in a tight grip, Evan hovered, uncertain of his place.

His gaze, however, took in the hand tucked into the crook of Stanford's arm. "You will make a statement immediately if you enter on his arm," he said quietly. "Are you prepared to do so?"

"I am," she said firmly. "I should take yours, too, if we could fit through the door."

"That might say something altogether different." At least she had surprised a smile. "If Ella does not mind, I shall guard your backs."

Evan proved to be right.

When they were ushered into the Viceroy's presence, it was to find him dressed as though he were meeting a foreign ambassador—complete with the royal sun and sash—and sitting by the fire, as before. A laden breakfast tray was set upon the low table, and Gloria saw immediately that it had been laid for two. A small nosegay of flowers lay next to a richly engraved box of gold, the contents of which no doubt contained an engagement gift of some kind. So, he had made an assumption, and as he rose and she released Stanford's arm in order to curtsey, she saw the moment when he realized he had made the wrong one.

"I was not expecting so large a party for so private an occasion," the young man said stiffly. He did not sit, so they could not either.

"I appreciate your willingness to receive us, sir," Gloria

said. "The subject of our conversation involves more than simply you and I."

"Does it, indeed?" His face became forbidding, remote … and Gloria got a glimpse of the man he might become twenty years from now.

If he lived that long.

For part of the reason for the bleakness of his countenance was its striking pallor. What had been pale yesterday looked positively gray today. His hands trembled, and even his hair seemed to have lost its luster. What could have happened between sunset and sunrise to have caused his condition to worsen so?

But that was not a question for this morning's visit. Her task now was to provide an answer. "I first wish to assure you that I am honored beyond measure by your considering me suitable to be your wife, to say nothing of your Vicereine."

"So you should be."

The next sentence was checked upon her tongue before Gloria recovered and went on. "I wish nothing more than to be the instrument of your happiness, but—"

"Then do so." He took a shuddering breath. "Send these people out of the room and make me the happiest of men."

"—but I cannot change the choice my heart has already made," she concluded softly. Defying all protocol, she crossed to him and took one cold hand in her own. "Some day, you will learn to care for someone as I care for my husband." Her voice was pitched low, but Stanford's ears were sharp. Her words were for both men, even if they were spoken only to one. "I would never want to stand in the way of your happiness—the kind of happiness I know now. I cannot leave my marriage, Felipe, not even for the glorious future you have promised me and your country." She took a breath to steady herself. To say words that would be shocking in any other company. "It is consummated."

His eyes widened. "But—I was told—" His gaze found that of Evan, who flushed and looked at his feet.

"He told you what he knew to be true. But I am telling you the truth as it is. I am fully Captain Fremont's wife, as he is fully my husband. And I choose to remain so, with your leave and good wishes."

She could see the whites around his irises now, hear his labored breathing. Would he fly into an apoplexy? Would he strike her in a fit of temper? Should she flee?

But no. The days of flight were over. Instead, she gripped his hand more tightly and had the distinct sensation that she alone was holding him upright.

"You have—done this—last night? After my proposal? In defiance of my promise to annul your marriage?" He was gasping now.

"I have, dearest Felipe." Somehow, her voice remained as gentle as it was steady. "And some day you will know what it is like to be loved—and to love in return."

"But I wanted that with you!" He moaned—

—his eyes rolled up in his head—

—and he collapsed in a dead faint at her feet.

CHAPTER 5

"Felipe!" Gloria dropped to her knees beside the young man's prostrate form and found the pulse in his neck that told her she was not—thank the heavens— responsible for the death of a prince. "Someone—we must help him."

Evan knelt beside her. "Allow me." With skilled hands he examined the still form, opening the sightless eyes and touching the back of his head, clearly feeling for lumps. "We are fortunate the carpets are thick. He has sustained no injury of that kind. Fetch me a cloth and some water, if you will."

Ella leaped to the low table, where a damask napkin and the contents of the teapot were dragooned into use. But still the young prince did not regain consciousness.

Nausea rolled in Gloria's stomach at the thought of what could happen if even the least of the Viceroy's retinue entered the room. They would be arrested on the spot—and if he died, executed with equal dispatch.

"Let us lift him on to the sofa, and remove his jacket so that his breathing is not constricted," Evan instructed.

As Joe cradled the Viceroy's upper body and Evan took his feet, Ella gazed at them curiously. "Joe, what an extraordinary thing—you could pass for his brother. I've seen the resemblance before, but side by side ... Gloria, do you see it?" She appealed over her shoulder as she moved cushions under his head. "So close together as they are?"

Gloria had seen the resemblance, too, but even with the contrast—one healthy and tanned, one pale and sickly—their bone structure was visibly alike. And the set of the eyes, too. The length of their lashes, and the shape of their lips.

A sudden question whisked across Gloria's mind with the speed of a swallow swooping in to its nest. "Joe, what do you know of your parentage?" she asked slowly. "Ella has told me that Clara, Mother Mary's right hand in the village, is your own mother."

He nodded, and held the Viceroy's upper body so that Evan could remove the ornate jacket and the sash, and loosen the collar of his shirt.

"What of your father?"

"No offense, Senora, but we have bigger problems to deal with at the moment."

"I am quite aware of that. But the resemblance between you and the Viceroy is uncanny. It cannot be accidental. What if—" She hardly dared say it. Joe was not a large man, but he was definitely a private one, and she did not know how well he would accept her prying.

Joe rose to his feet while Evan continued his examination. "If you must know, my mother was a cook in the royal residence in San Francisco de Asis. She was raped, and when she came up pregnant, she was fobbed off on a single man from San Gregorio. They remained in the Viceroy's household until I was four, and when the old Viceroy went on a progress with his household and grandees, her husband beat her and left her for dead near the mountains. The witches found us and took us in."

Gloria's heart squeezed with sympathy for Clara, who had endured horrible trials of which she had never once spoken. All Gloria had known of her was her good humor, her care for the witches and the rivermen, and her obvious affection for Mother Mary.

"The man—your true father," she said slowly, "could it have been the old Viceroy? For you and the prince are about the same age. If the Vicereine was … unreceptive … due to her own pregnancy, could he have abused the staff to fulfill his own selfish needs?"

Joe only shrugged.

"Gloria, is there a reason you are questioning this young man about his antecedents instead of focusing on the imme-diate disaster?" Stanford's tone held humor, but it was forced. "At any moment we will be interrupted, and I am sure no one here is unaware of the consequences."

"He is going to die of whatever poison they have given him if we do not do something," Evan said tersely. "He needs a doctor, and I do not trust his own. I believe they have been steadily poisoning him for months."

"And I can imagine whose gold they are taking to do it," Stanford said. "It is very convenient, is it not, that the Ambassador should be far away from San Luis Obispo de Tolosa, looking after the needs of the kingdom? What a tragedy for the de la Carrera family, to be responsible for the death of the Viceroy in their own home. When de Aragon bullies the Council into appointing him Regent, they will be disgraced and will likely have to forfeit their lands and stock. To him."

Evan stood now, too, his fists clenched. "Yes. How very convenient. But how inconvenient that he did not take Gloria into account."

"He does not even know I am here," she pointed out.

"He may not—but I suspect by now he does," Evan said. "He may capitalize on your presence."

"You're speculating," Joe reminded them. "We need to do something. How are we going to help him? We can't just leave him here to die and run. I don't much fancy the Ambassador getting his hands on this kingdom."

Another idea was already forming in Gloria's brain, this time with the majesty and force of an eagle beating its way into the sky. She drew in a breath at the prospect—at the sheer foolhardiness of it—at the amazing success of it should she and the friends around her have the courage to act.

"Gloria?" her husband said, holding out a hand as though he thought she might faint, too. "What is it, dear?"

"I know what to do," she breathed. "But you will think me utterly mad."

"It will not be the first time," Evan said, pressing the damp cloth to the Viceroy's forehead. The eyelids of the latter flicked and twitched, as though he were dreaming.

"That is true. And we did succeed in stopping that train," she reminded him. "This time, however, we will have the advantage of no air pirates to deal with."

She was gratified to see him grin in appreciation.

"What are you thinking, Senora?" Joe said. "Do you mean

to spirit him out of the window to a doctor who isn't in the Ambassador's pay?"

"No. I mean to bring him back to health and announce my engagement to him, while Evan takes his friend Joe to the doctor—or better yet, to the witches, where he will not only be safe, but will have a fairer chance of recovery."

"What in the world …?" Ella looked completely staggered. "You are not suggesting that they switch places? My—my Joe and the Viceroy?"

Gloria beamed at her quick apprehension of the kernel of the plan. "I am indeed. Joe, you and I shall secure that annulment, announce our engagement, and then stop this war once and for all. You may not be able to halt the work on the dam, but you can certainly recall the rancho troops that have mustered in the water meadows and send them back peacefully to their fields and fiestas. Then, Evan and his friends can ensure an accident occurs to level the dam, with far less loss of life. Why, we could have this kingdom set to rights and on its way into the nineteenth century inside of a month."

Three men gaped at her. Four, if you counted the unconscious form on the sofa.

"You are insane," Joe finally croaked. "Mad as a spring rattler."

"Now, now," the captain protested. Then he added, "May I register a protest? Must the annulment be part of the plan?"

Gloria took his arm and folded both hands about it as she gazed up at him with her heart in her eyes. "I am afraid so. And if Joe and I must go through with a wedding—plans for which I suspect are already afoot—then it must be perfectly legal. I cannot be a bigamist."

"Why not?" Joe asked no one in particular. "I cannot be a prince."

"Then unless you can think of a better plan, we are doomed," she told him bluntly.

A brief silence fell as the captain, Evan, and Joe exchanged agonized glances.

"It is utterly mad," Evan said at last. "But when have we encountered rationality and order in this country?"

"De Sola," Joe said. "And Isabela seems more sensible than she looks. Can we find aid in those quarters?"

The captain shook his head. "I doubt it. Both have far too much to lose."

"And we don't?" Joe asked. "If we're found out, it's death for all of us. I'll just be first in line."

"But Joe, think," Gloria said urgently, unwilling to release her husband's arm. She settled against his side, wondering wildly if this would be her last opportunity to do so. "If there is even a remote possibility that you are the Viceroy's half brother—though illegitimate, you are a threat to the Ambassador's plans every moment you live and breathe."

"No, I'm not."

"He knows you exist, that is certain," Ella said slowly. "Who else could have persuaded a San Gregorio man to take Tia Clara to wife save for the grandee of San Gregorio? What if he wanted to keep the old Viceroy's bastard under his own eye in the palace household? He could not have predicted that the man he sold your mother to would turn out to be a brute, nor that she would go to the witches rather than return to the palace."

"I'm no threat to him."

"If the Viceroy dies and there is no heir of the blood royal except for you, you might be," Gloria told him softly.

"So what you're saying is I'm damned if I do, and damned if I don't." Joe's voice rose in pitch with his agitation. "What if all I want to do is board a ship and go to the Antipodes?"

"Then I will go with you," Ella said. "But if you agree to our sister's plan, you could save thousands of lives—including those of your mother and mine."

Joe gazed at her, his mouth trembling with the force of his emotion. "I do not want to marry her."

"I do not want to marry you, either," Gloria assured him. "I am perfectly happy with my marital arrangements as they are. But as it seems to be my fate to marry my way to peace, I would rather you than the real Viceroy. At least I may count on you not to wish to produce heirs."

Evan covered his mouth on a strangled sound. Beside her, the captain swayed as though in a high wind.

"And how shall we resolve the situation when the real Viceroy has recovered?" her husband inquired after a moment, when he seemed to have collected himself. "It is one thing to change places, but what will happen to you when we must change back? For surely we must."

"I have not thought that far ahead, exactly," she admitted. "I confess that the urgency of our present situation has rather blotted out pieces of the larger picture."

"Let us jump off that bridge when we come to it," Evan suggested in his practical way. "It is a fact that he will die if he does not receive immediate care. It is also a fact that royal engagements can last up to a year, and there may be no need for Gloria to marry anyone."

"Except me, a second time," the captain put in.

"Except you, a second time." With recklessness born of the knowledge that time had run out, she rose on tiptoe and kissed him to seal the bargain. Then she turned to Joe. The trembling in his mouth had progressed to hands and even knees now. "We are open to any and all alternatives," she prompted him softly. "No one can force you to do this."

"Only my own conscience," he said on a groan. "And our lack of a better plan."

"Cheer up," Evan said. "If he recovers within the week, he can take his place again, and Gloria can find a reason to break their engagement."

"If we are not assassinated first," Joe pointed out.

"Take care not to eat or drink anything that others have not tasted first," Evan said. "I have a feeling that death comes by stealth and by law in these parts, not by the hiring of assassins."

Gloria had had enough of assassins to satisfy her for eternity. But Evan was likely right.

"How will we get him out of the house and down to the train?" Ella knelt by the sofa and patted the Viceroy's hand, but he did not wake. "He cannot walk in this state, and it is a long way to carry him."

"First of all, Joe must put on the prince's clothes, in exchange for his own," Evan said. "I will find Isabela and ask her to arrange a cart for my translator, who had too much to drink last night and is now feeling ill."

"I will meet you at the train," the captain said. "Tell Riley nothing. I trust him in a fight, but not with information he can sell. Ella, see to it that—"

"Ella stays with me," Joe said flatly, then a moment later amended it to, "and Gloria will need a maid."

"I was going to say, see to it that Gloria's trunk is collected and brought here," the captain said.

"Why?" Ella wanted to know. "If she is to marry the Viceroy, she will have seamstresses at her beck and call to make her trousseau. She must not be seen in a secondhand fiesta dress or an out-of-date bonnet any longer."

But Gloria had already perceived what her husband meant. "But can they make me a ruffled skirt and a man's waistcoat?" she asked with a smile that trembled at the corners. "I am the iron dragon, am I not? If Commander de Sola's dream comes to pass, I should not like my things on the other side of the country."

Joe was already tearing off his jacket. "If you all will excuse me, I need to change."

Politely, Gloria encouraged the others to give him privacy while Ella assisted him out of his clothes and into those of the Viceroy.

Gloria picked up the gold box on the table next to the nosegay of flowers. "I hardly dare look at this, but it seems we must costume ourselves for the play."

She opened it. Her husband peered over her shoulder and whistled.

Evan's breath left him in a long sigh as she drew out a gold ring set with a large sapphire flanked by four diamonds. Around the hollow where it had been in the box, lying on a bed of black velvet, was a necklace of sapphires and diamonds, and a tiara that would have given Queen Victoria herself a moment of envy.

Gloria slid off her wedding ring and handed it to her husband. "Keep this safe."

"Until we are together again," he promised in a tone husky

in its intensity, and slid it onto the smallest finger of his left hand.

Then she put on the Viceroy's ring and removed the shabby bonnet with its silk roses from her head. When it was set in place, the tiara sat upon her golden hair like the rays of the sun, enclosed by an arc of diamonds. Sapphires and emeralds formed the band at its base, to symbolize the earth and sea, she supposed. The tiara was a clever recreation of the flag of the Royal Kingdom.

The gift of a prince.

The crown of a princess.

The last thing in all the wide world that she wanted.

A small sound escaped Ella's lips, and the three of them turned from the vision in the mirror.

Joe stood there, splendid in the Viceroy's dress uniform, the scarlet sash pinned with the royal sun. Even the boots fit him, polished to a shine, with silver spurs at the heels.

"Shoulders back," the captain reminded him. "You are a prince. You own everything your eyes can see—you command the very lives of your people and have been brought up from birth to believe it to be your divine right."

Joe mumbled something, but straightened his shoulders and lifted his chin.

"That is downright eerie," Evan said. "I have been sharing a cell with you for weeks, and I hardly recognize you."

"Let us hope it works the other way," Joe told him, relaxing into familiarity once again. "I suggest that while Gloria and I are making our announcement to the family, that you spirit the—er, Felipe—er, Joe away while everyone is distracted by the happy news."

"Right," Evan said briskly, coming to himself. "I shall find

Isabela at once." A bell rang in the courtyard, its sweet sound shivering into silence. "There is the bell for breakfast. The family eats together alone. It will be the perfect time for me to have a word with her while the rest are enjoying the nine days' wonder."

Gloria turned to her husband and buried her face in his neck, breathing in the scent of clean cotton, sweat, and gear oil for the last time. "I love you," she whispered.

Before last night, she had never said those words to anyone. Their magnitude almost frightened her.

"And I you," he whispered into her hair, his arms tightening around her. "No matter what happens, we will be together again."

"Promise me." A wild urgency in her heart made her add, "I cannot live unless I know this mad situation will not be forever."

"I promise. For I cannot live either, unless my ring is back on your finger and your heart back in my care."

"It will always be in your care."

And then, the tears trembling on her lashes, she pulled away from the man she loved and crossed the carpet to the man to whom she must engage herself. She could not look into Ella's face, for if she did, both of them would break down.

Instead, she took a deep, steadying breath and slipped her hand into the crook of Joe's arm. "Shall we?"

And at his nod, the cogs and gears of their outrageous plan ground into inexorable motion.

CHAPTER 6

*E*van could not decide which he wanted most—to run for the train station, or to run for the water closet where he might vomit in peace.

Captain Fremont hoisted the Viceroy to a sitting position, and jerked his chin at Evan. "Get his other side. I'm sure you've helped a friend or two back to their rooms after they've had a drop too much."

He had—once. And he could not call those lads friends. They were laboratory assistants and nothing of a warmer nature had ever developed among them. Evan had always supposed this to be because of his diffidence and studious habits. If those lads could see him now...

Gloria and Joe waited until they were well along the colonnade before strolling behind them in the direction of the dining room. "You are supposed to be ill," Evan heard Gloria say. "Can you be proud and sick at the same time? We must have your recovery appear in stages. I do not wish to be responsible for miracles as well as dreams."

Evan couldn't hear Joe's reply, but he was sure it wasn't fit for the ears of a lady. Then again, Gloria had quite the vocabulary, so perhaps it was nothing she hadn't said herself.

Their little group parted ways at the main house. Joe moved as though to open the door, but Gloria clutched him back just in time for the majordomo to bow low and usher them through. That worthy individual gazed somewhere above their heads as Evan and the captain shared a sheepish grin and hustled the semiconscious prince up the staircase as best they could.

It wasn't easy. Evan was breathing hard by the time they were safely in his room and the Viceroy was laid out upon the bed with a pillow under his head.

"What if he comes around?" the captain said, hands on hips, as he gazed down at him, frowning. "What shall we do then?"

"If he did not during that confounded effort, then it is not likely he will in the next few minutes." Evan checked his traveling bundle, which contained nothing but his old prison clothes wrapped around some food he had secured just after dawn. "And once he does, he may not be up to much. Even walking might be difficult."

"On the bright side, anything he says may be put down to the ramblings of an ill man. Even if he declares himself a prince." The captain seemed to be talking himself into a positive view. This observation was confirmed when he ran a hand over his face. "Evan, what are we doing? Are we utterly mad?"

"Yes," Evan said bluntly. "We cannot possibly pull it off. But we are committed now—they will be going into the dining room at this moment."

"He is a good man, is he not?" the captain went on after a moment. "Joe?"

Evan saw at once the thicket the captain's emotions were leading him into, and dropped his bundle near the door. "I would trust him with my life, and in fact have done. Between him and Ella, she has just the friends about her that she needs."

"I know you are right. But the thought of leaving her in such a snake pit of dangers makes me ill."

Evan was not the sort of man to offer comfort of the physical kind, but he had learned a thing or two on this confounded voyage. He gripped the captain's shoulder, offering a sympathy he could not put into words. Especially to a man only yesterday he had resented and disliked. "She is the bravest, most capable woman I know, save one. If anyone can carry out a mad plan and make a success of it, it is she."

"That's not what you said a moment ago." With a wry smile, the captain moved, but not to reject Evan's offer of comfort. He gripped his hand instead in a firm shake. "But I appreciate the thought."

Evan had learned what friendship felt like. Could this be the unlikely beginning of another such friendship? Somehow the knowledge that the captain loved Gloria, and that she returned his regard, had changed his own feelings toward the man.

"Somehow, both are true," he confessed. "That we cannot succeed, yet if it is possible, Gloria will do it. My professors would be ashamed of me for such a featherheaded assessment."

"Your professors have not seen what you have accomplished." The captain smiled, though his eyes still held pain in their depths. "You had best get yourself downstairs to find your young lady and secure her assistance. The sooner we are on our way to the train, the better I will feel."

Your young lady.

There was no time to correct him, so Evan had a few stolen moments to savor the words as he hurried downstairs to the dining room. Isabela could never be his young lady. He had sense enough to know that. A country, a culture, an impending marriage all stood in the way, to say nothing of her own preference. She had been very candid about what she wanted from life, and every detail was so foreign to Evan that they may as well have been standing on opposite shores of the ocean.

If Gloria's plan worked, they would be, and that was as it should be.

But that did not stop another tiny, warm flame that flickered into life inside him, fed by the knowledge that someone had seen and understood Evan's shy, wordless regard for her. Her dark eyes and practical mind. Her humor. Her intelligence, hidden so carefully under her curls and silk. Her friendship.

But he could not think of all that now. What he needed from Isabela was her help—specifically, a horse and cart. He must focus his energies on practical things or the plan would be scotched before it even got under way.

He arrived at the dining-room doorway in time to see Joe clutch the back of the chair at the head of the table with one hand, as though to steady himself, and take Gloria's hand with the other.

"My most esteemed host and hostess," he said, not in the Californio tongue as might have been expected in the bosom of the rancho family, but in English, for Gloria's sake. "I have news of a most wonderful and personal nature."

"Your health is improving, Your Serene Highness?" Isabela's mother asked anxiously. "You seem better this morning."

"I am indeed better, kind lady." Joe inclined his head. "And part of the reason for that stands next to me."

All eyes turned to Gloria, who blushed and looked at the floor.

"Your Serene Highness?" Senor Ignatio, the head of the household, looked as though he didn't know whether to be embarrassed or delighted. Evan realized with a tingle of shock that they thought the prince had taken her—a married woman —as his mistress. Even for a people whose marriages and children and romantic entanglements were the currency of social interaction, this would be a bit much to announce at the breakfast table.

"Senora Fremont has discovered her marriage is not what it ought to be," Joe explained with aplomb. "I am having it annulled, and once that is done, she has agreed to marry me."

Dead silence fell, except for the clink of a fruit fork as it dropped from Beatriz's nerveless fingers.

"Sire?" Senor Ignatio choked. "Marry?"

"But she is not a woman of the *gente de razón!*" Beatriz blurted before her mother turned on her in a fury and shushed her.

Joe lifted his chin imperiously, and Evan could not help but admire him. "My intended is a gentlewoman of immense wealth and intelligence. In the Fifteen Colonies, she moves in the most exalted circles, and numbers among her friends those who enjoy the high regard of a queen. If this does not define a woman of the *gente de razón*, I do not know what will."

"Of course, Your Serene Highness." Senor Ignatio had finally recovered his voice—and his composure. "Allow us to be the first to offer you our congratulations and our most sincere wishes for your mutual happiness."

"Thank you," Joe said, and Gloria echoed him in a murmur that was most unlike her. "Until I have the bull of annulment in hand from Nuestra Senora de los Angeles, we will keep this secret, just among ourselves. It would not do for my lady's reputation to be sullied before she is free to accept my suit."

"Of course not, Your Serene Highness," Senor Ignatio managed. "You may be assured of our complete cooperation."

Again the regal inclination of the head. "And now, if you will send a collation to my suite, I wish to rest a little in the company of my intended bride. Dearest, do you prefer coffee or chocolate?" He lowered his voice tenderly.

"Coffee, if you please." Gloria clung to his arm like a morning glory. Joe, it was clear, was not the only one who had missed a calling upon the stage.

The family leaped to their feet as Joe and Gloria sailed out of the room, and Evan caught just the hint of a wink as the couple passed him in the doorway.

In the babble of shock and speculation that broke out the moment they were out of sight, Evan remembered that he had a job to do. He knelt next to Isabela's chair.

"Why, Senor Douglas. It seems you as well as I have been privy to a thunderbolt from the sky this morning."

"Yes," he said for want of anything better. "May I ask for your help with a certain difficulty?"

"Of course," she said instantly. "You have but to name it."

"My translator seems to be suffering from a complaint of the head, characterized by loss of the ability to walk or speak. I must take him to the apothecary. Might I borrow a cart and horse for an hour?"

"Apothecary? Are you sure he has not simply had too much to drink?"

Evan did his best to smile. "That could be—in which case the apothecary can help him. But I suspect it is something else."

Her smooth brow furrowed with concern. "May not one of His Serene Highness's physicians treat him? They are certainly closer to hand."

"I would not presume to ask His Serene Highness's staff for such a thing." Evan thought quickly. "He will be more comfortable at the apothecary's. He has but recently been awarded his citizenship after having been a vagabond and a prisoner. And beyond that, he is a man who does not like to cause a fuss."

"I had noticed," she said, nodding. "Come. We will go at once."

When her duenna rose with them, laying her fork down on a plate that had hardly been touched, Isabela waved her into her seat. With a rapid explanation in the Californio tongue that was mostly ignored in the spirited family discussion of the thunderbolt, Isabela ushered him out of the room.

Though small and encumbered by skirts, she was still quick, her shoes tapping on the flagstones as they crossed the courtyard. It was all Evan could do to keep up. At the stables, she gave the order to the groom in a tone that somehow managed to command as well as convey respect for him and the work he did for her family, though Evan could only understand about one word in three.

She turned to him and, slower now, walked beside him out of the stable block. "They will have the horse harnessed and in front of the garden gate in ten minutes. There is a track that leads into town without having to enter the mission gates or make a spectacle of oneself along the avenue. The servants come and go that way."

"You think of everything," he said with admiration. "Thank you."

"It is the least I can do for a guest who has fallen ill under our roof," she said with no little gravity. "We take the responsibilities of hospitality very seriously here."

"Then allow me to offer my thanks for that, too," he said, seizing her warm hand in both his cold ones. "For our business here is completed, and I return to the southeast of the kingdom on the noon train."

She stopped beneath an olive tree that provided a welcome, feathery shade. He should release her hand. She should release his. Both of them, it seemed, were perfectly aware of the *shoulds* of the case. And paid no attention whatsoever.

"You are leaving? This very day?"

"I am afraid so. Commander de Sola has given me my travel papers, and I have given him my word that I will return to assist with the work on the dam." Well, it wasn't a falsehood, exactly. He did plan to return, after the Viceroy was safe with the witches.

"But—but—" Now she did release his hand, to pace this way and that in the pool of shade cast by the tree, her skirts twitching like the tail of a cat. "It is so sudden. Why did you not tell us sooner? One cannot simply leave without a farewell dinner, or prayers to the saints in church for a safe journey, or—"

"Isabela—senorita—forgive me." He did not care about the farewell dinner, or the saints, but he did care about the disappointment and dismay in her eyes. "I am not familiar with the customs of this country. I merely thought to cause as little inconvenience as possible."

"You are a guest," she managed with some dignity. "Guests are never inconvenient. Besides, how can you leave your friend Senora Fremont when she—well, there will be much to celebrate in three days' time, once the bull of annulment comes through and we have had time to recover from the shock. Surely you can put off Commander de Sola until then?"

"Perhaps, but I cannot put off Joe. He needs care, and with medicine from the apothecary I hope he will be up to the journey."

"Is he going back to San Gregorio?"

Evan cast about for a suitable fabrication. "I imagine so, but he wished to visit friends first. To tell them the good news of his citizenship, I imagine."

"Oh, of course." She nodded, then her face clouded again. "But there is no urgency in that. He has friends here, too. Oh, senor—Evan—please do not rush off in this way. I—we may never see you again."

"If my friend is to marry your prince, there is every possibility we might see each other again."

It was all he could do not to repossess her hand. For that hand was all but spoken for by the Ambassador's pimply son, and he must not lose his head a second time in five minutes.

Five minutes.

The cart would be waiting at the gate in five minutes, and he still had to help the captain get the Viceroy downstairs and out the door.

"Please convey my heartfelt thanks to your parents for their hospitality," he said. Time, which had plodded so slowly in prison that every second became an eternity, seemed to be rushing past him with a sound he could almost hear. "Tell them that I must see to my translator, and that our business calls us away to the south."

"I will tell them no such thing." She folded her arms and pouted, which act was slightly marred by the trembling of her lower lip. "You must tell them yourself."

"Isabela, if we are to get to the apothecary and then to the station by noon, there is no time for protracted good-byes. And it is not as though we are the heirs to a rancho. They cannot care if two erstwhile prisoners depart their house. I should think they would be relieved."

She lifted her chin. "Then you cast aspersions upon their good character, and I am sorry I arranged the wretched cart for you."

That did it—he lost his head and took both her hands this time. "You do not mean that. Isabela, it is difficult for me to say good-bye. You have been so kind. At times your presence was all that kept me going."

"Was it?" Her frank gaze examined his face, searching out the truth.

Well, he could give her the truth of that, at least. He nodded, not daring to say more.

"Then kiss me good-bye properly," she said suddenly. Her fingers tightened on his as instinctively he drew back. "That is the price of my cooperation. If you are to leave like a thief in the night, then I will be a thief, too—and steal a kiss while I can."

"That would be—what about San Gregorio's heir?" For all he knew, a kiss was a contract, and she could be disgraced if it were discovered. Though no one besides themselves seemed to be in this narrow stretch of garden between the stable block and the house.

"I wish to be kissed by a man before I am sentenced to marry a boy," she said fiercely.

"Sentenced? But I thought you wanted to marry him. Didn't you say your ambition was to be second lady in the land?"

Her eyes compelled him to step closer, and she lowered her voice. "Now that Senora Fremont is to be the first lady, do you not think that things will change? The moment the royal heir is conceived, San Gregorio will return to what it has been for centuries—a rancho sleeping on the edge of the sea, with no pretensions to a throne at all."

"And where does that leave you?"

"Where I have also been for centuries—at my father's command," she said with some bitterness. "Do not mistake me —I have no wish to be allied with de Aragon and his warmon-gering, but as politics stand, Papa has no choice but to seek the alliance. As for me, I must go on acting the part of the butterfly among strangers."

"Am I a stranger still?"

Her skirts pushed softly at his legs as she gazed up at him. "I would never kiss a stranger—save for a dashing criminal who stole my heart and rode away."

"Now you are playacting again," he told her, a genuine smile coming unbidden to his mouth.

"Am I?"

She seized the embroidered lapels of his short jacket and pulled him toward her, rising on her toes. Her lips met his—so soft, so sweet—and parted just long enough for him to wonder if it were possible to become drunk on a kiss.

For he had never kissed a woman before. Oh, he had idly speculated, dreamed once or twice, but opportunities along that line had never exactly flung themselves at him. Not until now, with a girl he might not meet again until she was married.

When she released him, he dragged in a breath and wondered that his knees had not given out. "You—you seem to be quite skilled at stealing kisses," he finally said, when speech was possible.

"That was my first time. Was it acceptable?" she asked a little anxiously.

Her honesty took his breath away once more. "It was my first time, too, so I am no authority. But I can say that it was not at all like kissing my cousins. In fact, I … I believe I shall never be the same again."

"Truly?" Anxiety turned to a glow of delight in a second. "Shall we make a second attempt?"

The Viceroy—the captain—the horse and cart—all his most pressing concerns vanished like a wisp of mist under the heat of blinding day as her lips met his once more. An aeon passed in which stars whirled and galaxies formed … and he realized that he must breathe or he would be the one lying unconscious in the bottom of the cart.

"Isabela—"

"I know," she gasped. "I forgot to breathe."

"And I forgot my friend, for the moment. But he still needs me, and—and I still must go."

"One moment." She clutched his arm, and for a dizzy second he thought she meant to kiss him a third time. "I forgot to tell you. Why kissing you should make me remember, I do not know."

"It has rather rearranged my thinking. I would not be surprised if it has rearranged yours, too."

He had never seen anything so enchanting as the dimples at each corner of her mouth.

"You must not say such things. This is serious, and I can hear the horse leaving the stable."

He could, too, and the captain would be worried, thinking something had happened to him. "What, then?"

"I came down to the kitchen in the night because I could not sleep, and surprised one of the Viceroy's doctors in a welter of vials and grains."

That did not sound very newsworthy—certainly less important than a third kiss. "He was likely compounding a tincture. Considering what you and I both believe, I have advised the prince not to drink it."

"That was wise. For he packed up his ingredients and instruments hastily when he saw me, and bowed himself out of the room before I could say a word."

"Are they so secret?"

"When I took the lamp over to where he had been working, a few grains of rye had fallen on the floor."

"What tincture requires rye, I wonder? Besides whiskey, and he's not going to make that overnight."

"They were not healthy grains."

He stared at her, the first waves of horror washing over

him as she reached into the pocket of her dress and pulled out three or four grains of rye—distended, discolored, elongated with the fungus.

All thoughts of kissing fled as they stared together at the damning evidence.

"Ergot," he whispered. "We were right. I should have recognized it that first night when I smelled his glass." He closed his eyes in self-condemnation. "Why did I not take it to the apothecary sooner?"

"The Viceroy is going to die, isn't he?" she whispered, tears already starting in her eyes.

"No, he isn't," Evan said fiercely. "Not if I can get him to the train and—"

A second too late, he closed his mouth with a clack.

Her gaze fixed on his, Isabela stopped breathing.

The very sun stopped moving in the sky, and the cool breeze off the ocean ceased its whispering in the branches.

And then she exhaled, and time lurched into motion once again. "I knew it."

"You knew he was being poisoned."

"I knew it was not the Viceroy, there at breakfast with Senora Fremont."

"How?" Oh God, they were undone!

"It is Joe the translator … is it not?" She struggled for calm, to keep her breathing even, but he could see the effort it cost her. Anyone else would have fainted with the shock—or run screaming for the prince's guard.

"How could you tell?"

"I have seen the resemblance, but more than that—Papa and Mama may be willing to believe the prince has miraculously begun his recovery, because they are devout and see miracles everywhere. But I know how ill he was. A man does not recover so easily from ..." Her hand tightened, and she thrust the grains back into her pocket. "What are you planning to do?"

"To see him back to health." There was no point in lying, and no time to do so anyway. "You have been so good to help us. Are you going to tell your father?"

"So that the poisonous doctors in the Ambassador's employ can go on with their work? Hardly. No, I am going to hold that horse's head myself until I see my prince safely in that cart and away down the hill. You will tell me when he has recovered?"

"I will send a message. Coded somehow, in case it is intercepted." He did not know how he might do that from the river fastnesses of the witches, but now was not the time for doubt.

"I will wait for it." She took his hand. "Come. Stealing a kiss was only for practice. Now we are going to steal a prince."

CHAPTER 7

*G*loria was so frightened that the de la Carrera family would see through the hoax that her insides felt as though they had turned to ice water. It was all she could do to make inaudible replies, leaving Joe to carry off the deception. How he was managing it with such style and confidence was more than she could fathom, but here they were, safely back in the Viceroy's room, the majordomo fussing about with the tall porcelain pot of coffee and giving orders to the servants about the laying of the breakfast table. The earlier tray had been whisked away, the nosegay of flowers put in a vase on the table.

No one was the wiser. They had pulled off the first twenty minutes of a deception that could last a month—or a year.

Joe folded himself on to the sofa as though the effort of walking to the dining room had exhausted him—though perhaps it was merely the strain of acting. She had the presence of mind to say, "May I get you a cold cloth, Your Serene Highness?"

At his nod, one of the servants dipped a napkin in the chipped ice that cradled a green glass pitcher of freshly squeezed orange juice. She dabbed his forehead, hoping her features were arranged into a suitable expression of wifely concern, with no evidence of the hysterical gibbering that bubbled in her brain like a flock of panicked birds.

When the meal was arranged, she pulled herself together. "Thank you," she said to the servants, who bowed themselves out. When the majordomo made as if to serve them, she rose from the sofa. "I shall serve His Serene Highness, thank you, senor. His appetite, as you know, is delicate."

"Si, Dona—er, Senora—er—"

"You may call me Senora Fremont until the bull of annulment arrives. Oh, and should Captain Fremont wish to bid us good-bye, please show him in."

But Captain Fremont, as she was informed an hour or two later after she and Joe had demolished their breakfast, had been so overcome with grief at the destruction of all his hopes of happiness that he had left the house with Senor Evan Douglas and his translator, and the majordomo did not believe that he would be back. "He made some mention to Senorita Isabela of boarding the noon train, Senora, and since it has come and gone I can only assume that he was successful."

Thank goodness she was sitting, so that the blow of this news did not fell her like a tree.

He had gone!

Gloria had known he must—had known that the Viceroy's safety was the reason for this mad ruse—but still! Until now, she had not realized to the fullest extent how much of her heart she had given him for safekeeping ... and how hollow she felt without that vital organ. Now she was without his support, his unconscious grace, his humor, his silent confidence that simply got things done where other men would flail and bluster.

She was on her own.

No. She was not, and she must never forget it.

She had Joe and Ella, two stalwart friends who were risking their lives with every breath to help her in her mission. She must never think of herself as being alone again. Every thought, every movement must be carried out with the welfare of all three of them in mind.

"The poor man." She gave a wobbly smile to Joe. "I am sorry that your affection for me has meant such a reversal to his life."

"I am not." Joe squeezed her hand in acknowledgement of the smile, and pushed himself to a sitting position. "I am sure you wish to rest after such an emotional day. Senor, are there rooms prepared for my lady?"

"Indeed there are," he said. "The room overlooking the ocean, recently occupied by Senor Douglas and his translator, has been made ready for you." The majordomo bowed low. "If you will follow me."

All Gloria wanted was to kneel by the window and wonder how far down the track the train bearing Stanford and Evan and the Viceroy could be. Would they reach Nuestra Senora de los Angeles this evening? Would the train bearing the bull of annulment pass them going the other way?

But if she had craved solitude, her craving was not to be satisfied.

"Here you are at last," Ella said, closing the door firmly on the majordomo's bowed form. "We have been waiting for ages."

"Why? What is it? Do you have a message from the captain? Why didn't you come to fetch me?" Her questions tumbled out so fast the words practically ran together.

And then Gloria realized they were not alone, and snapped her mouth shut in case something far more condemning came out of it. She made as though to dip a curtsey to Senorita Isabela as she rose gracefully from the window seat, when the girl put out a hand to stop her.

"No, no, Senora. It is I who must curtsey to you." And she did, graceful as a bending willow. Then she dimpled with mischief. "Though the rules of precedence are so muddled at the moment that it is difficult to know for certain."

"What ... do you mean?" Gloria glanced at Ella for help, but her friend only shook her head, as though telling her, *wait —it only gets better.*

"For instance, as the wife of the captain for another day or so, you could expect a curtsey from an unmarried girl such as I. Though, since I outrank you here in the Royal Kingdom, that could be disputed. As the fiancée of the Viceroy, of course, you may expect every woman in the land to do you honor. But as the fiancée of Joe San Gregorio—why, you would be lucky to get a bob from a servant. It is terribly confusing, isn't it? Is it like this in the Fifteen Colonies?"

Silence fell, in which the girl's cheerful words seemed to clang in the air, like the mission bells.

Like an alarm. *Fear, fire, foes!*

Gloria stared at her, hardly able to comprehend—to believe she meant what she had said. "You—what are you saying, Isabela?" In her extremity, she used her first name.

The girl was lucky Gloria did not take her by the shoulders and shake a sensible sentence out of her. *"What are you saying?"*

"Simply that I know. It has taken me some hours to adjust to the discovery, I will admit. But I am all right now. Senor Douglas and *el Capitan* have safely boarded the train with—" Her voice dropped to a whisper. "—with our prince. I watched from the hill with the horse and cart we used to get him to the train, and saw it with my own eyes."

"You—" Gloria was going to be sick. She had made a pig of herself with the fresh orange juice, and now she was going to regret it. Deep, even breaths, that was the ticket. She must keep herself under control. "You know?"

"Oh, yes, as soon as you entered the dining room. Such a healthy-looking man could not be the Viceroy, despite the so strange similarity between them. Joe did his best to seem ill, but I see things that others do not."

"Clearly," Gloria managed. "What are you going to do?"

Should she offer money? What could she offer the daughter of a grandee, who had known nothing but luxury her entire life? Even one of the precious gold guineas in her corset was probably less than Isabela's pocket money for a month. What could she offer the girl for her silence? A place at court? A position of honor?

"Do?" Isabela looked puzzled. "Why, I shall put on my own domino and join the masquerade. Though I must say, I never saw such daring in all my life. I hope *you* know what you are doing."

"I do not."

"Then you will need help."

"And … and at what cost will this help come?" Gloria

braced herself. "I have only a little gold, but you are welcome to it if you will keep our secret."

The light faded from Isabela's face and she seemed to draw back, to take on dignity as a woman draws on a cloak against the cold. "Do you imagine me capable of blackmail?" The gentle consonants fell with the sting of hail.

"I only met you two days ago, so I have no way to know," Gloria said, shock making her rather more blunt than such a delicate situation called for.

Isabela lifted her chin. "Then know this—Senor Douglas trusts me implicitly. It was I who learned of the exact poison the doctors have been using on my prince. When I shared my discovery with Evan this morning, it became even more urgent that he take the prince into his care. If I trust him to do that, and he trusts me to keep Joe's secret safe, then what is your excuse?"

She might be small and dainty, and a little spoiled, and very young, but Isabela de la Carrera y Borreaga was no fool.

Gloria crossed the carpet to her, hand outstretched. "I have none. I spoke out of fear, not knowledge or suspicion, and I beg you to forgive me."

The tilted chin did not lower, but the dimples at the corners of her mouth flickered back. "I forgive you. And I in my turn must beg you to forgive me. Mama says a lady must control her tongue, and she is perpetually reminding me I am not a lady yet."

"I need to learn the same lesson," Gloria confessed. "We will help each other, then—with that, and other things."

"Agreed." Isabela smiled happily at her and Ella.

"You have not said what the poison was," Ella reminded their new ally.

"Ah. So I have not." She pulled something out of her pocket and showed them.

While Gloria gazed at three ugly, misshapen seeds in her palm without recognition, Ella drew in a breath. "Ergot. No wonder he was hallucinating and having such terrible dreams. To say nothing of losing his appetite and his vigor."

"What is ergot?" Gloria had never heard the word before.

"It is a fungus that grows on rye," Isabela explained. "When it is ingested, it produces effects that may be mistaken for— well, for being possessed of the Holy Spirit."

"I see." How horrible, to have one's mind nearly broken because of the ulterior motives of others! "You believe the doctors to have been administering it to him?"

"I know it. I caught one of them compounding the tincture late last night. He cleared away everything, but missed these few grains on the floor." She gazed at the damning evidence, then pocketed them once again. "I only hope that wherever Evan is taking him, there are excellent doctors."

"I believe there are," Ella said solemnly. "You will forgive me if I do not say the name of the town aloud, in case the worst happens and we are questioned."

"Of course." Isabela smiled. "Evan has promised to bring our prince back to us safe and well, and I trust him to keep his promise."

"In the meanwhile," Ella said a little hesitantly, "I wonder if I could impose on you for some help?"

"Of course," the girl said promptly. "You have but to name it and it is done."

"Joe—er, His Serene Highness, well—before he meets anyone outside the family, he needs lessons in how to be a prince. Do you know anything of that?"

"I thought he did rather well," Gloria put in. "I was paralyzed with terror, and he carried the entire performance."

"He did well," Isabela said, nodding, "but there is a great difference between the informality of a family meal and the kind of state engagements he will be expected to perform. I have had limited experience there myself, but luckily so has he. He has not even been on the throne a year, and with so much of the time spent in the sickroom, he has not been much in the public eye." She glanced at Gloria with a twinkle. "But with an engagement to announce, there will be more dancing and feasting and progressing about the kingdom than we have seen in many a long year."

Gloria's knees really did fold up this time, and she sank into a chair. "Thank heaven I have my friends about me." She reached for both girls' hands, and squeezed them. "For if I did not, I would not have the courage to attempt ... what we are about to attempt."

Ella looked pleased, and squeezed her hand in return. But the soft brown eyes of Isabela, inexplicably, were welling up with tears.

"My dear friend, what have I said?" Gloria asked anxiously.

"I—it is just that—well, I have never had a friend," Isabela said a little shyly. "I have my sisters, but I cannot say we have ever been friends, exactly. And there are the daughters of the other grandees, but they are so far away, and friendships often fade like flowers between fiestas. It feels ... strange ... to be called so. Strange, and wonderful, like so many other things that have happened today."

"Strange ... and wonderful," Gloria repeated. "I, for one, am happy to call the two of you my friends. If we are to pass through the fire like Shadrach, Mesach, and Abednego, then I am glad that of all women in this part of the world, I am in your company." She raised an eyebrow in Ella's direction. "Perhaps we might even call her sister, one day."

Ella's smile broke out in the sweet, irrepressible way she had. "I hope so. She would look lovely in red roses."

"What on earth do you mean?" Isabela demanded. "Red roses are for married love—certainly not for girls such as we."

"Ah, but for girls such as *we*, they are for blood, and sister-hood, and power," Gloria told her. "When the time is right, we will show you what we mean."

Ella nodded. "I wish I had my paint-box at this very moment. If Joe is to be made to look ill, it would have come in handy."

"Paint? You mean rouge, and kohl?" Isabela asked. "I am not supposed to know about such things, but Mama has them in her dressing-table. Would you like me to fetch them for you?"

"It will be a start," Gloria said after another exchange of speaking looks with Ella. "Before the announcement is made, we must transform my fiancé into a prince. But first, we will start with the magic of the paint-box."

THE NEXT MORNING, following the arrival of the train from the south, the bishop of Mission San Luis Obispo de Tolosa himself waited upon Joe and Ignatio de la Carrera. Gloria was already in Joe's sitting room eating the private breakfast that had appeared without its being asked for, following the pattern Gloria had established and the household had observed the day before. When the grandee and the monk were shown in, she dabbed her lips with a napkin and rose.

The two men bowed low to their prince, and Gloria curt-seyed to her host and the representative of the church, who held a leather folder similar to the one Joe had received earlier and which had accompanied the Viceroy on his journey to the river canyons.

"Your Serene Highness," the monk said, "I am honored to deliver to you the bull of annulment, signed by his grace the Archbishop at Nuestra Senora de los Angeles." With a bow, he handed it over to Joe, who unfastened the leather strings.

The thick paper was not as heavily decorated as his certificate of citizenship, but that was not important. What was important was that as Joe translated for her, his words dissolved the thing that had become most precious to her in all the world.

Know all by the law of the Most High and the will of His Holy Church and its representative on the earth, Carlos Felipe, Viceroy of the Royal Kingdom of Spain and the Californias, Defender of the True Faith, and General of the Armies of Heaven, that the marriage contracted by Gloria Diana Meriwether-Astor of Philadelphia and Stanford Fremont the Third of Santa Croce parish in this the Royal Kingdom of Spain and the Californias on the twenty-seventh day of February, 1895, is declared null and void for reasons of nonconsummation.

Let it stand as a witness that these persons have contravened the commandments of God to be fruitful and multiply, and are hereby deprived of the benefits of the sacrament of marriage and their vows rendered silent forevermore.

Signed this day in the presence of God and his servants, by the Archbishop of the Mission of Our Lady of the Angels.

Goodness. It took almost as many words to unmake a marriage as it did to create it. But in one thing at least it was utterly wrong. *Their vows rendered silent forevermore.* That was simply impossible. No matter what words she might be required to recite to Joe in the pursuit of her mission, her vows to Stanford were written on her heart, and they would never be silent as long as she was alive to remember them.

"Thank you, Your Excellency," Joe said, folding up the document and setting it aside. "I am both humbled and heartened by the church's support in this matter."

The monk inclined his tonsured head. "Your Serene Highness's wish to take this lady in marriage is worthy and good. His grace the archbishop, however, wishes to caution you against hasty decisions while you are unwell. Perhaps an engagement of some months may allow you to regain your health?"

"Perhaps it might, but … when you speak of decisions, what do you mean?"

"It is understandable that when you return to San Francisco de Asis and take up the reins of government, there will be many decisions which can be made by you alone."

"Of course. And I will make them with the support, encouragement, and advice of my bride-to-be."

The man's gaze flickered to Gloria and back again. "It might be wise to give the people a little time to absorb the happy news, sire. They are distracted by the preparations for war, and while a royal engagement will lift the spirits of even the most hardened soldier, we must remember that the kingdom comes first, and further changes may be best left to the future."

"I appreciate your advice." Joe inclined his own head

graciously. "However, it is my firm belief that one or two changes of an economic nature can only benefit the kingdom, especially one on the brink of war. We will make the formal announcement of our engagement tomorrow, if that is convenient for your household, sir?"

Thus addressed, Ignatio de la Carrera flushed with pleasure. "I can think of nothing more convenient, sir. The rancho will be roaring with joy."

Joe looked a little pained at the thought, and touched his forehead with his napkin. "Once we have announced our engagement, then, the next announcement will be that the skies shall be opened to airships."

"Sire!" The monk stepped back, as though Old Scratch himself had risen up through the floorboards. "That is blasphemy!" He closed his eyes and began to whisper what Gloria could only assume was a prayer for his prince.

"I am the Defender of the True Faith, Your Excellency. It is not likely that I would commit that sin. No, it is time that my kingdom came into the nineteenth century, with every mode of transport available to assist in the betterment of its citizens' lives. I will dictate my wishes to all the missions, if you will be so good as to send men with them."

"Your Serene Highness, I must protest! This goes against every tenet of our faith!"

"Not *every* tenet," Joe said gently. "Holy Writ cautions us not to fly in the face of God. It is only man, with his faults and poor understanding, who has translated this to mean we should not have airships. Nothing in the word of God forbids it, and—" He paused until the monk opened his eyes, clearly fearing the worst. "And I am under no obligation to obey the commandments of men. Only of the God I serve."

Gloria barely kept herself from staring at him in astonishment. Where had a rough-and-tumble man, the son of a witch, learned such things about Holy Writ? She must ask him at the first opportunity, for clearly there were depths to her *faux* fiancé that she had not appreciated before.

Certainly the bishop did not appreciate them in the least. "It is impossible," he said flatly.

"With God, all things are possible," Ignatio de la Carrera found his voice long enough to reply.

Joe beamed. "Exactly. That is the point of learning, is it not? To correct the old and misunderstood, and apprehend the new?" His gaze settled on the bishop, and Gloria felt the tension thicken in the air. "It is important to me that the holy brothers are in agreement with me."

"You will find it an uphill battle," the monk said bluntly. "This is too much—too sudden—it must be studied, discussed, a Council held—"

"It must be obeyed," Joe said quietly. "What I ask of the missions is little enough. An engagement. A few airships. I am not advocating witchcraft, you know."

The monk swallowed his horror that such a word had even been introduced into the conversation. "I—I did not say you were, sire."

"The wisdom of the holy brothers has been my mainstay since I took the throne. But if some prove themselves wiser than others, it is not inconceivable that they should be elevated to positions of greater authority. Do you not agree?"

The monk stared at him. Joe's gaze did not falter. Gloria and de la Carrera did not dare move. Or breathe.

At last the monk's Adam's apple bobbed, and Gloria dared to draw a breath. "Your Serene Highness is the anointed of

God, both by blood and by revelation," he said at last. "I will consult with the monks here, and send the messages expressing your wishes. But sire, I beg that you prepare yourself for the reluctance of those ... less visionary."

"I shall," Joe assured him. "Your loyalty is a gift from God, and deeply appreciated."

Gloria had no doubt that a generous donation to the church would be forthcoming, and possibly a promotion to a mission more prosperous and influential even than this one. But it was a low price to pay to make the bishop of San Luis Obispo de Tolosa the narrow edge of the wedge.

For once their plans were under way in truth, airships would be the least of the country's concerns.

CHAPTER 8

*T*he last time Evan had been in the river crossing of
Santa Croce, he had been operating the behemoth
in the firm belief that his pursuit of Gloria would soon find
her, if not well, then at least alive. Now, here he was in the
company of her husband and the Viceroy, who could be said
to be alive, if not well.

He was breathing. That was something.

The boy who looked so much like Joe had slept all the way
across the country, though Evan suspected it was not true
sleep at all, but a state of semi-consciousness that was frightening in itself, since he murmured and flinched as though he
were seeing terrible visions. With every mile the train
progressed away from the coast and its chain of missions,
Evan gave thanks on one hand and prayed on the other that it
would go faster—faster.

"Come," Captain Fremont said as the train finally rocked
to a standstill at the station. "This is just a whistle stop. We do
not have much time. Riley, we must leave the bags to you."

Fortunately, they did not have much in the way of luggage. One canvas holdall contained all their effects, leaving both Evan and the captain free to manage the Viceroy on and off the trains and into seats next to a window, where he could slump against the isinglass and give a fair impression of a man asleep.

"There is the *Queen*," the captain said with visible relief. "They got our message. A more welcome sight I could never hope to see, save that of my wife with my ring on her finger once again."

Evan had to agree that the sight of Gloria and Joe safe and well was nearly all he could ask for in this life, too, except perhaps another glimpse of Isabela.

"I dunno why we're putting up with him," Riley grumbled. "If it was me, you'd have left me in San Luis to sleep it off."

"If it was you, you're right," the captain said cheerfully, his shoulder under that of the Viceroy. With Evan on the boy's other side, they walked him through town toward the moorage on the river. "But Joe is ill, not drunk, and he's too valuable to Evan here to leave him lying about like unclaimed luggage."

"It's not catching, is it?"

"Not at all," Evan assured the man. "He suffers from an affliction of the brain, with results similar to being struck on the head. That is why he cannot wake up."

Satisfied that his own brain was in no danger of catching something nasty, Riley bounded up the gangplank and into the small crowd of the riverboat's crew, who were waiting at the rail.

"Welcome back, Captain!" a man called from the wheelhouse, having already begun the ignition sequence for the great steam engines in the rear. "We'll have her under way in a jiffy."

"The faster, the better," the captain called back. "We've got a sick man here who needs Clara's care without delay."

The captain guided Evan and the Viceroy into a cabin at the stern, and with no little effort, they got him laid out in the bunk tucked into its snug cabinet. "Is there anything else we can do for him?" The captain was breathing as heavily as Evan himself, with the effort of having hefted someone the length of a country over two days.

"I do not think so," Evan said. "I believe the best thing for him is to rest undisturbed."

"He won't have any trouble with that. Come. I have an itch to take my own wheel again and pretend that I have some control over something."

Under the captain's experienced hand, the riverboat pulled away from the dock and was soon churning its way upriver. The banks turned to walls, which soon turned to cliffs. Had Evan guided the behemoth through that twenty-foot pool there, or gone ashore at that grassy inlet where a fall of rock had formed a meadow over the centuries? Had that been where he had sat and rested, while a boat that might even have been this one passed him without his realizing what it was?

For the river was considerably deeper. Then, Evan had been able to walk in the middle of it for some miles, but now he doubted it would be possible for even five. How were the witches' villages constructed, and where were they located that they were in such imminent danger of being flooded?

An hour before sunset, he had his answer. With a shout, someone in the crew waved at something overhead. In a massive hollow that had been weathered out of the cliff nestled a village like a toy in a child's hand. Evan gazed upward, astonished, at the series of stone houses and towers, from one of the windows of which fluttered a red cloth.

The riverman must have a sweetheart there.

But they did not stop. On the contrary, the engines worked mightily against the stronger current, the great bronze and iron wheels in the stern turning and meshing and heaving them through the water at a pace faster even than a steambus on a straight road.

They passed under an arch of red rock, rounded a point, and Evan caught at the rail as the captain pulled back on the four acceleration levers and cut the engines. They coasted past what was clearly a quay, or a series of them, one holding nothing more than a tubular metal tank bobbing in the wake of their passing. Then, with the skill of a dancer turning his partner on the ballroom floor, the captain brought the riverboat about in midstream and nosed it up to the quay facing downstream, as neatly as you please.

Already there were people streaming out of the doors and hopping over the low stone walls of the village, which tumbled from its original hollow in the cliff down a slope to end in a series of terraces and sunning decks, much in the style of a Greek village Evan had once seen an etching of in a magazine. With a tingling sense of shock, he realized that these were not people—they were skeletons—no—impossible. Skeletons could not move with such grace and speed, nor snatch up their ruffled skirts in order to run.

Las brujas.

Evan let out the breath he was holding. At last, he was seeing the legendary witches of the river canyons with his own eyes. Women who struck terror into the hearts of the Californio soldiers, though the latter would be the first to laugh with false bravado and say, "They are just women, the dregs of society."

They did not look like dregs. They looked positively terrifying.

And now the excited, streaming crowd parted to allow two women to descend the stone steps of the terrace closest to the water. One was tall and majestic, with the figure of a woman of some years and experience, an embroidered silk shawl over her shoulders and wrapped around her waist. The other was perhaps a head shorter and several pounds rounder, but no less the recipient of respect. Both wore crowns of red roses— and with a second shock, Evan realized where he had seen flowers arranged in that manner before.

At the ball at the rancho. Both Gloria and Ella had worn roses just like this. Did that mean they were witches, too? Why had they not told him?

But there was no time for questions. He jogged down the corridor to the captain's cabin to find the Viceroy exactly as he had left him, twitching and moaning. Captain Fremont came in and leaned over him, his face grave. "Let us get him ashore as quickly as we can. And do not forget to call him Joe."

"That should not be difficult. Every time I see him I think it is Joe."

"Good. There is time enough once he is recovered to allow a very few to know who he really is."

"Agreed."

They got the limp form upright between them, their shoulders taking his weight. The most difficult bit to manage was the gangway, where the captain went down first, being the taller man. The Viceroy's dragging toes had barely made landfall when Clara gasped and ran to intercept them.

"Who—who is this? Is it—? Can it be my—?"

Smoothly, the captain said, "This is Joe, your boy, Clara, come back to you after all these many months of imprisonment. He needs your skill immediately."

"What is wrong with—him?" Clara had turned white, her fingers cupping Joe's chin as she tried to pry open one eye. "Captain, please! What has happened?"

"He has been poisoned, ma'am," Evan told her. "Tincture of ergot. Can you help him?"

"Help—! Santa Maria and all her holy angels, there is nothing I would not do for my own—son! Come quickly. Bring him to my stillroom. We have no time to lose."

When he had deposited Joe's limp body on the cot in the neat chamber, Evan stretched his back and looked about himself. Shelves lined the walls, filled with bottles of liquids— yellow, green, brown, and red—and boxes and small bags that must contain seeds, bark, and powders. The ceiling beams had been made from individual logs, and from them hung bunches of herbs and the garlands of dried red chile peppers the Californios called *ristras*.

As Clara hurried from one shelf to another, she said over her shoulder, "And who are you, sir? How were you able to diagnose his poison?"

"My name is Evan Douglas, ma'am, and while I am a doctor by education, I have never practiced. Well, until I came out here, where it seems there is far more demand for cures of the body than cures of the mind."

"This is a hard country for those who do not respect it. Evan Douglas, are you? The ways of the Mother are mysterious indeed. Hand me that jar of salve, there at the end of the second shelf."

Evan fetched it for her. "He purged himself at the beginning of our journey two days ago, and he has not eaten anything since."

"I am not surprised. What do you know of ergot?"

Evan had been racking his brain over that very question since the moment Isabela had shown him the swollen grains back at the rancho. "I cannot remember much other than that it produces visions and stomach pain, and restlessness, all of which I have witnessed on the train. And constriction of the veins, if I am not mistaken. Some have been known to lose their limbs for lack of blood. Many die. Hence our urgency in reaching you instead of depending on the Californio apothecaries."

"No one is going to die on my watch," Clara said grimly. "Come. Our task is to restore the blood flow and to help him breathe. If you will prepare a tea of willow bark and ginger, I will apply this salve to his chest. You will find a kettle kept expressly for medical use in my kitchen next door. The steam engine that heats the village keeps it on a low boil constantly, for just such times as this."

While she unbuttoned the Viceroy's shirt, Evan loped out and found the kitchen. And then … for one stunned moment he forgot the urgency of his mission, and stared, unable to believe the evidence of his own eyes.

A woman in pants was bent over the boiler, clearly in the final stages of a repair. Or a theft. For she lifted a pipe bent in a double angle in the manner of David lifting the head of Goliath, while steam issued with a hiss from the aperture where it had been. "Aha! Got you. And no one will miss you, either, once I stick a bit of hose in there."

Wrench in one hand and pipe in the other, she turned to meet Evan's astounded gaze.

"Why, Evan! Where on earth did you spring from?" Alice Chalmers demanded. "Say, you ain't going to tell anyone I'm taking this part, are you?"

"No." It was all he could do to manage one word. So many questions crowded his tongue that he couldn't manage another.

"I'm building a submersible so we can blow up the dam— you may have seen it out at the quay. At the moment, it's just a boiler, but give me a few days with it and I'll surprise you. But what are you doing here?"

Under this fresh shock, his powers of speech came back. "You're alive! It is a miracle—I saw the Californios shoot down your ship. How did you survive?"

"By the skin of our teeth, as usual. What do you mean, you saw it? Where have you been all this time?"

"Attempting to rescue Gloria, and getting tricked by the Californios into walking their behemoth across the border. Being clapped in gaol. And being forced to work on the dam." Where he might have related this with some bitterness before, now all he could say was, "Alice, *I'm* going to blow it up, with the help of the behemoth."

"Are you, now? Maybe we'll both do it, one from each side. Is Gloria with you? She left here a couple of weeks ago with Captain Fremont. Have you seen them?"

"Yes. And no, she is not with me, though the captain is. It is a very long tale that I promise to tell you. But just now I must get what I came for without delay. You will be here when I return?"

"If I'm not, I'll be down at the water, or in the room where Ian is recovering. One of the witches shot him a few days ago. He's on the mend, but he's at that stage where everything hurts and nothing is right, so I'm glad I have the submersible to work on."

Most of this went straight past Evan's ears. "I will come find you as soon as I may."

Feeling rather as though someone had punched him in the belly—Alice and her crew were alive! And had saved themselves without his help!—he wrapped a cloth around the handle of the kettle and carried it into the stillroom, where Clara had finished administering the salve and was measuring ingredients for the tea into a trim brown teapot that would be at home in any English cottage.

"How will we get him to drink it?" Evan asked. "He has not regained consciousness."

Clara's brows were pinched, her eyes worried. "We must use a siphon once the mixture steeps and cools. His natural urge to swallow will assist us from there."

With gentle dexterity, she got the tea down the Viceroy's throat using a siphon with a long hose that might once have been a part of a riverboat engine, while Evan held his head. Then they laid him down, Clara plumping the pillow as though he were a child.

"Rest, *mi'jo*," she murmured. "Rest and I will return in an hour to give you more."

Mi hijo. My son.

"In the meanwhile, we must keep him warm." She tucked another quilt around him, this one embroidered with cheerful flowers. "And I must check on my other patient, too."

Evan accompanied her out of the stillroom and into a room down the corridor, where Captain Ian Hollys was sitting up in bed looking like a very grumpy bear.

"Devil take it, Clara, I must get up or I will simply go mad." His gaze collided with that of Evan, and he added, "Well, I'll be a swinging rope monkey—Mr. Douglas. Where did you spring from?"

"Alice's very words. I am very glad to see you alive, Captain."

"I am glad of it, too, though at some moments more than others. Can you convince this termagant here that I am perfectly capable of walking about, since she pulled the bullet out of my shoulder, not my leg?"

"He does not need to convince me," she chided him, checking his dressing with a no-nonsense skill that Evan envied. "You may get up for dinner, and not before."

"But—"

"Be quiet, or I will reconsider."

Fuming, Ian subsided. "You will allow Evan to stay, will you not? I am sure he has a tale to tell, and I could not be more anxious to hear it."

"He may stay for an hour, at which time I will need him to help with my other patient."

"What other patient? Has that she-wolf Gretchen been shooting every man she sees?"

"My translator," Evan said, before the captain's temper could get the better of him once more. "He has a brain fever. We have been carrying him on land, by train, and by riverboat for two days, all the way from San Luis Obispo de Tolosa."

Clara's eyes widened. "So far! You value his life very much indeed."

"I do." Best to keep it simple. "As do you, if I may be so frank as to say so."

But she only gazed at him for a moment in a most puzzling fashion before rising from the side of the bed. "One hour," she reminded them both as she passed under the curtain hanging across the aperture in the rock.

"If you see my wife," Captain Hollys called after her, "please send her in. I am sure she would like to hear Evan's tale as well."

"We will all hear it at dinner," Clara called from some distance down the corridor.

Even so, ten minutes later Alice pulled back the curtain and in came Jake and Benny Stringfellow with her.

"Look who I brought," she said, smiling.

"Mr. Douglas!" Benny exclaimed. "Ent I glad to see you! We thought you were dead."

"So did I, many times." He ruffled the boy's hair. "You've grown two inches, I'm quite certain. And Jake." He shook hands with Alice's navigator. "I'm glad you all are well. I saw you shot down over the mountains and feared the worst."

"For a few moments there, so did we." Jake returned his handshake with a firmness that surprised Evan. It was the grip of a man, not a boy any longer. A capable, quick-witted man whom Evan had no doubt could hold his own with anyone, whether it was in a room or a battle.

"Have you seen Gloria?" Jake asked. The man fell away for an instant, revealing the boy who had always had a soft spot for a woman out of his reach. "They told us she was married. Is that true?"

"Oh yes." Then he corrected himself. "I mean, she was. She is not married now. She is going to marry the Viceroy."

"What?" Four voices rose and cracked in utter disbelief.

"Come," he said, and settled on a carved trunk for want of any other seat. "Let us hear each other's stories, from the moment we last glimpsed each other during the Battle of Resolution. I am quite sure that there are parts on either side that we do not wish the entire village to hear."

CHAPTER 9

*J*t had been a long time since Alice had been struck speechless, but when some three-quarters of an hour later Evan finally got to the part where the Viceroy demanded the annulment of Gloria's marriage as the price for stopping the war, she sat there like a frog on a log, her mouth open in astonished dismay.

She was not alone. Jake had turned white, and then flushed a dangerous shade of red. "She ent going through with it, surely?" he croaked. "What did Captain Fremont have to say about this?"

"We were not privy to that," Evan said, "but wait until I tell you the next part."

"I don't think I'll survive the next part," Alice said faintly. What kind of man was this Viceroy to ask such a thing of a woman? Whether Gloria had married her riverboat captain as a means to an end or not, you just didn't go about annulling people's marriages to get your own way.

"It was Gloria's idea," Evan began. "You see, my translator Joe—"

"Yes, tell me about your translator Joe." The cool voice from the door made every head swing to look at Mother Mary, who came in with Clara and Captain Fremont. The two women did not look happy, and the captain was clearly trying to communicate something to Evan with eyebrows and fingers, but the latter only gazed at him in confusion.

"Go on," Clara said in that same cool, dangerous tone, most unlike her usual warm practicality. Alice had spent plenty of time in this sickroom, and she figured she'd seen Clara in any number of moods. But not one like this. A woman in a mood like this could pick up a pistol and shoot you without even giving you a reason why.

"I—I—why, you know, ma'am," Evan stammered. "Your son—we brought him across the country so you could treat him for ergot poisoning."

"My son."

Evan gazed at her helplessly. "He said he was your son. By the old Viceroy. Who took you against your will. Is that not true?"

"Shut up!" Mother Mary snapped. "How dare you!"

Poor Evan. He looked as though he was about to cry.

"*Madre*, perhaps you could tell us what is wrong?" Captain Fremont said gently.

"What is wrong is that you're lying to us, and I won't have it," Mother Mary said, her cheeks flushed with temper.

"Who is that boy in there?" Clara demanded of Captain Fremont. "Because he's not my son. I don't have a son. I have a daughter. You promised to bring both our daughters back to us, and you've broken your promise!"

Now even Captain Fremont was at a loss for words. "But— Daughter? Joe said he was your son."

"Where is she?" Clara practically shrieked.

"Who?"

"My daughter! The child of the old Viceroy, may his soul rot in hell for all eternity! The stepchild of that San Gregorio murderer, may he join him in his agony!"

"I ... I don't know any daughter." Both Evan and the captain looked about them, as though they wanted to take a step back, but in a room this small, there was nowhere to go. Nowhere to hide. Nothing to do but weather the storm of maternal rage—the most potent, unpredictable kind of all.

"Oh, for the Mother's sweet sake," Mother Mary said, clearly attempting to control herself. "Honoria is Clara's daughter. She was shanghaied in Santa Croce a year ago, where she had been masquerading as a man in order to stay alive while she spied out the land for us. The first we heard of her in months was a letter from Ella a few days back saying that she was calling herself Joe and acting as your translator."

Now Evan looked like the frog on the log. His mouth opened and closed, but no sound came out.

"Honoria?" Captain Fremont whispered. "That was *Honoria?* I have not seen her in a couple of years, but still, I would have known—it's—"

"Impossible," Evan finally got out. "There must be some mistake. I lived in the same cell with Joe and two other men for weeks. I would have known if he—if she—if it was a woman. For heaven's sake, he relieved himself into a bucket in the corner, right in front of me!"

Clara marched out and came back a minute later with a device that looked like a fine leather cucumber attached to a hose. She was in such a state of emotion that it trembled with the force of her grip. "May Lin made this for her, so she could go into the country as a spy and pass for a man. She has done it before—my warrior daughter, who can wrestle a man to the ground with one hand and shoot a deer with a pistol in the other." She flung the device into the corner. "Now, tell me once and for all where my daughter is, and who that boy is in my stillroom. Because I have a guess, and I for dang sure don't want to be right."

Evan and Captain Fremont exchanged a glance, and this time it seemed as though the message was communicated clearly. "That boy in there is Carlos Felipe, the Viceroy of the Royal Kingdom of Spain and the Californias," the captain finally said.

Mother Mary seemed to sag as all the breath hissed out of her lungs. "You've kidnapped the Viceroy?" she gasped.

Sitting on the bunk next to Ian, Alice fumbled for his hand and gripped it as though it was her only anchor in a fierce current. They were all about to be swept away. What in the name of heaven had Evan and the captain done?

"And Honoria? Ella?" Clara croaked. "If he is not in his palace where he belongs, and they are not here in the village where they belong, then where are they?"

The captain took a deep breath. "They are with Gloria, at the house of the Borreagas in San Luis Obispo de Tolosa. My wife and your daughter are very likely getting ready to announce their engagement and stop the war."

"I CANNOT DO THIS," Joe moaned for the third time, his forehead on the cool pane of the window. He even banged it a little in his distress. "How can I carry off this bamboozle? How can I fool anyone? And how can I announce our engagement when it is the last thing either of us wants?"

"Both of us want to stop the war," Gloria reminded him, also for the third time. "Courage, my friend. It is lucky you are supposed to be so ill and can retire early without saying much. But still we must put on a good show—still we must dance."

"I am a terrible dancer."

"I am not," she assured him. "Never fear, I will not allow you to put a foot wrong."

"Neither will I," Isabela put in, having given up the lessons in protocol for the time being. She knew an astonishing amount for a girl so sheltered, but not everything that a prince could be expected to know. The rest—politics, dealing with the Privy Council, military maneuvers—he would learn on the fly, much as the Viceroy had likely been doing for the months he had been on the throne. "But I must say that there will be many more ladies who will require your notice this time. The invitations have gone out to every rancho in the kingdom by train and fast rider, and I cannot imagine that much but illness or death would prevent everyone's coming. Such a fiesta has not been seen in two generations."

Joe groaned and scrubbed his face with both hands. "I will never remember them all."

"You are not meant to. That is why your majordomo will be at your elbow in the receiving line, whispering the names of the families. Just be glad this is happening at short notice. If you had to sit through the *cuento* that the singers are no doubt composing for the occasion on top of it, you might fall asleep —and that would be dreadfully bad manners."

"Buck up, Joe. It is time to dress." As Gloria and Ella left the room, the majordomo and his staff streamed in, ready to dress and lecture and inform poor Joe of the protocol of such a momentous occasion—one that had not taken place in the kingdom in twenty-five years.

Following the announcement to the family, Gloria had been offered a staff of her own, but she had gratefully declined. The fewer people who had close access to them, the better, and Ella's skills as a lady's maid were not to be discounted. All those hot afternoons playing dress-up were certainly standing them both in good stead now.

The one thing she had accepted was the offer of the skills of every single seamstress connected to the rancho, the mission, and the village below. No more secondhand dresses for her, no sir! It had only been a matter of a few days, but already she had enough ball gowns, day dresses, riding habits, blouses, and underthings to fill six leather-bound trunks. She had taken the reins there, bringing the fashions of London and Philadelphia into the Royal Kingdom with a sheaf of sketches and strict instructions as to décolletage, length of trains, appropriate fabrics, and trims.

The fiesta dresses were lovely, but one could not wear ruffles and ribbon trim every hour of every day. A linen skirt notable more for its stylish cut than its embellishment said a lot about a woman's opinion of herself—and thus influenced the opinions of others.

Tonight, for this momentous occasion, she had chosen a midnight-blue silk cut low in the bosom to accommodate the royal sapphires, trimmed in lace and illusion so fine it looked as though a cloud had settled about her shoulders. Ella set the sun tiara upon her hair and pinned it in place, then gently turned her around to face the cheval glass.

"If anyone was born to be a princess, it is you," Isabela said with admiration. "How I wish I had golden hair!"

Gloria stared at the stranger in the mirror with her uptilted chin and breathtaking jewels.

"But you and I both know I was not," she said softly. "I am simply the daughter of an arms dealer, attempting to deceive your family and all these well-meaning and honestly happy people."

"But you'll look wonderful doing it."

"I cannot go out there like this. Not without my roses, to remind me of who I am." She passed an arm about Ella's shoulders. "How can we accommodate both roses and diamonds?"

There was a question she'd never thought she would ask in a million years. Until this moment, she had never worn diamonds—her mother had always said they were only for engaged or married women. *Pearls are suitable for girls*, whispered her long-ago voice in Gloria's mind, and then faded.

For she was not a girl anymore.

Ella gazed at her thoughtfully. "We could tuck them in the back."

"But I wish them to be seen. They are part of us. They mean something—and when I lose my courage, I need to be able to see them."

"We could paint up." Ella grinned audaciously, and Gloria believed she half meant it.

But Isabela was cut of more practical cloth. "As far as everyone knows, you will be Vicereine. You could wear a canvas coat and riding boots to your engagement party and they would accept it. And at the next fiesta, everyone would be wearing canvas and leather."

"So then ... how many people among the rancho families are aware of what the roses mean?"

"All of them—the women, at least," Isabela said, to Gloria's astonishment. "Men do not pay attention to the adornments of women. Have you not seen our embroidered blouses?"

"Of course." Most of the women wore them for everyday, with bright sashes and the ruffled skirts, in a constantly moving panoply of color. "But what does that have to do with—"

"It is our language of flowers," Isabela said. "It is how the women of the various families identify one another—and how we find our friends. It is how we speak to one another when words may not be used. Red roses mean love unto death, which I expect is why the witches wear them."

"But the rancho women? Surely they do not think themselves witches."

"You might see more than you think if you look closely at the embroidery," Isabela said. "You might find women loyal to the witches' cause, though of course to say so aloud means treason."

Gloria turned to Ella. "Why did you not tell me this?"

"I thought you knew. You borrowed my blouses, all embroidered with roses and other flowers. If roses mean something in our hair, then of course they mean something on our clothes."

"Well then." Gloria made up her mind. "If I was determined before, I am implacable now. We will simply make some adjustments to this tiara, and incorporate the roses into it. Let us experiment, shall we? I shall be very interested to see what fashions this will set."

"You might get more than you have bargained for," Isabela warned, helping Ella to lift the tiara off without damage to Gloria's crown of braids.

"If anyone can manage it, it is Gloria," Ella said loyally.

So it was that when Gloria met Joe at the top of the hacienda's staircase and they heard the blast of trumpets outside that was to announce them, his eyes widened. "Are you mad?" he whispered as they descended slowly, her right hand lying regally upon his left.

"I am perfectly sane," she whispered back. "I have never been one to cause a sensation, but then, usually all one wants for that is an opportunity."

The double doors were flung open and the lights and lanterns, the enormous crowd, the sound of music, all stilled into silence as Ignatio de la Carrera y Borreaga took a deep breath. His voice, as resonant as that of any Shakespearean actor on the London stage, projected all the way into the third balcony—or in this case, the gardens.

"Ladies and gentlemen of the Royal Kingdom, *gente de razón* and loyal subjects all, may I present His Serene Highness Carlos Felipe, Viceroy of the Royal Kingdom of Spain and the Californias, Defender of the Faith, and General of the Armies of Heaven ... and his intended bride, Miss Gloria Diana Meriwether-Astor of Philadelphia!"

The orchestra crashed into something joyful and Sousalike which Gloria deduced must be the national anthem. Under the singing and the cheers, she was deeply aware of the astonishment, the stares, the whispers as one woman turned to another, then another.

For in front of the rows of sapphires and emeralds signifying land and sea were pinned the red roses of love unto death ... which could very well be interpreted as a woman's feelings for her husband-to-be ... or as a silent rallying cry for independence, for female power, for a call to sisterhood.

Gloria smiled brilliantly, inclined her glittering head, and floated down the steps on Joe's arm, nodding to left and right as they proceeded to the receiving line.

She knew, as did every woman who had ever embroidered a flower on her blouse, that she had just thrown down the gauntlet.

Issued a challenge.

Made her position crystal clear.

It was only a matter of time before someone took up the challenge, and as His Excellency Augusto de Aragon y Villarreal, Ambassador to the Fifteen Colonies, bowed low in front of them, she knew exactly who that was going to be.

CHAPTER 10

"Your Serene Highness," the Ambassador said, including every last flourish that court etiquette demanded. "My surprise and delight know no bounds."

Why? Because you expected the Viceroy to be dead? Gloria did her best to keep her thoughts from her face, but she was not sure how well she succeeded.

Joe inclined his head. "I am happy you were able to come, sir, and leave the affairs of state temporarily. You are acquainted, of course, with my fiancée?"

The Ambassador's dark, liquid eyes with their disarmingly long lashes took in Gloria from her hem to the starry curve of the tiara. "I am," he said with admirable brevity. "I am very happy to see that rumors of your death have been greatly exaggerated, senorita."

Since you started them after failing to capture and kill me, I am sure you are. "I was fortunate to have been rescued after being swept into the river, sir. I can only attribute my good fortune now to the will of God."

"Some mighty hand has certainly been at work," he agreed smoothly. "One marvels at such power. Perhaps, if His Serene Highness will permit, you might favor me with a waltz this evening?"

So you can grill me like a fish? "Certainly, sir, though of course the Viceroy comes first in this as in all things."

"Of course," he murmured, and moved along the line to greet the family.

The challenge had been accepted, then. Neither she nor Joe had failed to notice the hitch in his gaze when it had reached her hair—a hitch that would not have been explained by the sight of the tiara. Jewels the man had to be familiar with. Roses he was not—at court, at least.

He was not alone. Gloria made careful note as the members of the Viceroy's cabinet and council were introduced. The eyes of some were raised to her own. Others raised theirs no higher than her bosom. And a few took in the roses, including the master of Carmel, who was also the Minister of Defense, with a degree of puzzlement and a sudden cooling of the temperature that told her this man at least might be either better informed or more observant than the average landowner.

When at last the reception line dwindled, the orchestra struck up a *contradanza*, which was similar enough to a reel or the English set dances she had learned at St. Cecelia's Academy for Young Ladies that Gloria felt quite comfortable at the head of the set. As the caller announced the figures and Joe translated, she whispered back, "I thought you were no dancer?"

"I'm not," he said. "But these are country dances. Everyone learns them at fiesta—even the Viceroy. I hope they play a very slow waltz, though, or I'll embarrass both of us."

Gloria found herself enjoying the dances, though occasionally Joe would turn in the woman's direction. That was quickly mended, though, for he was both graceful and light on his feet—and any lapse in memory could be attributed to his recent illness.

Joe made sure his endurance appeared to flag, though, after he had satisfied protocol by dancing with his hostess and the wives of at least three of the cabinet ministers. Then he retired to a small room, where both Gloria and Isabela saw to it that refreshments were brought in for him. She would have stayed had not the Ambassador followed her in.

The less time he spent with Joe, the better. "The waltz is next, Your Excellency," she suggested. "Since His Serene Highness wishes to rest a moment, perhaps we might take this opportunity?"

She now outranked him, and so he could not refuse her. With a graceful bow, he led her out on the floor, and inside of eight bars of music, he commenced to exact his revenge.

"May I say once again how delighted I am that you have not only survived, but ... how shall I put it ... come out on top as no woman in this country could have," he said pleasantly, holding her with utmost respect and guiding her expertly about the floor. They were attracting admiration already, and she must spar and riposte as best she might in full view of hundreds of people.

"However crudely put, I appreciate the sentiment," she said.

"How did you do it?"

"How does anyone fall in love?" she said with a smile. "One meets, one speaks, one cannot be parted. Is it not so?"

"One works very quickly when up until recently, one was married to another man."

So you know about that. What an excellent spy network you must have! "That, I must confess, is all His Serene Highness's work. He has quite swept me away."

"There are many grandees here who have all they can do to bow to one who has aspired to what rightly might be the honor of one of their daughters."

She allowed him to twirl her about and catch her again. "They may take it up with the Viceroy if they dare. But to no avail, I am afraid. He is quite fixed in his purpose."

"And what is that, pray? For I find it difficult to believe that a young man so recently ill and on the point of utter consumption by visions from God can now be thinking of marriage and children. Especially with a—forgive me, senorita—a foreigner."

"Perhaps the same God he worships has blessed him with a return to health. And I believe it is quite natural for a young man to think of marriage."

"Natural," the Ambassador repeated. "His recovery is quite astounding—perhaps not natural, but a miracle of San Luis, who was so poor yet so holy."

Does he suspect that it is Joe and not Felipe? No, surely not. "I quite agree," she said, devoutly hoping that her high color would be interpreted as the result of exertion and not alarm. "We must be sure to make a gift of gratitude to the saint."

"Perhaps you will do it when you leave and proceed north

to San Francisco de Asis. For of course you must. It is the seat of his government, and he has been away too long."

"Of course." *It is the center of your power, you mean, where you have many allies and we have none. And you sent him away so that you could poison him without guilt.* "But His Serene Highness must be fully recovered before he travels, as I am sure you understand. That does not mean he cannot govern, of course. Why, with his ministers here for the celebration, he might accomplish much of what must be waiting in San Francisco de Asis for his return. For of course there are matters that require *his* approval, not that of—" *Lesser men.* "—mere landowners, be they ever so noble."

"You have a quick apprehension of the responsibilities of princes, senorita."

"I have been well trained by my father."

"Ah yes. With this news of your engagement, I suppose the matter of the missing arms and mechanicals is now moot, is it?"

She barely resisted batting her lashes at him. "Why, I do not know that they are missing. I imagine they are still where you left them at Resolution. Goodness knows they are too heavy to be moved without the right equipment. Do you have plans to return on *Silver Wind* to collect the remainder?"

Any satisfaction she might have felt at batting the ball into his court was dashed a moment later as he said, "I have already dispatched troops. It is a small matter, and I am needed here."

"Oh? Not for much longer, surely, since the Viceroy is recovering more and more each day. I am sure he would have wished you to attend to the matter personally, as it was your commission from the beginning."

His eyes narrowed and he would have replied, but the music came to an end and he was forced to bow gallantly instead. "Perhaps you might honor me with another, senorita? I am anxious to continue our conversation."

Her smile held more relief at the conclusion of this round than politeness. "Perhaps later in the evening, sir. I must return to His Serene Highness in case I may perform some small service for him."

To that there was nothing he could say, and she sailed away, acutely conscious that to right and left, people were bowing and curtseying as she passed, as though her tiara were already a crown.

Let that stick in his craw and choke him.

"YOU MUST RETIRE SOON, before the Ambassador backs you into a corner," Gloria told Joe a few minutes later, in the quiet safety of the Viceroy's private parlor. "He smells a rat, though he cannot see one, and we would be foolish to oblige him."

"I agree." Joe ate a handful of dates with evident enjoyment. "I've missed these. Mama used to dry them for us."

Gloria did not think her tight stomach could manage even one. "He wants you back in San Francisco de Asis, so we must stall as long as possible."

Joe's intelligent gaze met hers. "I agree, it would be fatal to go. While I spent the first few years of my life in the palace, I do not remember much. At least here we have an ally, and some familiarity with the country."

Isabela dimpled at him. "I would suggest a relapse, but your recovery has been visible. And I am sure playing the invalid is irksome."

"It is. I am trapped in rooms when all I want to do is leap on a horse and ride as far away as I can." Joe's gaze turned to the window, but with the darkness outside and the lamplight within, all he could see was his own reflection.

"I have a suggestion," Gloria said. "The whole cabinet is here with their wives and families. What is to stop you from taking up the reins of government right here? We must be about the business of stopping the war."

Joe considered this for a moment. "You're right. It's going to be an uphill battle, but better here than there. The farther I must go from the river and home, the more danger we will both be in."

"And if we spend many days in building alliances and coercing people and arguing over dinner, it is the business of government and no one may question it without seeming negligent themselves."

Isabela cocked an eye at her. "You sound as though you have experience in such matters."

"Only in sitting on my father's right while he harangued the captains of industry at our dinner table. I watched him play one man's ambition and greed against another, never dreaming I might have to employ such tactics myself one day."

"I am glad one of us can—I am handier in a bar brawl than arguing at a table." Joe looked glum. "So of the cabinet members, which do you think might be most sympathetic to our cause?"

"I do not know, never having laid eyes on them before tonight," Gloria admitted, "but I will say that the Minister of Culture seemed to be honestly pleased that you were recovering and had found a woman to stand beside you."

Joe nodded. "Isabela, what do you know of these men?"

"I know that Papa and the Minister of Culture—Senor Peralta—correspond regularly, and he and his family visit more often than the usual once a year. He plays the cello while my father and mother sing."

"Are there others on equally good terms here?"

She named three more—the ministers of Education, Roads, and Cattle.

"The Minister of Cattle?" Gloria repeated. "That does not seem to be a title to carry much distinction."

"Oh, but it does," Isabela assured her. "Cattle—beef—is our principal export, and what sustains our lifestyle on the rancho. Without cattle, what would we grow?"

"Oranges? Wheat? Something of that nature?"

"There are not enough people in the Fifteen Colonies and abroad who enjoy oranges to make it profitable," Isabela said. "But imagine a table without beef. Unthinkable."

Gloria had never given it a thought. In Philadelphia, Paris, or London, one's cook went to the market and came back with a roast, and that was the extent of her experience with beef.

Ella, who had come in with the food as though to serve it, said, "We manage quite well without beef on the river. There is not much grazing land on the mesas, and chickens and pigs are better at surviving."

But Joe was not thinking of cattle, pigs, or chickens, it was clear. "So we may possibly count on four out of twelve. I believe we had best get to work as soon as may be. Isabela, would you ask your father to bring Senor Peralta here? We shall begin with him."

She slipped out, and in less time than it took for Joe to peel a prawn and eat it, Ignatio de la Carrera was bowing himself into the room, Senor Peralta on his heels.

"Your Serene Highness, it gives me great pleasure to see you so well," the minister said, taking in the napkin with which Joe wiped his fingers, and Gloria sitting beside him as though supervising the consumption of each morsel.

Which she was. They had fed a bit of everything to the cat in the garden, so far without ill effects. And Gloria had seen the sealed bottle of wine opened in front of her.

"Thank you, Minister," Joe said. "I think it must be the sea air and the beneficence of San Luis himself. Please, both of you, be seated."

The men settled on the sofa opposite, so comfortable in one another's company that Gloria could almost relax.

"I understand that members of my cabinet wish me to return to San Francisco de Asis, where there are weighty matters of government to attend to."

"True, Your Serene Highness, but no one wishes to interrupt your recovery with a journey, now that it has begun," the man assured him.

"Just so. I wonder if you would approach each of your number quietly, Senor Peralta, and advise them not to partake too heavily of their wine this evening. I wish the cabinet to be convened in the morning in order to receive the news you have for me, and to make you all cognizant of my own plans."

Peralta's eyebrows rose. "Of all things—save the news of your wedding, sir—that would please me most." He glanced at Gloria with a smile.

She returned it—a real smile, not the Vicereine's smile she had been practicing all evening.

"But surely you do not mean to interrupt the celebrations of your engagement, sir?" de la Carrera protested. "The singers have arrived, and tomorrow night will perform the *cuento* of your romance with the lovely Senorita Gloria. And then there is the rodeo, and at least three more balls—"

"My dear friend," Joe said, looking alarmed, "I may be recovered enough to sit in a chair and speak to my cabinet, but as for sitting in the sun to watch a rodeo—or listening to all seventy verses of the *cuento*—my heart fails me at the thought."

"We have many weeks in which to celebrate," Gloria put in with a combination of deference and reason that seemed to allay the initial shock at her speaking at all. "The reins of government have been slack for too long as it is. I have encouraged His Serene Highness to put the Royal Kingdom first before his own natural inclination to celebrate our joy with his people."

"Of—of course," Peralta said, blinking rapidly. "Admirable. Wonderful. *Si*, I will see that it is done. We will convene here, then, at ten o'clock?"

"Perhaps your lady might arrange breakfast?" Joe suggested to their host.

"Of course."

They bowed themselves out and Joe took a deep breath of both relief and determination. Had she not been corseted so tightly, Gloria might have done the same.

"That's one hurdle over," he said. "Now all we have to do is tell them how their lives are going to change. Do you suppose they'll throw rotten fruit at us, as though we were in the stocks?"

"Mama does not serve rotten fruit," Isabela said crisply,

rising to her feet. "If you do not mind, I want to go and dance, though the partner I most wish for is not here."

"The partner I most wish for isn't here, either," Gloria told her, taking her arm and walking out with her. "Let's see how long I can avoid the Ambassador. Do you think that if I dance with every grandee in the country, I can pull it off?"

$\mathcal{G}$loria dressed carefully for the cabinet meeting. She fully expected that the ministers would insist she be dismissed from the room, but the real Viceroy would never have allowed it, and she and Joe would begin as they meant to go on.

For as long as they were able to go on.

Her skirt was an elegant sweep of biscuit linen, her blouse a wonder of delicate organza, which she and Ella had stayed up late the night before embroidering with white-on-white roses.

"They mean innocence, or they mean death," Ella had explained.

"They are not used for a wedding?" Gloria snapped off a length of silk with her teeth.

"Not here," Ella told her. "And not among us. Death is the last purifier, you see, returning every man or woman to the innocence with which they arrived in the world."

Gloria tucked one of her red roses into her crown of braids, and took courage.

The cabinet members filed into the Viceroy's sitting room and seated themselves around the table that the servants had brought in earlier. The majordomo had produced seating cards, and set a discreet diagram near Joe's elbow. Gloria was half convinced they believed him to have lost his memory—which was turning out to be to their advantage.

Joe cleared his throat, and the men at the table ceased their breakfast conversations and scraping of chairs. Opposite him, at the foot of the table, the Ambassador had taken his seat as though this were his customary place. The man whose card had been there hastily found another seat.

"Thank you for joining us here today," Joe began. "And for attending these celebrations of our engagement." He held out a hand to Gloria, and she sank gracefully into the chair at his right hand. "The future Vicereine and I welcome you, and thank Senor de la Carrera y Borreaga for his unstinting hospitality. Please, help yourselves to more coffee."

"Is ... our future Vicereine to join us today?" one of the men asked in surprise.

"*Si.* If you please, we will conduct our discussions in English so that she may apprehend everything fully."

"But, Your Serene Highness ... this is most irregular," the Ambassador said in dulcet tones. "And no doubt extremely dull for the young lady. Perhaps it would be best if she met with the wives of our ministers? For everyone knows," he said with a smile, "that as many decisions are made in the drawing room as in the council chamber."

"The decisions to be made here today require her presence," Joe said shortly, and signaled for the coffee to be poured.

"I am sure that the reason for this will soon become apparent," the Ambassador said, even though it was clear Joe did not intend to pursue the subject. "Perhaps we are to discuss the next fiesta—or the fashions of the eastern seaboard?"

Joe allowed the question to hang in the air until the serving maid—Ella—had poured his coffee and stood silently behind them both.

At last Joe said, "I have received word from Nuestra Senora de los Angeles that the missions' ban on allowing airships in the Royal Kingdom's skies has been lifted."

A renewed silence met this declaration, as though this were the last thing the ministers had expected to hear. Perhaps they really had thought she was there to talk about fiestas.

"Lifted?" Peralta finally repeated. "Is that even possible?"

"It seems that a delegation of monks was tasked to determine whether Holy Writ actually forbids man to fly," de la Carrera, briefed earlier by the bishop, said smoothly. "As it turns out, it does not. The legends of the Greeks would teach one not to attempt to fly too close to the sun, but fortunately, we do not base our eternal hopes upon mere tales."

"Airships are now permitted to fly here?" one of the ministers repeated. "But we have none. What good is such a thing?"

"You will see much good come of it in the future, sir," Gloria said pleasantly. "In fact, His Serene Highness has already decided that the ships of the Meriwether-Astor Manufacturing Works might be the first to cross the mountains and bring equipment and trade to the Royal Kingdom."

"Of course he has," murmured de Aragon.

But the elderly minister was not satisfied. "How can this be? How can a thing be a sin for generations, and then overnight be as acceptable as a train journey? What will we tell the people?"

"I doubt they will be too concerned," de la Carrera said. "But it is certainly known that diligent study of Holy Writ produces a knowledge of the will of God. With deeper knowledge comes conviction ... and change."

The man subsided, shaking his head. Clearly Joe had been very clever in soliciting the approval of the missions first. It had spiked the cabinet's guns before they even had a chance to fire. Gloria wondered how many roadblocks of this kind they were about to run up against.

The mention of trade led quite naturally into a discussion of the expansion of the Royal Kingdom's interests abroad. Which quite naturally was the bailiwick of the Ambassador to the Fifteen Colonies, Augusto de Aragon.

Sadly for him, it was also Gloria's bailiwick. She had not often had reason to be thankful for her father's grudging, often unpleasant insistence on her presence during his board meetings. Her own short-lived experience at the head of the table before her journey out to the Wild West had been nearly as humiliating. But now, the tactics she had learned and the sheer bullheaded determination she had inherited came to the fore, as though her mind had been keeping them in reserve for just such a moment.

When he boasted about river shipping, she pleasantly pointed out that the dam was even now flooding the towns where his as yet unpurchased boats and barges might take on coal and kerosene.

When he suggested moving the towns, she countered with

a reminder that he was massing troops to attack the Texican Territories, the only land to which towns might be relocated.

When he blustered and pounded the table and urged the Viceroy to annex the Territories and be done with it, Gloria calmly reminded him that their neighbor had airships equipped with bombs, and the Royal Kingdom did not. "And which side, Your Excellency, will come out the victor against such odds, both physical and moral?"

He glared at her while several members of the cabinet gazed out the windows and one or two smothered smiles under the guise of dabbing their lips with embroidered handkerchiefs.

"As the future Vicereine has so ably pointed out, sirs, it would be folly to go on massing for war. We do not need to take from our neighbors when we have ample resources with which to trade with them," Joe said, capturing the gazes of each man in turn. "Before I gather all the landowners together this evening to command that their forces stand down and return to their ranchos, I would like to know I am assured of your support."

The Ambassador leaped to his feet. "Sir! I protest! The gold—"

Joe gazed at him with pity. "We are not pirates, Ambassador, to take gold by force instead of by trade and commerce. Your ideas belong in the sixteenth century, sir. In fact, I am no longer convinced that such ideas best serve the Royal Kingdom, since no one has ever been able to find these miraculous caches of gold. Do not try my patience further. There may be a more forward-thinking man here better able to build bridges with the leaders of both territory and colony."

Spittle had formed in the corners of the Ambassador's lips,

and he shook with the force of a towering temper barely held in check. If his dress sword had been to hand instead of lying in the rack in the corridor, Gloria had no doubt that he would have drawn it despite the certainty of execution to follow.

"With respect, sir, you are making a mistake. We will be left vulnerable to—"

"To whom?"

"The Texicans, of course!"

"Once the skies are open, it will be obvious that there are no armies massing, no weapons being deployed, no dam being built."

"The dam is being built! It is half its planned height already." His hand firmly on a fact he could prove, he flung it at his prince with satisfaction.

Peralta cleared his throat. "The dam must be finished, sir, if your plans for commerce and trade are to be carried out. I am willing to call off our plans for invasion, for the cost to us would be horrendous, and our children's children would still be paying the bill fifty years hence. But the dam must be completed if the Royal Kingdom is to enjoy the prosperity that you and the future Vicereine envision."

"Despite the danger to life and limb along the river?" Gloria asked. "Would it not be better to pour the Kingdom's resources into building airships instead, to take the cargo where it must go?"

"There is nothing along the river but witches and half-breeds and *los indios*," declared the Ambassador with contempt. "Jackrabbits and vultures. Nothing we may concern ourselves with. Certainly nothing that might stand in the way of Your Serene Highness's plans."

Oh, he was clever. And they were trapped, if the nods of

approval around the table were any indication. For who would build the airships? They could not do it here, with not one trained mind in the entire country. They would have to hire engineers, or pay the Meriwether-Astor Manufacturing Works to do it, and that might take longer than they were willing to wait.

Whereas the river was already there, and rising daily.

"If the men of the ranchos are to be demobilized," the Ambassador went on, "then might I suggest they augment the workforce now laboring at the dam, that the work might be finished twice as quickly?"

He was the very devil!

Gloria exchanged a glance with Joe. They had won the war —or stopped it, at least—but the battle for control of the river would not stop. It would go on even more quickly unless one of them had an idea in the next few seconds.

"I will not allow conscription of free men." Joe's tone was deadly quiet. "If the men wish to work for a fair wage rather than return to homes and fields, then the ranchos will support them as they would have had they gone to fight."

This took the cabinet members aback. How clever Joe was! If he could not stop the work, then at least he could throttle the number of men who might be permitted to go, and slow it down. And there was another advantage—when Evan succeeded in blowing up the dam, even fewer lives would be lost.

"The dam and trade on the river were my father's dream— not mine," Joe said. "Air travel is the standard in this modern day and age. Are we all agreed that this should be put to the grandees—that they should choose whether their men should be better employed building a dam, or learning to build airships?"

They looked at one another, and before the Ambassador could speak, Peralta nodded. "Your Serene Highness, these are weighty matters. If all the grandees are to agree, it will take time."

"How much time?"

"If you progress from one rancho to another during the period of your engagement to our future Vicereine—" He bowed in Gloria's direction, and she inclined her head in acknowledgement. "—then you may bring your powers of persuasion to bear. In this manner, it may take no longer than a year to reach consensus."

Gloria stared. *"A year?"*

Peralta nodded. "Certainly. Such changes cannot merely be conceived and carried out. It will take time for new laws to be written, for our prince to show himself again, to gather the approval and support of the people, who barely know him."

"We do not have a year," Joe said, frowning. "I will speak to all the landowners here, which account for more than half the country, if what our host tells me is correct?"

De la Carrerra nodded. "Only a few are missing from the northernmost reaches of our land, where I believe the snows have prevented their coming to celebrate your engagement."

"Then I wish the grandees to reach agreement and the laws rewritten within a month."

"Sir, that is impossible." For a man who was ready to march across the mountains and take what wasn't his, the Ambassador was awfully willing to delay his sovereign's wishes.

"I do not wish to rule by fiat, as my father did," Joe said

with dignity. "I wish to rule with the support of cabinet and people. At the same time, I will not brook delay. Our country has languished in the backwaters of the world for long enough. The landowners will reach agreement on three things —stopping the mobilization for war, changing the laws to outlaw conscription, and choosing commerce by air or river —within a month. If they do not, I will begin insisting upon ... contributions ... to the treasury from each rancho owner who drags his feet."

Once again the exchange of glances. Then Peralta said, "Nuestra Senora de la Soledad will support you, sir."

"As will San Luis Obispo de Tolosa," said de la Carrera.

Joe smiled. "Excellent. That is two out of twenty-one." He stood, held out a hand to Gloria, and raised her from her chair. Every man at the table rose, too. "I thank you for a most illuminating meeting, and look forward to your company this evening, when I address the landowners."

They bowed as Joe and Gloria sailed out of the room.

It was not until they reached the safety of the gardens, far from listening ears, and were strolling arm in arm among the orange trees, that Joe leaned close to whisper in Gloria's ear, "We are in trouble."

"We don't have a month," Gloria whispered back. "All the witches and the people in every town on the western reaches of the river will die, because you and I both know the work on the dam will not stop."

"Evan and Barnaby are bound and determined to blow it up. I expect news of an accident any day."

"But if we do not get our way with the airships—yet—what if we can find a way to stop the work before the rancho men come expecting their wages, and there are twice as many lives at stake? For truly, if the real Viceroy has consensus among his people to do the right thing, would that not be a better situation for him to return to when he is well?"

"Yes … but the question is, how? They can only see prosperity in the use of the river, not the skies."

"You will have to make your case to the landowners. I will tell you as much as I can about airships this afternoon. Then, when the dam has its accident, they will have a plan to fall back on, and you will look like a true leader."

"Or a madman who has blown up the Ambassador's dam. I wouldn't put it past him to accuse me of it."

"Of course he won't."

But even as she said the words, Gloria wondered if she might be wrong this time.

CHAPTER 12

*Somewhere along the Rio de Sangre Colorado de
Christo
Three weeks later*

nxiety rolled in Alice's stomach as she stared down into the swirling waters of the mighty river that both sustained and threatened her, the man she loved, and her hosts, *las brujas*. She stood, not on the stone pier where she had begun work on the submersible, but two levels higher. Her original moorage was now under water, and the submersible, which she and Ian had nicknamed the *Chaloupe*, after the dinghy-like glass-and-iron bubbles used to travel back and forth to Gloria's undersea dirigibles, now rested on what had been a sun terrace. They had floated it in four feet of water.

"We must act without delay," she said to May Lin, who was working with her.

"I agree." May Lin shaded her eyes to gaze down the

canyon. "My calculations tell me that at the current rate of rise, the water will begin to flood our storage rooms in three days. I have told Sister Clara to begin moving the animals and the food to the upper levels. At this rate we will be living on the mesa before we know it."

"The water is getting more dangerous, too. It is not running freely through the sheer rock canyons, but has slowed, becoming more powerful. More unpredictable. This little tub has only the most rudimentary steering. I don't much care to be dashed against the walls on the voyage down. Not with a hold full of explosives."

"Our original plan of using the spider's legs might have to come out again."

"I think you're right. We're going to need something to fend us off the rocks and give us some stability." Alice glanced at the younger woman. "May I take this opportunity to tell you how much I've enjoyed working with you? Just in case—you know—Ian and I don't come back."

May Lin's face softened into a smile. "It is mutual, Alice Chalmers. I think we have done some good work here. And you will come back. You are one of us now."

Alice touched the silk roses braided into her unruly dust-colored hair. She had declined to be painted for Ian's sake—the inability to tell one witch from another without careful observation made him tetchy—and though his wound was healing well, he was plenty tetchy enough. She did not think he would appreciate his wife's adopting the custom of the country quite so thoroughly. But the roses were a different matter.

The roses meant she belonged—something she would not have believed even a fortnight ago. Gretchen had taken herself off on another spying mission and good riddance. Though they had come to a kind of uneasy peace, Alice still didn't trust her, and if Ian had a lightning pistol to hand, he would probably shoot her on sight.

"Alice, what are you going to do with the mechanicals aboard your ship?"

She turned back to the *Chaloupe* and resumed screwing the isinglass window into the bow. It hadn't been easy cutting an aperture into the end of the boiler-turned-submersible, but they had to see where they were going.

"I've had so much to think about lately that I haven't given them much thought, to be honest."

"If the Californios do attack, the mechanicals cannot be used for battle here in these canyons. They are designed for charges on flat ground."

"So I risked my ship for nothing?"

"I do not believe anything we do is for nothing. But perhaps they could be put to good use ... as pack animals. To help our people travel to safer places if blowing up the dam does not work."

"If it doesn't work and I don't come back, you're welcome to them."

"In any case, I believe they should be unloaded. We can make *Swan* flightworthy if she is not burdened so heavily."

"Can you?" Alice's gaze swung back to May Lin. "But we can't inflate the last gasbag."

"Not with proper gas, no. But we can certainly repair the holes and fill it with ordinary air. She will not fly so high, but she will lift."

"Your pumps will burn out before you can get enough air in those bags."

May Lin dimpled. "Not my pumps."

Hope swelled in Alice's chest at the thought of *Swan* airborne again, heading across country as fast as her propellers would take her, to … where? Realistically, they could not moor in Santa Fe, because of the price that no doubt was still on her head. And how could they return to Philadelphia without Gloria? The crazy masquerade she was embroiled in might be discovered at any moment, and then how would she escape to freedom?

But May Lin was waiting for an answer. "I have a lot more to learn from you, I can see." May Lin smiled again. "But oh, I wish we had some news from the Royal Kingdom! It's been two weeks since Captain Fremont and Jake took Evan downriver to Santa Croce and the dam. He promised he'd bring word about what's happening."

Benny Stringfellow's head popped up from behind the submersible's stern, where he was testing their welds for leaks. "We could send a pigeon, couldn't we?"

Alice shook her head. "They need a destination with a magnetic code to fly to, like an airship."

"Are airships the only things with codes? Because the Lady sends hers to Carrick House."

"Illegally, my lad," Alice reminded him fondly.

"Who is this Lady?" May Lin asked. "Is that not your title among the English?"

"It is, but … he means a good friend of ours. She has shared many an adventure with us—including one in Resolution, where I met her." Which was probably the understatement of the century. But now another memory was served up from the depths of the cogs and wheels in Alice's brain. "She told me once that the Meriwether-Astor pigeons had basic instructions to fly to M.A.M.W. ships. Others could be added, but all the company's pigeons have that same feature. Wouldn't it be nice if their codes also included things like the behemoth? Then we could talk with Evan directly."

May Lin's gaze became fixed on the sandstone cliff opposite, as if her mind had gone into complex calculations. Then she blinked. "Do we have a Meriwether-Astor pigeon on hand?"

"Sadly, no. If we did, we could turn it loose and see if it goes to the nearest thing Gloria built."

"There are crates of things in *Swan*'s hold," Benny pointed out. "Maybe there's one in there. I can look. I'm finished here, Captain—can't find a single leak."

Alice had nearly run out of things a twelve-year-old boy could do, and since Jake had gone, Benny had stuck to her and Ian like glue. For which she could hardly blame him. In a howling wilderness, you stuck with the things that made you feel safe. Checking for leaks had been just the job for him, and this was even better.

"That's a good idea, Benny. See what you can find. We're nearly finished with the *Chaloupe*. All I have to do is load her up with the explosives and then May Lin and I can attach the spider's legs."

He put away his tools and scampered up through the terraces to the rock chute where the stairs to the top of the mesa were concealed. He and Jake went up and down like a pair of jackrabbits, but it always made Alice a little queasy, and she avoided looking down. Opening those crates would keep him busy for a couple of days, and it wouldn't hurt to know exactly what they had on hand if push came to shove.

Ian came out on to the sun terrace the next level up, and leaned over to see them. "How is it going?"

"Nearly done. May Lin helped me with the rudders and the vanes, and this window is in." She sloshed over to the steps with her own tools, climbed out, and rolled her pants down. The stone was warm under her feet, but it wouldn't last long once the sun set. "How do you feel?"

"I want to tear off this sling and throw it in the river. I am healed, Alice, no matter what Clara says. The wound has only a small scab, and I can put up with stiff muscles."

"Keep exercising them." She joined him with a kiss, and he lifted his left arm out of the sling and slipped it around her. "I like this kind of exercise. I advise ten repetitions daily."

"Is that all?"

She slipped both arms around his waist.

"I don't like this silence," he said, echoing her earlier thoughts. "And I don't like the fact that the Ranger ship has never returned."

"You want me to be captured?"

"You know I don't. But if I were in command, I would have landed to give a downed ship aid, at the very least."

"I expect they're nervous about the witches."

"And with good reason. But the witches cannot prevent air surveillance. Its commander ought to have looked for signs of life."

"Well," Alice said, finding it very comfortable leaning against him, even if her feet were bare and beginning to get cold, "if they haven't come back in three weeks, it's not likely they're going to. Maybe some air pirate has decided he wants to keep Ned Mose's legacy alive, and is giving them trouble in Santa Fe."

"We know nothing here, and it makes me uneasy. Communication among friends is as vital to success as communication among a fleet's ships."

"We're spread so far apart," Alice agreed softly. "With his papers and his skill with the behemoth, Evan might be relatively safe, but I'm afraid for Gloria. Something is bound to go wrong."

"What is this about Gloria?" A new voice came from the doorway behind them, and Alice turned to see the young Viceroy. Carefully, he made his way down the steps to them.

"Felipe," she said, slipping from Ian's one-armed embrace to offer him a helping hand. "Are you sure you should be outside?"

"If I do not get up, I will go mad," he said simply. "If Captain Hollys may do so, then I will, too."

"Well said," Ian told him. "We are not children."

Alice bit back a comment about fractious and disobedient men delaying their own recoveries by not doing as they were told. Such an opinion was not likely to help.

"I am glad to see you outdoors," she said instead. "Your strength must be coming back, and we want to get some color into those cheeks."

"I feel as unsteady as a new lamb," the young man admitted. "But do not tell Tia Clara."

"It's still a miracle to me that once you regained your senses, you recognized her," Alice said. "What a memory you must have."

"It is no great feat when in the entire course of your life, you have received kindness at the hands of only a very few," Felipe said wistfully. "When I was young, in the palace at San Francisco de Asis, she would allow me to help her in the kitchen, making cakes and bread and all manner of delights. Those are the only happy memories I have of that place."

Alice thought of her own childhood, fraught with peril and the uncertain temper of a brute who would as soon wallop you as look at you. The only place where she had found that kind of safety and kindness had been in the house of the desert flowers, with her mother.

Now May Lin joined them, stripping off her leather gloves. "Felipe," she greeted him. "I am glad to see that you are going to recover. Sister Clara has not lost a patient yet, and we now know much more about ergot poisoning than ever we did."

"I am happy to be of service," the prince said with a smile and a bow.

Alice was glad to see a glimmer of a sense of humor. Between him and Ian, the past few weeks had been quite a trial. No one minded their tongue around the Viceroy, which to her surprise, he found refreshing. His thirst for truth after a rule marked primarily by lies and betrayal had turned into an asset. She had never realized before how much she had taken for granted the honesty that was common currency among her friends and loved ones.

"May I give you any assistance?" Felipe asked. "Though I am quite certain it is treason to ask such a question of you all in connection with that little engine there."

"A prince may not commit treason," Ian reminded him. "He simply changes his mind."

A shadow passed over the young man's face. "I am quite sure Ambassador de Aragon would not agree with you. After finding the gold cached in your caverns here, this dam was his pet project."

"I am sorry to disappoint him," May Lin said tartly. "We were just lamenting the lack of news from beyond the mountains ourselves."

"Had I not been in two places at once, I might have sent a message from Santa Croce and had the entire court come to brief me."

"I still find it astonishing that you are so sanguine about our deception, sir," Ian said. "I suspect that most men in, er, your position would have hunted out the axe first and asked questions later."

"Ah, but I do not appear to be remotely like most men in my, er, position," he said with a wry twist of his lips. "I am simply happy to be among the ranks of the living. And even more, to know that the woman I loved and trusted as being the next thing to a mother is alive as well. You cannot know how I felt when I opened my eyes in my right senses and recognized Tia Clara."

"Oh, I think I can." Ian took Alice's hand. She squeezed back.

"Our lack of news becomes even more frustrating when we remember that at some point we must switch you back, Felipe." May Lin leaned upon a stone wall, her gaze leaving him with reluctance and fixing itself upon the rush of the river through the canyon's walls.

"It is something I have thought upon for many an hour during my convalescence," he admitted, apparently not possessing Alice's sharp eyes and the newlywed's nose for possible romance among other people. "As soon as I am able to travel, I suppose I must return to San Luis Obispo de Tolosa, provided, of course, that Gloria and Joe—"

"Honoria," May Lin corrected him.

"—and Honoria are still there. For all we know, they could be in San Francisco de Asis by now."

"I would not be, were I she," Ian said.

Alice nodded in agreement. "They'll do everything they can to stay as close as possible to where you are. In fact, I wouldn't be surprised if Gloria expressed a wish to see the dam herself."

"The only question is whether it is there to be seen or not, when they come," May Lin said. "I would prefer not, and the sooner the better. Already we have had messengers from some of the villages downriver, asking for refuge."

"I had no idea when I agreed to the project just what it might mean," Felipe said. "I feel as though I ought to apologize to every refugee who comes."

"We must keep to a minimum those who know who you really are," Ian cautioned him. "Outside of ourselves and Mother Mary, you must continue to be Joe, Evan's translator."

"I understand. I must also remember to keep his—my— papers upon my person, for the happy occasion when we do meet and resume our proper identities." He sighed. "I hope he is enjoying Gloria's company, at any rate. I should have done so, in his place."

Alice watched as May Lin schooled her face to smooth-ness. Then the young woman frowned. "Ship ho," she said suddenly. "Riverboat."

Alice grabbed the canvas tarpaulin and flung it over the submersible. Once it was secure, she pulled on her stockings and boots. The boat had to be bringing news—to navigate this particular stretch of river took skill and a certain amount of nerve brought on by urgency.

Witches began to appear in doorways and on terraces as the sound of the paddles striking the water became audible, echoing and multiplying between the smooth canyon walls, and by the time it docked, nearly all the village had come down to welcome it. Clara joined them on what was now the bottom-most terrace as Mother Mary progressed majestically to the gangplank.

Alice didn't recognize the captain—he was not the same man who had helped bring Ian here. But she certainly recognized Gretchen as she disembarked with another man and only one of the witches who had gone with her days ago. And then—

"Jake!" she shouted, and waved until he looked up.

With a lift of his hand, he jogged up the steps and straight into Alice's hug.

"We'd nearly given you up," she said breathlessly as he released her, then shook hands with Ian. "Benny will be so upset he wasn't here to greet you. He's up on the mesa."

"I'll see him at dinner. We have news. Hello, er ..." After a moment, he stuck out his hand for the prince's clasp. "You probably don't remember me. I'm Jake, Captain Chalmers's navigator on *Swan*."

"I am happy to make your acquaintance, sir. I am ..." He glanced at Alice. "Joe."

"It's all right, Felipe. Jake is safe as houses. I trust him with my life—and you can, too."

Jake looked pleased, and then shook the prince's hand a second time. "I'm very glad to see you up and about. It was touch and go for a little while."

"I am very glad, too. I hope ... we may be friends."

Alice could count on the fingers of one hand the number

of times Jake had let himself go enough to smile as unabashedly as this. "I would like that … Felipe."

"And now we must hear the news," May Lin said. "Look, Mother Mary is coming up here with Riley and Fitz."

Riley, Alice had been given to understand, had been with Gloria's party when she had set off to find the Viceroy, and had gone with the man who was no longer Gloria's husband when they had escorted Evan downriver.

"Jake," she said quietly. "Where is Captain Fremont?"

"He's—"

But Mother Mary had begun to speak. "We are all anxious to hear what you have to say, and then we'll feast. That way, there will be fewer supplies we'll have to move to the upper levels tomorrow."

Riley spoke up so the witches ranged along the walls could hear. "Santa Croce is all but inundated. The church is on an island and most of the townsfolk have moved down to the water meadows."

"On the bright side," Fitz said, turning his bowler hat around in his hands, "conscription has been outlawed, so folk who moved there can pursue their own trades without fearing they'll be seized and made to work on the dam."

Alice nudged the Viceroy. "That's Gloria's work. I'd bet my ship on it."

"Well done, Gloria," Ian murmured.

"And that isn't all," Riley added. "Airships can fly into the Royal Kingdom now."

"*What?*" Alice gripped Ian's arm and made him wince. It was the one in the sling. "Sorry, darling," she whispered. "Jake, is it true?"

"It is," he said in a low tone. "I don't know what good it

does them, since no one knows about it outside their borders, and there's no one to build them on the inside."

"Still," Ian said, "once we have *Swan* flightworthy again—"

"Exactly," Jake said with satisfaction. "We can go and get her if everything goes to Hades in a hand basket."

"Airships." The Viceroy sounded rather pained. "I had hoped to be the one to introduce them to the country. How did she get around the missions' objections without me, and their belief that airships fly in the face of God?"

"The Church once believed the world was flat," Ian pointed out, "and changed their minds once they knew better." He chuckled. "I must say that girl is much more persuasive than I ever gave her credit for."

"I should simply have issued a command," the prince said with dignity. "Persuasion would not have been necessary."

May Lin shushed him, since Fitz had begun speaking again.

"All the grandees from every ranch were required to attend the Viceroy at San Luis Obispo de Tolosa and agree to these changes to the law, or be forced to pay a fine," he said.

The Viceroy's mouth opened and then closed with a click, as though he had remembered just in time that he was supposed to be Joe.

"Many of them did agree, and it's official—the rancho troops have been sent back to farm and family, unless they want to work on the dam for the wage they would have received had they been soldiers."

"Genius," Ian said.

"So the war is over, then, before it began?" Sister Clara called from their terrace. "Can it be true?"

"Unless something has changed in the two days it took us

to fight our way upstream, it is true," Fitz said. "And we all know how slowly the Royal Kingdom changes."

"Until lately," Felipe muttered. "I cannot believe she has taken such advantage of my absence."

May Lin leaned close enough to say with quiet ferocity, "But you knew her goal—to stop the war that both your fathers began, and to save countless lives. She made that plain to you, did she not, before you asked her to marry you?"

"Well ... yes ... but it does not follow that I would have granted her *carte blanche* to do it."

"Then you would have deceived her and broken her heart."

Even though he now insisted on the truth while he was among them, Alice had a feeling the young Viceroy hadn't been prepared for *that*.

"You do agree that we have to destroy the dam, don't you, Felipe?" Alice's voice was a little sharper than she had intended it to be. "Since your recovery began and you saw what was at stake, you haven't changed your mind?"

The Viceroy pulled himself to his full height, somewhere between that of Alice and Ian. "Would it change your plans if I had?"

"No, but we would far rather have your support than your condemnation."

"It will be seen as an act of war by your Ambassador, unless we succeed in making it look like an accident," Ian said. "The last thing we want is to start the war all over again, with your forces taking the field against those of the Texicans."

"A battle my forces would almost certainly lose." Felipe's face, which still had not filled out, looked bleak. "I have seen the differences in the technology and the skill in spycraft which the witches possess. Somehow, book learning about historic battles and fencing lessons do not seem an adequate response." He gazed at Mother Mary, who was deep in conversation with Riley and Fitz. "I do agree that the people along the river must be saved. But can we not simply regulate the water flow and leave the dam as it is?"

"Who will be in charge of such regulation?" May Lin asked.

Again, her penetrating insight left him speechless. For the peoples along the river needed the water levels back where they had been. The people west of the mountains would profit by a river running high enough to take a boat well into the heart of the continent. It was a stalemate, and Alice's little *Chaloupe* was going to break it.

"If the men of the ranchos come to the dam to work," Felipe said, "they will die in the flood. If we must accomplish this thing, it ought to be very soon."

"Within three days," May Lin told him. "We will have the spider's legs attached tomorrow, and the day after, Alice and Ian can take it downriver."

No one noticed Gretchen until she stepped out from between Felipe and Jake. Such was her ability to sneak … or as Felipe put it, her *spycraft*. "The day after tomorrow? Even twelve hours is too much. Tomorrow night, no later. The dam is seventy-five percent completed, according to the laundress I spoke to in what is left of Santa Croce. The men from the ranchos are already arriving, and the work is going even faster. They are forced to actually feed the builders now, you see."

"What do you mean?" Felipe demanded. "Of course they must feed them."

"The conscripts are—how do you say it? One step from

starvation. The Viceroy's army is not known for its care of those men, only its soldiers."

"Disgraceful," muttered Felipe, to whom this was clearly news. "Changes must be made."

"Oh, they will," Alice said cheerfully, lest Gretchen think this was an odd thing to say. "The *Chaloupe* will see to that."

Gretchen dared a glance at Ian. "Captain Hollys, I—I am glad to see you on your feet again."

Stiffly, Ian nodded.

"Please accept my apologies again for—"

"I did the last time you offered them." Ian straightened his spine. "We are fighting on the same side, *Fraulein*. Let us put the past behind us."

She slipped away as unobtrusively as she had come.

"She is very good at that," May Lin said. "So, tomorrow night? We shall have to make an early start of it."

Alice could not reply. By the time the moon rose again, she and Ian might no longer be alive.

CHAPTER 13

*S*ix months ago, if someone had told him he would be working for an enemy army, in the company of the husband of the woman he had once had hopes of, and enjoying himself, Evan Douglas would have told them they were utterly mad. Would have said he chose his company better. Would have said he didn't even *know* any women of whom to have hopes.

How his life had changed! Well, as a schoolboy he had craved adventure. Now that he had it, he would give almost anything to be back in the schoolroom, the bespectacled professor he had always vowed he would never be.

Almost.

For despite the harrowing dangers he had been exposed to hitherto, there was something very rewarding about operating the behemoth—it made him feel capable. Powerful. And rather possessive of its huge, awkward iron self. Even if all he was doing was lifting horizontal beams into place.

For despite the familiarity of the work, everything was

different now. Joe was gone, and in his place working the behemoth's arms was Captain Fremont. The guards who had shared the pilot's chamber were gone, and in their place was a modicum of trust. Commander de Sola had not actually believed that he would keep his promise to return, and in his astonishment, he had removed the guard and moved Evan, Fremont, and his old cellmate Dutch into the soldiers' dormitory. While it had far less privacy than the gaol cell, it did have the advantage of a bed and sink—two gifts for which Evan had learned to be grateful.

Carefully, Captain Fremont dropped the beam into its trusses and lowered the behemoth's arms. Evan turned them about and they stumped back in the direction of the staging yard to fetch the next one.

"I must say," he said over his shoulder to Fremont, "I am still having difficulty understanding why you choose to stay when you could be piloting your own steamboat and taking orders from no man."

"I am not certain myself," the captain admitted, swinging down from the gunner's chair, his sailor's legs adjusting easily to the movement of the behemoth. "But I suspect that this feeling in my gut is simply a need to be on the same side of the mountains as Gloria. If there are fewer obstacles between us, then there is less to prevent my reaching her should she need help."

Evan couldn't help but admire such reasoning, since he shared it himself.

"I might ask you the same question," the captain went on. "Any other man would have broken his word and taken the first train to Reno, Santa Fe, and beyond."

Evan chuckled, his legs moving in an even rhythm that

caused the behemoth's mirrored movement to eat up the distance far below. "Perhaps. For I would be free ... but friendless and alone. Better to be foolish and honorable and close to my friends. And as you say, available to help should I be need—"

Something hit the side of the behemoth with a clank.

Their stride faltered as Evan lost his rhythm. "What was that? Are we being fired upon?"

"That, or someone threw a rock—though few men have an arm strong enough. If you will stop, I will investigate."

Evan brought them to a halt and Fremont scrambled out of the hatch and down the iron ladder built into one leg. After a wait of some five minutes in which Evan tried unsuccessfully to see what was going on below, he heard scraping sounds. In a moment, slightly out of breath, the captain hauled himself through the hatch once more.

In one hand he carried a familiar brass shape. "I have no idea what this is, but I found it between the behemoth's feet. Its nose seems to have got a bit crumpled from the impact."

"Good heavens." Evan unbuckled himself and crossed the few steps to take it from him. "Have you never seen a pigeon?"

"Only the feathered kind. What is it?"

"It's an airborne messenger. It carries correspondence between airships."

"That explains it. I haven't been in an airship for a decade, much less seen one of these in use. The little blighter seems a bit confused," the captain observed wryly. "There are no airships in the Royal Kingdom's skies despite the reversal of the laws against them. Not the most helpful of laws, I must say."

"Give Gloria time." Evan opened the cylindrical compartment tucked below the wings and propellers, and in front of its engine. "This must have blown off course. Let us see to whom it was sent and release it on its way."

> *Evan Douglas*
> > *Behemoth*
> > *Evan, if you get this, please reply soonest. We think all Gloria's pigeons go to things her dad made. This is an experiment to see if it will find you. If it does, send it back—it knows the code for Swan.*
> > *We hope you are well. We are all fine.*
> > *Yours faithfully,*
> > *Benjamin Stringfellow*
> > *Gunner second class, Swan*

"For heaven's sake," Evan said blankly.

"Who is it for? One of the Ranger ships?"

"No, for us. Look. Our address is *Behemoth*. I must say I prefer that to Colliford Castle or Orpington Street."

Fremont scanned the crumpled sheet with its blotted handwriting and chuckled. "That little scamp. How did he discover such a thing?"

"I don't know. We had no pigeons aboard *Swan* that I know of, and this one looks very new. I suppose if it knows how to find the behemoth, it must have been in a crate with the mechanicals."

"Wherever it came from, I'm deuced glad to see it. It means we can communicate with Alice, at least. Though I would much rather we had thought to equip Gloria with a mechanical, so that I might write to her."

"We must certainly keep it a secret—any correspondence going to the witches will undoubtedly be considered treasonous. We will lay hands on paper and ink at the first opportunity and send our reply."

That evening, when most of the soldiers were enjoying games of cards or contests of athletics in the parade yard, Evan and the captain availed themselves of a pencil and paper. Other men wrote letters, so this was nothing unusual. Their advantage was that now they need not wait for a train or a passing friar in order to communicate with the outside world.

> *Benjamin Stringfellow*
>
> *Gnr 2nd Class, Swan*
>
> *Delighted to receive your letter. Further examination of the behemoth reveals a communications cage behind the gunner's harness, which this unfortunate bird missed. Apologies for damage. We've done our best to repair. Fremont is with me. We are well and have been promoted to sleeping in the dormitory with the soldiers. Best to avoid sending during the day to prevent discovery. We hope your captain has been busy and await news every day. Nothing new from the north save that more men come daily to work on the dam. Time grows short in that regard.*
>
> *Yours ever,*
>
> *Evan*

A moonlit stroll took him to the storage yard, where the sentry recognized him, nodded, and allowed him through the gate.

"I noticed some stiffness in *El Gigante's* joints earlier," he told the man. "I'll just do a bit of maintenance now, so I don't lose the time tomorrow."

He carried a mechanic's bag with an oilcan on top of the pigeon, its spout poking out rather conspicuously, so the sentry merely nodded and closed the gate. Evan scrambled up into the pilot's cabin and gave the pigeon its instructions to return to *Swan*. When he released it through the communications cage, it would know to return to that specific location on the behemoth's body. He watched it fly away, his only hope that the sentry would not see it, become alarmed at something else flying in the face of God, and shoot it out of the sky.

The night remained quiet, however, and he nodded to the sentry as he left once more, his bag of tools somewhat slimmer ... and his heart considerably lighter than it had been since his last sight of San Luis Obispo de Tolosa and the people he cared about therein.

CHAPTER 14

"*A*lice—Captain—you cannot do this to us."

Alice's blood turned to ice at the anguish in Jake's voice. She felt sick at the thought of what they must do, and yet … "I've got to, Jake. Don't you see? It was my idea to run the *Chaloupe* into the flow regulator, so I can't very well hand off the job to May Lin or Mother Mary."

"Hand it off to Gretchen," he said bitterly. "No one will miss her. We're your crew. How can you leave us behind?"

A suspicious sheen glittered in his eyes in the light of the lamps, and the lump in her own throat nearly choked her. "Because, my dearling, someone must stay alive to tell Claire what happened. Someone must look after Benny, and get him back to London. You are that someone. Ian and I are braving this task together because … well, because whatever happens, I must be with him, and he with me."

"And you expect me to let the both of you go, just like that?"

"Too many lives are depending on us," she told him gently.

"And I suspect you'll have a tussle with the witches if you try to follow us."

"I can't believe this of ye. We're a flock, Alice." His voice broke, and so did her heart.

"Jake—"

But he had already twisted away from her, pushing through the silent crowd gathered to watch their departure, and collecting Benny on the way. Her last sight of her navigator and gunner were their shadows as they disappeared into the vertical chute of rock where the spiral stair lay concealed in the darkness.

Were they really going to attempt that climb, grief-stricken and blinded by emotion? But there was nothing she could do now—except hope the witches wouldn't find their lifeless bodies at the bottom in the morning.

Mother Mary touched her arm, making her jump. Her nerves were stretched thin, and the bone-deep desire to flee right along with Jake wasn't helping.

"Our prayers go with you," Mary said. "Our sisters have been praising your courage."

"Foolhardiness, more like," Alice mumbled. "Two of the people I care about most just ran away from me, angry."

"Great things have been accomplished by people whom others called fools—we live with that. And the boys will not be angry forever. We will look after them."

"I know you will." Alice was not the sort who indulged in demonstrations of affection outside of those she considered her immediate family, but this might be the last opportunity she would ever have to connect in the most basic of human ways. She hugged Mother Mary. "Try to get them to forgive me."

"They love you, sister. They likely already have."

May Lin crawled out of the *Chaloupe*. "It is ready, Alice."

"Then I guess we are, too."

Ian gripped her hand and helped her in, then settled into the rudimentary harness next to her while May Lin slammed the hatch shut.

As submersibles went, it was about what you'd expect from a boiler fitted out with a viewing port that had been salvaged from a capsized Californio boat, and only the most basic of steering mechanisms. They had air, but not a lot. Gretchen had estimated it would take six hours to reach the dam.

Six hours of navigating underwater, at night, in an unfamiliar vessel.

Six hours of contemplating their own insanity.

Six hours of being together, possibly for the last time.

Helping hands shoved the *Chaloupe* away from the makeshift pier, the current caught them, and they were under way. Alice could not even look over her shoulder for a final glimpse of the village, for there was nothing behind her in the dark but explosives. And while it was true that a recovery party would venture down to the dam in the morning, there were no guarantees that she and Ian would be in any shape to greet them.

She shook off such unpleasant thoughts and forced herself to do her job. In the upper reaches of the river, they could coast along on the surface. She must keep them from crashing into the walls of the canyon, using the controls for the spider's legs. She imagined that, from above, they looked like a very clumsy version of those insects that skimmed the water of a pond.

Ian gripped the navigation wheel with both hands, his sharp gaze on their course. "Mother Mary tells me that the Californio lookouts are posted about a mile upstream from the dam. A fallen tree across the canyon is our landmark, and where we must submerge."

"I'm not looking forward to that. Give me a big sky and a lot of clouds, rather. You can keep your water vessels."

"You will hear no arguments from me on that score."

"We've yet to have our first argument," she pointed out, somewhat wistfully. "But I suppose that in the next six hours, anything is possible."

"As if I should wish to argue with the woman who is roped to me." He glanced at her next to him, their shoulders pressed against one another in the cramped space, a rope connecting them to each other so they were not separated in the water. "Perhaps we might discuss the wallpaper in the receiving room at Hollys Park. That always put my father in a towering temper—it is seventeenth century, you see."

"High time it was replaced, then," Alice said promptly.

"You and my mother would have seen eye to eye."

"I should have liked to have met your mother, and thanked her for doing such a good job in bringing you up."

"I should have liked you to have met her, too." He steered around a double outcropping of rock that forced the river into an S-curve. "Ah well. When we are home again, you shall meet my aunt Dorothea. You will either love her or hate her. No one seems to fall in the middle. It is to be assumed that my uncle falls on the loving side. Papa fell on the other."

"You are gossiping, Ian Hollys, in order to take my mind off this little excursion."

"I am indeed. Sadly, my gossip is rather out of date now. I wonder how Claire and Andrew are?"

"I would give a lot to see *Athena*'s shabby old fuselage in the distance, for true."

"You will some day, I promise. We are not going to die, Alice. The plan is straightforward."

"It's the execution that worries me."

"Ah, but the execution is in our hands. My greatest concern is for your safety, and yours is for mine. As long as we both crawl out of that water together, hang the dam."

"Have I told you lately how much I love you?" Alice said softly, hoping her tone would make up for the fact that she must not take her eyes off the walls of the canyon.

"And I love you. I am sorry now to have been such a bear during my convalescence—you would think that having my own mortality cast in my face by our friend Gretchen would have made me both sober and silent."

"You're a man." Alice leaned her head on his shoulder briefly, her hands never leaving the levers. "You can't help it."

And so the moon rose and travelled across the sky, and the stars wheeled a little farther in their nightly arc, while Alice and Ian spoke of things both heartfelt and inconsequential. *Of rope and string and sewing thread,* as the childhood rhyme went. *Of cake and pudding and sopping bread.*

And then a narrow horizontal shadow passed over them, blotting out the light of the setting moon for less than a second as the current carried them under it. Without a word, Ian set the vanes to vertical and they sank beneath the rolling surface of the water, plunging into gloom. The small engine that propelled them was only enough to keep them ahead of the current. It was of no use in taking them upstream again.

There was no turning back now—not that there ever had been a chance to do so.

Suddenly a bolt sliced the water ahead of them, like a spear made of bubbles. Then another, and another.

"Ian! We've been spotted—they're shooting at us!"

"So much for Gretchen's information," he said through his teeth, taking the *Chaloupe* deeper. "I would not put it past her to have added an hour to the travel time she told us."

"She has no reason to do that, and there's only been the one fallen tree," Alice said, but her mind was focused wholly on peering through the murk. "Can we risk turning on the lamp? We have to find the bottom in any case, and we've less than a mile."

The lamp in the rounded nose of the boiler didn't do much good, but at least it illuminated the rocky, jagged floor of the chasm enough for her to keep them from hitting it and risking a puncture in their iron cylinder. She hoped that it was also not enough to be seen under all the weight of water in what had fast become not a river, but a deep lake.

"Engines reversed," Ian said tersely. Construction rubble came into view—broken rocks, scaffolding, buckets. Now the current pushed them against the sheer wall of the earthwork and cement that rose out of sight in the darkness.

"That current is rather stronger than I expected," she said, her arms aching with the effort of holding the legs steady on their task. If she had had a spare moment to think about it, Alice would have been gibbering with fear. But it was all she could do to keep the *Chaloupe* creeping along the base of the dam, searching for the aperture containing the flow regulator.

It seemed an eternity until, on the right, a wall rose to box them into a corner.

Ian swore violently. "We've missed it. We're on the right bank, directly beneath the guard tower."

She would not commence gibbering now. She would not be sick. She would take a deep breath and grip the controls and get them out of this fix before someone saw the glow deep under water—or the guards upstream got the message to the tower that they were under attack.

Slowly ... slowly ... they turned the *Chaloupe* about and crept back the way they had come. How long was this wretched dam? Did it even *have* a flow regulator? Were they going to die here, drowned by water spraying in through multiple bullet holes?

"There." Ian let out a breath as though he had been holding it. "Slowly, now. We don't want to overshoot it. Our mistake has cost us precious minutes."

By now, Alice's hands had frozen into claws on the levers that controlled the spider legs. She hardly dared breathe as she crept up to the aperture built into the base of the dam—a tunnel that narrowed into a spillway on the other side. According to May Lin's information, which was several months old, the aperture contained a huge butterfly valve that turned back and forth so that the flow could be shut off altogether.

"Brace the spider legs on either side."

Slowly ... do not make a mistake ... allow for the pressure of the current ... that frighteningly strong current ...

"Legs braced," she whispered.

They clung, splayed across the hole like a spider in the center of her web, the legs braced on either side. May Lin had calculated that the legs would hold in this position for less than five minutes before they collapsed from the pressure and the *Chaloupe* was swept into the tunnel and wedged fast.

Which was the plan, but still ... it was a dadblamed terrifying plan.

"Right, then." Ian released his harness and swung himself over the floodgate into the rear, where he ignited a lamp in which was wound two feet of fuse. "Alice, are you ready?"

Ready to drown? No. Ready to go with him, come what may? "Yes."

"I will open the hatch. We must get out and close it again before the water fills the forward chamber, goes over the floodgate, and douses our fuse."

"The hatch will hold for twenty seconds, no more," she reminded him. "It was the best I could do on short notice."

"It will work. Come, a kiss for luck."

The kiss was worth the seconds it cost. Then, Ian shoved on the hatch while Alice braced the iron arm that held it open. Ian hauled her out through a torrent of ice-cold water, and her boot heel barely cleared the hatch before the arm failed and it slammed shut with a hollow sound that echoed weirdly underwater.

The cold was paralyzing, but she could not gasp. Immediately the current pushed her against the earthwork, flattening her and pulling her legs into the aperture. No! If she were to somersault forward, she would be sucked in and heaven knew what was on the other side. A cliff, perhaps. Clawing, crawling crabwise, half swimming, they struck out for the surface in the general direction of the left bank.

Ten seconds.

She was already running out of air thanks to her frantic

swimming—and the current—all that rushing water leaping headlong through an aperture too small—

Fifteen seconds.

Alice's concentration narrowed to the dim form of Ian beside her, swimming against the current with Olympian strength and getting absolutely nowhere. She paused just for a split second to orient herself—to gaze frantically upward as though she might be able to see the surface—*you fool, Alice*—

The merciless force of the water grabbed her. She was sure she screamed, for her mouth filled with water and pushed the last of the air out of her lungs. Headlong, she was sucked past the *Chaloupe*, grabbing fruitlessly at anything—a spider leg—a vane—only to have it torn from her hands by the current as it carried her into the tunnel. From the drag on the safety line, Ian was being pulled willy-nilly behind her—paying with his life for her mistake!

Twenty seconds.

She would drown and Ian would drown and no one at Hollys Park would ever know what had become of them—

With a crunch, the spider legs collapsed and now they were being pushed forward by the bow wave, deeper into the tunnel, as the *Chaloupe* did what she had designed it to do and rushed forward into the aperture. With a grinding scream, the little vessel wedged itself tight into the tunnel.

Ian hauled on the rope and her head broke the surface like resurrection morning. With the force of the outflow temporarily plugged up, leaving a few inches at the top in which to breathe, she dragged blessed air into her lungs, her head spinning, stars whirling in her vision—

"Alice, swim!"

She didn't know whether she was up or down, but somehow, between the drag of the security line at her waist and the water under her, she oriented herself and swam after him with all her remaining strength. She still could not touch the bottom, but allowed the current to take her down the tunnel until a half-circle of lighter gloom appeared a distance ahead.

"Valve!" she croaked. "Stay left."

If they passed through it one on each side, the security line would snag and they would be trapped, flapping hopelessly, one on each side of the valve, until they drowned.

Ian struck out for the left side and in seconds, they had been swept through and out into cold space.

Alice screamed, a high, keening sound as she fell, not knowing what in the name of heaven lay beneath them. Yet somehow Ian hauled on the line and yanked her against him, cradling her so that they would land with her body uppermost.

Her heart broke with love for the man who, even in this dreadful extremity, would put her life before his own.

With a splash that deafened her all over again, they landed in a broad pool. Fortunately, their feet were forced up and they skimmed beneath the shallow surface, their bodies pummeled by the fall of water from above. If they had landed just a centimeter differently, they would have clocked their heads on the rocky bottom and been washed down the water's course to drown, unconscious and very probably dead.

They passed on either side of a submerged rock. The security line caught and both Alice and Ian jerked to a halt. Instinctively, she put her feet down and found solid ground.

"Up here!" Ian gasped, scrambling up the bank and hauling her up behind him like a trout on a line. They collapsed in the mud, gasping and shivering. Alice went into his arms and wrapped both hers around his back as though she would never let him go.

"We're alive!" she groaned. "I don't know how."

"We're not supposed to be on this side," Ian said grimly, his teeth chattering with the cold of the April night. "The *Chaloupe* will go up at any moment. We were supposed to be on the other side, above the maelstrom. We must get out of the way."

But there was nowhere to go. Over his shoulder, Alice's frantic gaze took in the sheer cliffs and the guard tower at the top of the dam. The massive bulk of the earthwork, looming into the sky. The channel of the creek below the dam that was about to be filled with tons of water that they would have avoided had she not taken that brief second to rest and been caught like a bit of soap in the drain.

They could run, climbing over the rocks in the riverbed, but the water would catch them in seconds.

As though Ian had also realized that this was it—this was the end of their journey together—he passed an arm about her and squeezed her tightly against him.

From far away came the sound of thunder, and the ground shook.

Ian sucked a final breath into his lungs and pointed. Far above them, the dam's lamps seemed to shudder. The sound of the river became a triumphant roar, and then with a *boom!* like the very trumpet of the archangel Gabriel signaling the end of the world, the dam collapsed in on itself with slow unwillingness.

The hungry river leaped into the gap with a roar.

And as it did, the stars were blotted out.

Something landed heavily on the rocks beside them. Alice

dragged her gaze from the spectacle of her own death to see what poor creature had fallen to share in the end of the world.

"Bloody hell, get in!" Benny Stringfellow screamed from a basket, both hands outstretched.

Ian leaped up and flung her over the gunwale by main force. Alice landed in a heap in the wicker bottom, then jumped to haul on the back of his shirt and drag him over the side. Even as she did so, the basket swung into the air and began its ascent, and the momentum flung Benny against her, weeping.

"We thought you was dead—we couldn't see you—oh MarymotherofGod, it's too late!"

Alice had enough sense remaining in a mind wiped completely blank with surprise to fling herself to the opposite side of the basket from Ian, so that they did not overbalance and tip themselves out. Her eyes widened as they rose one agonizingly slow foot at a time, and she could see.

More and more of the earthwork whirled away into the widening gap in the dam until with a final crack, the last remaining buttress fell into the maelstrom and the crunch and snap of agonized rock breaking into pieces filled the night. The roar of the river took on a deeper, even more terrifying note as the water was flung through the narrow gap and leaped into space over the place where they had just been crouching, lunging past it for the plains below.

The guard tower that had been attached to the north side of the dam keeled over like a woman in a faint, the men inside screaming as they plunged into the frothing monster of water. On the south side, as the basket crested the chasm, men poured from the gatehouse and out on to the mesa, panicking and running through the sage and pinon pines in every direction.

The basket rose through the air and reached its docking station in the stern of the ship. *Whose ship? For this can't be Swan—have Benny and Jake gone a-pirating? Is it the Rangers, returned to investigate at last?*

"Jake," she said in a high, unnatural voice as he stopped the winch. She did not think she could climb out of the basket under her own steam. The only thing holding her up was her death grip on the gunwale.

But he did not answer. He was gazing down through the hatch, his mouth agape, as the enormous bottled-up river behind the dam pushed the last of man's efforts to control it out of its way and poured through the canyon like the wrath of God unleashed upon a disobedient humanity. It crashed through the turn in its former course, throwing up water so high against the cliffs that Alice felt the spray of the torrent upon her face, blown back by the wind.

"*Swan*, gain fifty feet and proceed westerly at five knots," Jake ordered the automaton intelligence system.

Swan! But how...?

There was no time for talk, or even for joy. *Swan's* vanes and propellers took them higher, widening the panoply of disaster unfurling below. The river reclaimed its dry course, crashing around curves and spilling through canyons that had never felt such an onslaught since the day the earth had formed. And now, as they proceeded westerly, Alice realized with horror the full extent of what they had done.

In the distance far below were the water meadows, where the turns and crescents of the river flattened and became civilized enough to support plant life, water birds, animals ... and the town and military fort that had sprung up in the valley. Ranged in rows outside the town were the white tents of the Ambassador's forces, still asleep in the grey hour before the dawn.

Alice clutched the rail as the river, flouted by men for long enough, roared and lunged into the valley to devour the innocent and defenseless.

CHAPTER 15

*D*uring that day's work, both Evan and the captain had had difficulty concentrating on their tasks. One eye always seemed to be cast toward the sky, searching for a glimpse of the pigeon, and the other toward the guard towers, from whence it would certainly be shot down if it were seen. But as the sun set, both men glanced at one another and wordlessly resigned themselves to another stroll in the dark to the equipment yard, for which they would have to come up with another pretext.

But no pigeon came.

Evan went to bed with an odd feeling of anxiety, which prevented his sleeping well, though his bunk was not uncomfortable. When he started awake in the darkness before dawn, he could tell by the harsh breathing of his companions that he was not alone.

"What was that?" Dutch muttered. "Something has happened. An earthquake?"

Captain Fremont was already throwing on his clothes.

"Get dressed," he said tersely. "That was an explosion, if I'm not mistaken. Dadgummit, that young rascal could have told us!"

"You do not think—" But Evan couldn't finish. Surely Alice and the witches would have warned them before blowing up the dam. Surely they would have waited until their friends were clear of danger.

By now the soldiers had been roused by the urgent summons of a trumpet in the parade ground, and in the melee of yanking on boots and locating arms, Evan, Dutch, and Fremont were utterly ignored.

"Come," Evan said, grabbing Dutch's arm and beckoning Fremont around the side of the building. "To the behemoth. No matter what happens, we must stay with it."

They could hear de Sola calling for his sword in the officers' quarters, and Evan felt a moment of guilt for not joining him. For really, what could the three of them do? They were not about to fight the prisoners, whom the law now regarded as free men but who were too important to the construction to set free, should they take this opportunity to stage a coup. The three of them could not take up arms and march, for this was not their fight.

While the likelihood of fighting was low, the danger to life and limb if the dam had collapsed was extremely high.

They ran to the equipment yard to find the trumpet had already caused the sentry to desert his post. Evan swarmed up the behemoth's leg and inside, where he ignited the boiler and prepared for movement. The captain heaved Dutch into the pilot's chamber and scrambled in behind him.

"Find a security line and attach it," he ordered. "We may have a bumpy ride."

Dutch held a finger in the air. "Listen."

Evan flipped open the vents on either side of the viewing port, and cranked the isinglass outward.

Once, as a child, his grandmother had taken him to Scotland on holiday. Shivering, he had attempted to build a sand castle on the beach in a howling gale while she walked up and down attempting to convince them both they were enjoying themselves. The sound of the wind roaring over the waves, whipping them into a frenzy, had soured him on oceans forever.

That same sound now froze his blood. "The water!" He cranked the viewing port closed like a madman. "Close everything and brace yourselves!"

There was just enough steam pressure in the boiler to allow Evan to raise the behemoth from its resting position and brace its legs, knees bent, trunk angled forward, like a pugilist taking the measure of his opponent. In the distance, dawn broke over the eastern peaks and he saw the steam loader—that very vehicle they had once imagined could toss rail cars at the dam to damage it from the outside—fling its arms to the heavens as it was engulfed and went over backward. Evan had no doubt that the piles of iron rails, containers of cement, and heaps of lumber were being scattered willy-nilly as though they weighed nothing. And perhaps this was what saved them to some extent, for as the water expended its force on the heavy equipment, it was slowed down. However, the millions of gallons behind it had no such compunction.

"Cast off—here we go," Captain Fremont muttered, as he and Dutch hung onto the truss on either side of Evan, their security lines attached to their belts.

The water meadows were engulfed in the maelstrom and a huge wave struck the palisade of the equipment yard with a crash. Down it went and disappeared in the swirling muck. The behemoth shuddered as the wave hit it, and the water climbed its legs as though the machine were getting into the bath. Higher—higher—

Don't let it reach the boiler, Evan prayed. *We shall be helpless to come to the aid of all these poor people—*

The behemoth rocked under the onslaught, and Evan controlled the walking apparatus with all the strength in his body, making tiny adjustments to the behemoth's stance in an effort to help it bear up under the strain.

And then the land itself came to their aid, spreading the water far and wide, cupping it at the foot of the mountains and throwing it back into the riverbed, the lowest point in the valley. The main force of it thundered away to the south after taking a careless swing through the water meadows, leaving a mile-wide path of detritus and death in its wake.

Within minutes, the wash of water receded to the behemoth's knees, and at the same time, the pressure in the boiler reached working levels. Dutch seemed to force his jaws to relax by sheer effort of will, and hoarsely said, "Thanks be to God for His protection."

"Thanks be to the Meriwether-Astor Manufacturing Works for building such a sturdy machine," Fremont managed, surprising a huff of a laugh out of Evan, who had honestly wondered if he would ever be able to laugh again.

Then the magnitude of the disaster sobered him, and he brought the behemoth to a full standing position. "Come," he said. "Let us see if we can save some lives, now that ours have been preserved through the grace of God and no efforts of our own."

"I have an idea," Fremont said. "Allow me to grasp that corner beam of the palisade. Perhaps we can encourage men to climb upon it. If they also climb the legs, we might save twice as many."

"An excellent plan."

And so, with Fremont working the pincer arm, they hauled the sole remaining corner post out of the ground and set off toward the main encampment. The streets of the town were running with two feet of water, but to their amazement, it seemed that the little adobe buildings were tougher than they looked. Not a single plant remained, though one or two of the older trees still stood. The church bell began to ring the alarm, so it was clear that at least one of the friars had survived.

"We will bring any survivors to the mission," Evan said. "Surely someone will be able to render medical aid—and if not, I will leave the behemoth to the two of you, and do it myself."

"But I have only had a day or two of experience at the walking controls," Fremont objected from his perch in the gunner's chair. "I cannot do it!"

"It is amazing what we are capable of when we must do something," Dutch told him. "For now, let us concentrate on our task."

The behemoth waded into the water meadows, which were ten feet deep in muddy water and debris. Men clung to bits of wood, to swimming horses, to doors and furniture, waving frantically. From the hatch, Dutch leaned out and encouraged them to climb on to legs and beam. Some brave souls pushed unconscious comrades onto the beam before them, and climbed on themselves, clinging and screaming in terror as the behemoth lifted them into the air above the flood. Evan's brain calculated angle, weight, and speed with lightning rapidity, the fear of what might happen if he made a single error with so many lives at stake forming a cold weight in his stomach.

They sloshed back to the mission with thirty men, lowering the beam and kneeling outside the gate so that the survivors might climb down. Then it was back into the water with cries of thanks and grief ringing in their ears.

On the fourth trip, it became clear that the water was receding. The able bodied formed ranks, and Evan was relieved to see that at the head of one such rescue party, about to set off, was Commander de Sola.

He cranked open the vents and leaned into the communication horn. "Ho, Commander! I am glad to see you are among the living."

De Sola shaded his eyes and gazed upward. "And I am even more glad to see you and *el Gigante*. I have never seen such heroism in all my years, senor. You shame me."

Heat crept into Evan's cheeks, which was a change from the bloodless fear in which he had been operating since the moment he had been startled awake. "Not at all, sir. I had a means to help at my disposal, and it appears that God might have been merciful as well."

"Truer words have never been spoken. I will leave you to your good work, and we will follow to see if any are yet alive in the shallows."

If it had been possible to make the behemoth snap a salute, Evan might have done it. As it was, he could only turn them about and stump off into the water, wading along what had been the access road toward the riverbed.

"At least we can be thankful our friends acted at night," he said. "Imagine what would have happened had the dam been swarming with hundreds of workers."

"I am sure they took that into account," Fremont said from the gunner's chair. "But the Californios have paid an awful price all the same—and when an investigation is mounted, there will be another price to pay."

"Perhaps there will be no evidence left," Dutch suggested from the hatch, where he hung outside and waved men toward them.

"I do not think the Californios will need evidence in order to find someone to blame," Fremont said. "Dams do not simply fail without reason."

"They will blame engineers such as myself," Dutch predicted. "I do not wish to be executed after surviving such an ordeal as we have survived this morning."

This awful possibility clung to Evan's thoughts like a particularly unpleasant cobweb even as they delivered dozens of men to safety, even as the day wore on and the water receded more and more. For such a dreadful event must have a cause, and whatever else they might be, men like de Sola and Ambassador de Aragon were not stupid.

Questions would be asked, and answers demanded. And it was not likely that he and his friends would like what would be found. They may have been successful in saving the witches and all the inhabitants of the river's banks and tributaries, but at what cost?

Evan was very much afraid that it would not be long before they found out.

CHAPTER 16

*G*loria lay in bed, watching the sky lighten with the sunrise, wondering if she dared get up. Twice this week she'd flung off the quilt and stood, only to be assaulted by such dizziness that she'd fallen back to the mattress, reeling and practically in a faint.

Now, added to her fear that her ruse with Joe would be discovered was the fear that she herself was being poisoned. They had been so careful, testing everything they ate, eating only foods that were shared with the family, drinking wine that others had tasted first. But even the wine had lost its savor and tasted flat.

Something was wrong—and yet when she looked in the mirror, she did not look ill. Other than lately, her color was good, and her hair seemed willing to behave when Ella put it up, which was not like it at all. Her eyes were not hollow, as the Viceroy's had been, nor did she dream violent and otherworldly dreams. Perhaps those were common only to the advanced stages of ergot poisoning. How long did the process take? And what should she do if every precaution could not save them?

Someone knocked briefly on the door and then Ella came in bearing her cup of chocolate—an indulgence of which Gloria had grown very fond. Ella closed the door with her hip, shutting out whomever might be listening in the corridor. "Are you awake, sister?"

"I am, but I'm afraid to get up."

"If you do not, you know the Ambassador will drag you out by main force. He is determined to get you and Joe on the train to San Francisco de Asis today. You have been lucky that the fainting spells have held him off for as long as they have."

Gloria did not remind her that they were not indeed a strategy. They were real.

With another knock, Isabela came in. They had turned the first hour of the morning into an agreeable custom of feminine conversation and plans for the day before she joined Joe for breakfast in his parlor. No one was allowed to interrupt them; in fact, Gloria rather suspected that Isabela's parents encouraged it, in hopes of a place at court for their youngest daughter since she had become such a confidante of the future Vicereine.

What they did not know was that Isabela yearned every moment for news of Evan, and as his irregular letters came only to Gloria, the girl had taken to visiting with the post in hand. In the absence of a letter, that had grown into a daily visit that all three of them looked forward to, almost like a breakfast for the soul. And through Isabela Gloria kept up to date on the movements of the women of the kingdom.

For her wearing of roses on the day her engagement had been announced had blazed through the kingdom in a silent wave that even now still lapped upon the shores of this house. She might meet a maid or a laundress in a corridor and see a rose discreetly tucked in a cotton cap, or a band of them embroidered on the brim, and a smile and a glance of encouragement would pass between them. She might walk with Isabela and Ella along the avenue, or to the mission for Sunday service, and exchange a nod with a woman in a beribboned black dress with a rose in her hair. Should she need a message passed from rancho to rancho, there was a hidden chain of unremarkable, unmemorable women who could cause the smallest of her wishes to be carried out.

With every glance, every smile, she acknowledged the silent sisterhood of the Royal Kingdom—women who had no voice yet managed to speak. Whose only loyalty was to husband, father, and prince, yet managed to rebel. Whose only tasks were in hearth and home, yet still wove a tapestry of loyalty and communication throughout the kingdom that resulted in help where it was needed, a letter passed where it must, a request given and granted.

In these weeks since Evan and Gloria's erstwhile husband had taken the Viceroy to safety, she had learned the true extent of the horror in the old Viceroy's and the Ambassador's treatment of Joe's mother. For Clara had been isolated from the community of women, and once abandoned in the desert, they had not been able to find her. If it had not been for the witches... Gloria thought of Joe, whose bravery and confidence continued to amaze her, and shuddered.

"Are you going to be sick?" Ella asked anxiously.

"No, I—" And then, as though Ella had spoken the nausea into being, she put down her cup abruptly and bolted for the water closet.

When she returned, pale and chilled, she could not face the chocolate, and pushed it away.

Ella and Isabela exchanged a wide-eyed glance, and Ella covered her mouth as though holding back a torrent of words.

"What is it?" Gloria said, rather irritably. "I cannot be expected to be perfect all the time. Inform the Ambassador I am ill and will not be able to travel today. If he puts up a fuss, show him the chamber pot."

Isabela's eyes danced. "My dear friend, you are not ill."

"I certainly am!" Gloria said with some indignation. "Would *you* like to see the chamber pot?"

"That is one of the signs, sister," Ella said. "You are with child!"

Gloria's jaw dropped for a moment before she collected herself. "Balderdash. Good heavens, I am an unmarried woman."

"You are now. But last month you were not," Ella informed her.

Gloria's ability to think ground to a halt, and memory flooded in to take its place. Memory of the one night she and the captain had spent as husband and wife in every sense of those beautiful words. The one night that was all she had to cherish in the face of the long months of the masquerade that was saving the young prince's life. One night that it now appeared would change every single night to come for the rest of her life.

"Surely not," she whispered. "It cannot happen after only one night."

"It can happen after only one *time*," Ella said. "Just ask Tia Clara. The old king had her once and when he found out she was expecting, he cast her off to the beast from San Gregorio."

Gloria had been wife to her husband more than only once during that wonderful night. Good heavens. Could it really be so?

As though someone had draped a warm blanket about her made of the finest, most fluffy wool, joy bubbled up and spread from her heart to her fingers and toes, warming her and bringing a smile to her lips. "I shall be a mother," she whispered. "I shall have our child—the captain's and mine!"

The two girls flung themselves upon her with hugs and kisses of congratulation, until at last Isabela drew away. "How long have you been having these spells, Gloria?" she asked.

"Why—why, I hardly know. I am not an expert in these things at all. I have never even spoken with a woman who was expecting. In Philadelphia, you know, one doesn't go out in public once one begins to show. But ... I suppose a week?"

Ella did some rapid calculations. "Then we have a month or two before it becomes noticeable."

"And you will bear the child in the winter. Near Christmas," Isabela put in.

Christmas! Could any gift be more wonderful? She and the captain—

No, she and Joe—

"Oh, dear heaven above." The blood seemed to be draining out of her head, and with one look at her face, Ella leaped to the pitcher and poured her a glass of water. Isabela brought over the basin, just in case. She drank the water down. When she could speak, she said aloud the thing that it was clear the girls had already concluded. "Joe. We—we must marry immediately, mustn't we?"

Isabela nodded slowly. "You must—and well before you begin to show. Within the month. Otherwise ..." A new thought seemed to strike her rather unpleasantly. "My dear, you will fail the doctor's prenuptial examination."

"I shall not have the wretched examination. We discussed this before. Joe will simply tell them it will not happen."

"They make everybody have it."

"Then he will tell them that we—we anticipated the wedding." Gloria lifted her chin defiantly, feeling herself blush at saying something so unladylike. "Or he can change the laws."

"You may change many things, but I am not certain you will be able to change that," Isabela said sadly.

"At the very least you must announce a date," Ella said. "We will solve the examination problem another day."

"You are right." Isabela straightened her back and became her usual practical self. "Today, it is urgent that the date be set. You cannot be exposed to gossip, and there must never be a whisper that the child is not the Viceroy's. Thank heavens the real Viceroy had your marriage annulled for non-consummation, and not some other reason. If it had not been approved by the church and announced in every congregation, you would be in a pretty pickle now."

"I am in a pickle as it is," Gloria retorted. "I do not wish to marry Joe. I want to find Stanford and marry him—again!"

"Also a problem for another day," Isabela told her. "Now, you must dress and tell Joe. Then go to the bishop and request that he set an early date. That is how it is done here."

Gloria's brows knit in an expression her father would have recognized as mulish, but deep down she acknowledged that Isabela was right. Much as she hated it, she must still keep up this charade. But …

What would happen when the Viceroy returned to find

her married to his half brother and expecting a child? For when they switched places, what would happen then? Would she have to stay married to him? For heaven's sake, would Stanford's child inherit the kingdom? Would she be forced to leave him or her here in order to be with the man she loved? No, that was mad. This was the point at which her plan had failed before. And she had as useful an answer now as she had then—which was to say, no answer at all.

"I must speak with Joe. Help me dress."

In ten minutes, she was dressed in a dark green linen skirt and a lacy blouse embroidered at high neck and cuffs with pale green leaves. The observant eye would note they were the leaves of briar roses, but just to be sure, Ella tucked a silk one into her coronet of braids.

Then she forced herself to walk calmly along the colonnade to Joe's suite of rooms, instead of doing what she really felt, which was picking up her skirts and running helterskelter in a panic. The guards at the door bowed as they did every morning. She smiled as she did every morning, and waited for them to announce her.

And then the door closed behind her and she did what she had never done—she burst into tears. They welled up with no warning, spilling down her cheeks in a torrent.

"Gloria!" Joe snatched up a damask napkin from the table, on which breakfast had already been laid, and pressed it into her hands. "What's the matter? Are you ill?"

"I wish I were," she wailed into the spotless cloth.

But she must take herself in hand. This was no time to break down—not after all they had been through. And besides, poor Joe didn't deserve to be afflicted with a snuffling mess. None of this was his fault.

She blew her nose and he pulled out a chair for her. "What has happened? Have you had news?"

"Only of—of a personal nature." She hiccupped and willed herself to speak coherently. "I thought I was being poisoned—fainting in the morning, being ill, things not tasting as they should."

His brows rose. "I thought you were doing all that on purpose. Stalling. So we wouldn't have to go to San Francisco de Asis."

"That was a side benefit."

"You are not being poisoned, surely? For if you were, I would have all the same symptoms. We eat everything together."

The thought of him having such symptoms made her smile, and he relaxed a little, though he could not know the source of her humor.

"That would be impossible. You see, Isabela and Ella have just now informed me that I am expecting a child. Who could imagine that the symptoms would be the same as poisoning?"

His face went utterly slack.

In the ringing silence she went on, "They also inform me that it is now a matter of some urgency that we marry. We must go to the mission at once and ask the bishop to set an early date."

"But—but we do not want to marry. Each other."

She nodded, and squeezed the long-fingered tanned hand lying on the tablecloth. "I know. This is where my plan broke down before, do you remember? We thought we could figure it out as we went along … but no one anticipated *this* turn of events."

"No. Are—are you sure?"

"Quite sure. I have no experience along these lines, but you may rest assured that every woman in this house has, whether directly or in their endless preoccupation with marriage and children. Isabela and Ella have no doubt I am expecting ... and I am sorry that it means we must take this charade farther than we want to." She hesitated. "I know your feelings for Ella. Just as I want to be married to the captain, I know you would much rather be married to her."

His face, which had gone pale at her revelations, now flooded with color, and he pulled his hand from under hers. "Ella and I will never marry."

"Not if we have to go through with this, no."

"Even if we don't." He swallowed, then seemed to steel himself to go on. "Gloria, there is something I must tell you."

She could not read his eyes, but his mouth trembled. "Oh Joe," she whispered. Her stomach rolled with dread. "Please tell me you are not ill. That they have poisoned you despite all our precautions."

"No. I am not ill. But ..." He cleared his throat. "Gloria, I have been deceiving you. Deceiving everyone. I am not the Viceroy's bastard half brother."

It took her a moment to adjust her expectations of bad news to such an innocuous reality. "That does not signify. It is your resemblance to him that counts, not your relationship."

"I am his bastard half *sister*."

His words made no sense. In a morning that had seen her entire life turned upside down, she could not bear any more. "Joe, this is no time for levity and nonsense. We must come up with a plan, and I cannot do it alone."

"My name is not Joe," he said in the same flat tone. "My name is Honoria Luisa de San Gregorio, and I am a woman."

"No, you aren't," she objected stubbornly. Had he gone mad?

He rose and, to her utter astonishment, began to disrobe. "Joe! For heaven's sake, what are you doing? What if someone should come in? Stop it! Stop it at once!" She had no desire to see him unclothed. The only man she—

Gloria's frantic thoughts ground to a halt as his shirt came off. Then his belt.

Her very brain stalled.

Acknowledged the evidence of her own eyes.

She raised her gaze to that familiar face that from one moment to the next had become the face of a perfect stranger. Now it was her turn to be utterly bereft of speech.

Joe—Honoria—tucked in his—her—shirt and buckled her belt, then shrugged on the short black jacket. "I am sorry to have embarrassed you, but sometimes actions are stronger than words."

"How—how—all this time—Evan—the prison—"

"I wear a device invented by May Lin that enables me to behave as a man as long as I am able to remain at least partially dressed. So far, I have managed it."

"But—but—why—"

"Gloria, you know as well as I what can happen to a woman alone here. Someone had to smuggle information to the witches. Someone had to sow the seeds of revolution. It happens to be a talent of mine—and it was only once I was shanghaied to work on the dam that I could no longer do what I had been sent to do."

But Gloria could not think of politics when this revelation had much more personal consequences. "Does Ella know?"

Honoria's face warmed with humor, and her long-lashed

eyes twinkled. "Of course. We have loved each other since we were children. But of course, society being what it is, we can never marry."

Any student at St. Cecilia's Academy for Young Ladies knew that friendships among girls reached many levels of affection and intimacy. And during her sojourn with the witches, Gloria had learned that love came in many shapes and forms. Now that she herself had experienced the fullness of love, it broke her heart to know that these brave women, who had shouldered the burden that Gloria had thrust upon them with such grace and skill, could never know the fullest, most sanctioned of its joys.

But then, perhaps they had found joy another way. Perhaps there was more to love than a document that conferred a title and status upon one or the other. *Perhaps there are more ways to love in heaven and earth, Gloria my dear, than are dreamt of in your philosophy.*

"I am so sorry," she whispered. "I want to see you happy. You and Ella have suffered so much."

"Don't be sorry. Now that we have found one another again, we *are* happy. Simply being able to see her every day is a gift." She resumed her seat, and helped herself to a glistening wedge of orange.

Suddenly Gloria was ravenous. When they had eaten all there was to eat, she was about to return to the prickly topic of their marriage, when an idea struck her with blinding clarity.

"That's it!"

Honoria regarded her over the rim of her cup of coffee, which she preferred to chocolate. "Yes?"

"That's how we'll get out of it." She leaned in, her excitement bubbling into her voice. "I have not been able to figure out how we will manage the marriage when the time comes for you and the Viceroy to switch back."

"That has also been a concern to me."

"But you yourself have provided the key. When the Viceroy comes back, he will take your place, and we will tell him that you are not a man, but a woman. *That* marriage will have to be annulled and we will both be free."

Honoria's forehead crinkled. "It will not work. For his name will be on the marriage document. There will be no difference—except that at least one of us will be quietly removed and executed. You may be entitled to a state funeral, but it is certain that I will not."

Gloria nearly dropped her cup. "What? Why should Honoria not simply go about her business and take up her life again? Why should I not do so?"

"For a dozen reasons—such as impersonating a sovereign, aiding in a kidnapping, but most important, loving where it is illegal to love, or marrying someone whom you ought not to marry—which in this country is punishable by death."

Gloria's cheeks cooled to ice as her excitement faded and horror poured in. She had thought they were in a tight spot before. She'd had no idea that in revealing herself, Honoria's honesty could mean death to them both.

CHAPTER 17

*E*lla Maria de Balboa did not seem unduly bothered about the prospect of imminent execution when Gloria returned, shattered, to the privacy of her chamber. "I have looked *La Llorona* in the face a time or two before this," she told her, fishing the green linen skirt's matching jacket out of the closet trunk. "She has told me my time is not yet. Put it out of your mind and finish dressing. One does not pay a visit to the bishop in one's shirtsleeves, be they ever so prettily embroidered by one's friends."

"But—but Ella, oh, why did you not tell me?"

Ella gazed at her. "Because you would behave exactly like this. You are not going to give us away, are you?"

"Of course not. But it is so dangerous, this game we are playing!"

"More dangerous than carrying a man's child? I think not."

Gloria did not want to think about the actual mechanics of that just now. She had nine months to think about it, and to discreetly ask questions of Isabela's mother, who might possibly stand in for those she really preferred, namely Mother Mary and Tia Clara. At the moment, she just needed to get through this day. And then somehow come up with a plan to get through tomorrow, and the day after that.

Once she was suitably dressed, Isabela came in with a length of black lace. "You must wear the *mantilla* in the bishop's presence, Gloria. Wear it over your face the entire time to signify, er, blushing modesty."

Gloria sighed. "If I must. At the very least he will not be able to see my rose."

"He would not know what it meant in any case," Ella told her with some satisfaction. "Men have no business in the affairs of women, and prelates even less."

With these bracing words, Gloria went down to meet Honoria—Joe—dadburn it, the Viceroy. She must be very, very careful not to slip and address him as anything but Your Serene Highness, which would cover all contingencies. They had not even walked as far as the end of the gardens when Ignatio de la Carrera y Borreaga met them on an intersecting path.

"I have been checking my hydrangeas," he greeted them. "Another month and they will be in full bloom. Are you unescorted, Your Serene Highness?"

"By choice, my dear sir." Honoria smiled with real affection. "We are going to the bishop to set a wedding date."

Joy bloomed on the man's face, and he grasped the royal hand to give it a delighted shake. "I am so pleased. If I may be so bold, would you allow me to accompany you ... in a father's place?"

"We would be pleased and honored," Gloria told him. "Since neither of us has any experience in these matters, yours will be welcome indeed."

The broad avenue accommodated them three abreast, talking amiably until they reached the cool shadow of the mission. And then Gloria's hand tightened in the crook of Honoria's elbow as they heard an all too familiar voice.

"Why, Your Serene Highness," Ambassador de Aragon said smoothly, emerging into the sunlight. "What a pleasant surprise to see you and Miss Meriwether-Astor out of doors. Senorita, I trust you are feeling better?"

Trapped, Gloria could only say, "I am, thank you."

"Then perhaps your maids might be instructed to make your small household ready to travel soon?"

"We have other matters on our minds today, sir," Honoria said stiffly. "We are on our way to see the bishop."

"They are setting a date," de la Carrera said happily. "If you will excuse us, sir? Such a happy event must not be delayed by even a moment."

The Ambassador seemed to gather his wits with difficulty. "A wedding date? This is rather hasty, is it not? Why, you have not even set a date to begin your progress about the kingdom. Surely the kingdom must come first, before matters of a personal nature?"

De la Carrera chuckled. "How long has it been since you were young and in love, Your Excellency? Come, let us not keep them any longer. In any case, when His Serene Highness sets off on his progress, you know the date of the wedding will be the first thing his people will wish to know."

Outnumbered, the ambassador did the only thing he

could. He bowed ... and then followed them into the church. Gloria would much rather he had gone about his business out of her sight, but now was one of those times when she must choose her battles.

An audience was requested and granted with alacrity, and their little party was shown into the bishop's spacious west-facing study, where arched windows admitted views of the sea and, presumably, reminded man of his insignificance beside God's creation. "Your Serene Highness," he said, "you had only to send word, and I would have attended you."

"It is we who seek your approval, Bishop." Honoria handed Gloria into a studded Spanish leather chair that had probably come over with the *conquistadores*, and seated herself. The other three followed suit. "We wish to set a wedding date."

The bishop took in Gloria's suitably bowed head covered in its frosting of lace with approval. "Normally at this juncture I would ask the couple if they had the approval of their families, but that does not seem appropriate in this case."

"His Serene Highness has graciously allowed me to serve in the place of a father, though of course there is no replacement for our late lamented Viceroy," de la Carrera said. "I can say without hesitation that San Luis Obispo de Tolosa approves their decision. We consider Miss Meriwether-Astor a member of the family, and support her wholeheartedly as she contemplates this step."

"Then let the calendar of saints' days be consulted." From a shelf behind the ornately carved oak table he used as a desk, the bishop lifted down an enormous book whose pages were rippled and spotted with age. "What part of the year had you considered?" he asked Honoria. "Once Your Serene Highness's progress about the kingdom is completed, we might consider next February, when the weather can reasonably be expected to cooperate."

The Ambassador nodded with approval. "February would be an excellent time for a wedding. All the grandees and their families can be expected to attend after Christmas but before spring planting."

"We prefer April," Honoria said. "Or perhaps May, if we cannot be accommodated sooner."

"April of next year?" The bishop nodded to the clerk waiting beside him, who uncapped a pen and pulled a leather-bound diary closer.

"No. April of this year. Or May."

The bishop's hand froze in the act of turning a page in the saints' calendar. "I beg your pardon? This year, did you say?"

"Yes," Honoria told him as though this were nothing unusual.

"But it is April now." The bishop looked down at the diary, as though confirming the fact.

"I am quite aware of the date," Honoria replied. "I do not wish to wait. In fact, I have waited long enough. When I go on progress, I wish it to be with the Vicereine at my side, to introduce her to my people. Of course, the coronation may wait until after the progress."

"But—but Sir—"

"Your Serene Highness, there is absolutely no reason for such unseemly haste," the Ambassador cut in, as though finishing the sputtering bishop's sentence. "In fact, if you marry now, the people will most certainly look upon it with a degree of censure, as though you had, er, anticipated the ceremony."

"That has most certainly not happened!" de la Carrera exclaimed. "I can vouch for the utter rectitude of this young couple's behavior. My own daughter has been so much in Miss Meriwether-Astor's company that there has been scarcely a moment when she has been alone with the Viceroy."

"Young couples are notorious for finding moments to be alone," the ambassador said darkly. "Really, sir, I must protest, for your own good."

"I will decide what is for my own good," Honoria said with cold hauteur. "These inferences cast a slur not only upon the lady present, but upon me. I can assure you that I do not like the presumption suggested by censure from my subjects at all. I advise you to tread carefully, sir."

Ambassador de Aragon flushed as scarlet as the ribbon crossing Honoria's chest under her short jacket.

The bishop became very focused upon the ancient pages in front of him and hastened to proceed. "Your name-day saint, sir, is San Felipe Neri, the patron saint of joy. May I suggest that your wedding day be the same—the twenty-sixth of May? That would give the bakers time to create a cake, the messengers time to return with the acceptances of the grandees, and the dressmakers time to make our future Vicereine her wedding gown." He bowed in her direction.

As she graciously inclined her head, Gloria added up weeks with lightning speed. It would not be wise to quibble over the date, lest the Ambassador feel free to make more impertinent remarks. At the same time, on May 26 she would be eight weeks along. Would she be showing by then? Could they adjust the dress to hide it if she was? How she wished Isabela were here!

She turned to Honoria. "If May twenty-sixth holds meaning for you, sir, then it will mean everything to me."

It would also give them time to think of a way out of the fix that switching the real Viceroy back into his place presented.

Honoria took that as the approval it was meant to be. "Then it is settled. We will marry on San Felipe's day."

"At the royal chapel in San Francisco de Asis?" the Ambassador inquired, smooth as an assassin slipping a blade between the ribs. "As your forebears have done for generations?"

"Perhaps," Honoria said. "We have sent for my fiancée's private airship. Once it arrives, travel between the ranchos will become much simpler and more expedient. In fact, one could spend the night before the wedding practically anywhere in the kingdom, and fly to San Francisco de Asis in time for the ceremony in the evening."

The bishop mumbled his sentiments on that head in the Californio tongue—or perhaps he was imploring protection from a saint—as he slumped in his thronelike chair with a shudder.

A commotion broke out in the corridor, and the Ambassador, whom Gloria was quite sure had been about to make an additional disparaging remark, clamped his molars together and frowned in the direction of the clerk. But instead of opening the door to request propriety outside, the young man was thrown back as it was flung open with such force it nearly bounced off the paneled wall.

A monk burst in. "Your Excellency—Your Serene Highness —a messenger—"

On his heels came a man in military uniform, stained to the knees with what appeared to be mud. He snapped a salute and ignored everyone in the room but the Viceroy, who rose from the chair. "Your Serene Highness, I bring news in haste from the water meadows and Commander de Sola."

"I thank you for your haste. What has happened?" Honoria asked.

"Sir, the dam has failed."

"What?" Ambassador de Aragon lunged forward. "Impossible."

"Not only possible, it has been a disaster. We can only be grateful to God that it happened during the night, when all were asleep. Hundreds of additional lives could have been lost."

"How many were lost?" Honoria asked.

"Thirty-four, Your Serene Highness. Twelve soldiers, twenty-two rancho volunteers, and the rest conscripted—er, that is, involuntary labor."

Gloria, who had been frozen into the silence of shocked horror, sighed and found that her lungs could resume their work. *Oh, Evan. Thirty-four people.* Men who would never see their families again—many of whom had never wanted to be there in the first place. The innocent who had given their lives in order that many, many more might be saved.

Honoria crossed herself and bowed her head. "Send a message to all the missions for a special mass to be sung on Sunday for the souls of all who perished."

"It will be done, Your Serene Highness." Before the words had even escaped the bishop's pale lips, the clerk had begun to write.

Tears welled into Gloria's eyes and spilled down her cheeks. She pulled a handkerchief embroidered with yellow rosebuds from her sleeve and wept into it as though her heart were breaking. She could not help it—the tears seemed to come from nowhere, just as they had done earlier this morning. Embarrassed, she turned her face into Honoria's shoulder and attempted to get her emotions under control.

Part of it was grief for the lost men and for their families. Part of it was gratitude that the witches and the Navapai villages up and down the river would now be saved. And a part of it was awe that with one act, the Royal Kingdom's plans for commerce and the eventual annexation of the Texican Territory were now foiled, perhaps forever.

The silence in the face of her tears slowly changed from respect to discomfort. She must recover herself. After mopping her eyes, she blew her nose and sat up. "I do apologize," she murmured. "This news has me quite overcome."

Honoria patted her hand. "Would you like some refreshment, dear?"

"No, no. I am quite well now, thank you."

When she raised her gaze to those of the bishop and the Ambassador, the eyes of the former were filled with relief at not having to witness female vapors any longer. And the eyes of the Ambassador...

Gloria forced herself to remain still. To not flinch in the face of such naked suspicion and loathing. "You have done this," he whispered.

"Your Excellency?" the bishop inquired.

"You have done this," de Aragon said in a stronger voice, pointing at Gloria. "I do not know how, but through some nefarious and devil-inspired means, you have caused that dam to fail."

"Mind your tongue, sir!" Honoria said.

The Ambassador backed away until he was pressed against a heavy oak bookcase, his pointing finger now shaking—the very figure from a medieval painting of a visit from Old Scratch. "I see it now, as though God has caused the scales to fall from my eyes. You have never supported the late Viceroy's vision—his plans, so carefully constructed and carried out with years of effort. You said yourself that his dreams of commerce, of shipping and transport along the river into the heart of the continent, were old-fashioned and inefficient. You are the head of a company that uses airships, and in your manic determination to line your own pockets, you have made sure that the late Viceroy's dream would die and your godforsaken airships would take its place!"

"Silence!" Honoria snapped. "You go too far in your mad imaginings, sir. Have you no respect for the lives of your countrymen—to say nothing of my future bride?"

"I have all the respect in the world for the former," the Ambassador retorted. "But I am very much afraid that this woman—this viper whom you have clasped to your bosom— does not. In all likelihood it was she who paid spies and assassins to rig explosives and cause the dam to fail!"

"You are utterly mad," Gloria managed through cold lips. "You have shanghaied hundreds of men for slave labor. Say rather that someone with engineering skill has purposely built a fault into your dam, and you are reaping the bitter fruit of your actions!"

"Far from it," he snarled. "I am the only one in this room— in all the kingdom—whom you have not been able to blind with your simpering charm and your feminine blandishments that drip honey in the ears while they hold a dagger to the heart."

Now was not the time to point out his distressing mix of metaphors. Not when the confusion in the bishop's eyes could turn to suspicion and then conviction between one breath and the next.

"Enough," Honoria said. "You will cease these mad ravings and apologize to your future princess at once."

"Even Our Lord did not apologize when He spoke the truth, though it meant His death."

"Do not compare yourself to Our Lord lest you be guilty of heresy as well as treason," Honoria said in a tone hushed with the threat of power. "Upon your knees, sir, and apologize, or you may hope I will merely have you banished from the kingdom."

"Whereupon I would call upon all the leaders of the surrounding territories with whom I have been building treaties and agreements all these years, and ask them to join me in taking back the country from the worm at its heart."

"How dare you!" Gloria said on a gasp.

"I am not alone." The ambassador drew himself up with pride and looked Honoria in the eye. "There are those who share my dedication to your father—who would follow him into battle even as you shrink from it."

"Are you implying—"

"I imply nothing. I simply state that men such as I—many men—may fight for what they believe in, no matter how young and deceived their prince may be."

"Treason! Guards!" Honoria shouted. Immediately, the sentries standing in the corridor burst into the room. "Take him, and imprison him where his ravings cannot be heard."

"You shall not touch me," the Ambassador said with acid contempt. "Guards, take that woman. She has poisoned the mind of your prince and must be removed at once for his safety."

The six men moved several steps into the room in instinctive obedience before the one in front gathered his wits enough to realize he would have to go through Honoria in order to get to Gloria.

Honoria stared them down. "Think very carefully about the next movement you make, sir. Treason is found in actions as well as words."

Helplessly, the men looked to the bishop for instruction.

"For the love of all the saints, man, you must not lay a hand upon the anointed of God!" he snapped in exasperation. "Do as your prince tells you!"

As one man, they turned to seize the Ambassador. But he had already slipped behind them, and before they could cross the room, he was out the door. One of them drew a horn from a cord at his side and blew a blast upon it, and they tumbled out in pursuit.

But Gloria knew it was already too late. Ambassador de Aragon had connections and spies and men who were beholden to him in ways even she could not imagine. He would vanish, and then reappear when he was least expected, armed and dangerous, even if it were only with his poisonous tongue.

When the detachment of soldiers returned an hour later, it was to report that the Ambassador could not be found.

"Have the trains stopped at the stations before this one," Honoria commanded. "Search the town, the rancho, and the outlying farms. He is a traitor and must come before me in manacles to answer for his crimes."

But de Aragon had been too quick, his contingency plans too efficient. He had vanished like the morning mist heated by the rising sun. Gloria had no doubt whatsoever that, before the seamstresses could even finish her wedding gown, the country would be plunged into civil war.

CHAPTER 18

*T*hough she was in her own navigation gondola once again, her hands on the helm, Alice still could not quite comprehend the manner of their salvation. They sailed in a huge circle over the water meadows and watched the tiny figures below as what had clearly been rescue operations became salvage and cleanup operations. No one fired at them. No one paid any attention to them whatsoever, other than the occasional individual who shaded his eyes to look up at a sight he had clearly never seen.

"We've been working on *Swan* for days," Jake explained again. "While you lot were rabbiting about in the bush, Benny and me got the creases pounded out of her hull, and May Lin found us a propeller. It's the wrong size, and makes her list a little—"

"I noticed that," Captain Hollys said absently, his gaze on the vista below.

"But she's in a lot better shape than she was, all stove in and helpless up on that mesa."

"But the gasbag," Alice said. "I never would have believed it could be repaired."

"Nor I," Jake admitted. "But May Lin and Mother Mary are a pair of magicians, for true. Squirreled in those tunnels were a few lengths of silk. Mother Mary said they were for a wedding dress for someone, but I don't believe that. The stuff is peacock green."

"It looks a bit funny," Benny said, "and it's holding air, not gas, but beggars can't be choosers, innit?"

"No indeed." Alice rumpled his hair with affection. "I'm half tempted to promote the pair of you for bravery and skill beyond the call of duty—both for the rescue and for making our ship as whole as she can be outside of dry dock."

"That rescue certainly warrants it," Ian told them. "I have never been closer to a miracle than that moment, not even in the canal in Venice when the kraken had Claire and Lizzie in its coils. And it's down to you two."

Benny flushed with pleasure, and even Jake looked close to it.

"We weren't really running away from you that night, Captain," Jake said to Alice, his voice rough with emotion. "I hope you know now that we were running to get *Swan* in the air. We knew you would need a second if something went wrong, and *Swan* was all we had."

"That's more than many a man will ever have," Alice told him, heroically resisting the urge to kiss him upon the cheek, which would have embarrassed him so much he'd likely have fled the deck. "I feel a mighty need to offer our services down there. Those poor men don't deserve what we did to them. Our objective was the dam, but that don't mean we don't have their deaths on our hands. Maybe we could ferry a few to hospital, if they don't have the means to help them here."

Benny pointed. "Captain, look! Is that the behemoth? Cor, what a monster it is, for true!"

Alice leaned to look out of the viewing port. "Last I saw of that thing, it was aiming its great cannon at Evan and Gloria."

"It waved at us!" Benny bounced upon his toes and waved back, though it was unlikely the pilot could see him.

That decided the question. "If Evan is aboard, maybe he can turn that thing into a mooring mast and make himself useful."

Swan did not respond to the helm with her usual grace, but that was only to be expected. None of them had the trim of her yet, with the deck tilted from the too-large propeller on the one side, one gasbag full of air instead of its proper contents, and the forward vane crushed beyond recognition, but still … she was in the air. Alice reckoned that was one hundred percent better than being at the bottom of that riverbed, dead as a doornail.

In a banking turn, Alice brought her around and they sank toward the behemoth. Men scattered out of her shadow like sparrows from beneath a stooping hawk. As *Swan* settled into a landing position, the behemoth stumped over to meet her. Awkwardly, it reached up, its hooklike appendage snapping fruitlessly in the air.

"It's trying to grab the bow line!" Benny exclaimed in delight. "It's Evan. See him there in the viewing port?"

On the fourth try the mechanical marvel managed to wrap one of its pincers around the line, holding it taut as *Swan* floated gently to the ground. There wasn't so much as a bush on the flat, scoured clean by the rage of the escaping river, but when they leaped down, Benny and Jake managed to find a boulder to tie her two aft ropes to.

They disembarked to see Evan, Captain Fremont, and a stranger clambering down the iron ladder built into the behemoth's right leg. Evan's face was lit with delight as he hugged Alice and shook Ian's hand with vigor.

"I never thought—" He caught himself. "I mean, I am glad to see you. Fancy *Swan* being flightworthy again."

"Thank Benny and Jake," Ian said. "The good Lord knows we did, having seen more of the west side of your building project than we intended to." His long glance at the swath of destruction in which the behemoth had been working was enough to tell the tale, and Alice saw, not understanding, but confirmation dawn on both Evan's and the captain's faces.

The less said of what they'd done, the better.

She turned to the man who had been with her friends in the behemoth, but who now hung back, gazing up at *Swan*'s fuselage as though trying to remember where he'd seen it before. "Will you introduce us to your companion?"

"I wish I could," Evan said. "He was with Joe—sorry, Honoria and I in the gaol here. But he has no memory of who he is or where he comes from."

The man clicked his heels in the Prussian manner and gave Alice a courtly bow. "They call me Dutch, and I would be honored if you would address me by that name, too. I find I do not mind it so much on the tongues of friends."

She held out her hand and shook his. "Alice Hollys, and this is my husband, Captain Ian Hollys. My navigator, Jake Fletcher McTavish, and my gunner, Benjamin Stringfellow."

"These are names worthy of good men," Dutch told the boys, shaking their hands firmly. "But you have heard that the law forbidding flight is now repealed? Is that why so many of the Californios are treated to this so unusual sight?"

"We came to offer help," Ian told him with a glance at Evan.

"That I have no doubt will be gratefully received," Dutch told him. "Here is your welcome party."

Alice turned to see a company of horsemen riding toward them, their faces tilted up in astonishment at the sight of *el Gigante* holding *Swan*'s bow line the way a child holds a balloon at the fair.

"Senor Douglas," called the man at the head of the party, "I have seen you put *el Gigante* to use in many ways, but I confess I never expected such a sight as this."

His horse snorted and skittered as *Swan* moved gently in the wind, her shadow brushing it and frightening it as though its very shade were alive. The man must be an expert horseman, for he brought the animal under control with his knees alone, the reins loose in his hands.

Quickly, Evan made the introductions. So this was the Commander de Sola who had befriended Evan in the prison, whose dream Evan had interpreted and which had led in the end to the outrageous plan to switch the Viceroy with his half-sister. Had any two men been friends with such enormous secrets standing between them? What was the likelihood their friendship would survive the unveiling of even one of those secrets?

But now was not the time to wonder about that.

"We have come to offer our help," Ian said. "If there are injured men who need care that you cannot provide here, may we take them by air to a hospital?"

De Sola must have stiffened, for his horse danced sideways

and was again brought under control. "How is it possible that our suffering is known already east of the mountains?"

Here was a poser, but Ian was up to it. While Alice felt herself blanch at the word *suffering*, her husband said, "Anyone in contact with the river knows of it for hundreds of miles. The drop in the water level tells its own story. We assumed some disaster had occurred, and set out as soon as we could. As we crossed the mountains, we could see what had happened."

De Sola looked as though he was having trouble overcoming his astonishment enough to speak. "That is ... singular of you, Captain. Such generosity from citizens of a foreign nation is—Frankly, I am having difficulty believing it."

If you knew the half of it. Alice, keep your composure. There will be time enough for guilt and mourning later.

"In battle, sir, you know that the code of a gentleman in the care of the injured takes no sides. And while our nations are not at war, I believe that when nature itself goes on the attack, men from all walks of life may band together to help one another."

De Sola gazed across the water meadows to where the dam had been, and where there was now nothing except a rushing torrent, its roar faint in the distance. "If I could be sure it *was* nature, as you say, I would rest more easily," he said, almost to himself. "There will be questions."

Now Alice's blood halted in her veins altogether, and it was with an effort that she kept her gaze upon him and did not glance at her companions like a guilty bandit. Beside her, Benny shifted, and she laid a hand, heavy with caution, upon his shoulder.

"If we may be of assistance," Ian went on as though he had

not heard, "I hope you will allow it. Where is the closest military hospital?"

"We have none such." De Sola brought his attention back from wherever it had been questing. "The missions possess apothecaries and doctors who can provide expert care. How many men can your ship take?"

"A hundred at least." Ian glanced at Alice for corroboration, and she nodded.

"We have that and more," de Sola said sadly. "Some we can care for here, but the men most severely injured will be glad of your help. It is not likely they would survive two days on the train to Reno, which is north and east of here, and where the most skilled of our doctors are."

"We can make the journey in two hours," Alice said.

He shook his head in amazement. "How can such a thing be possible? Never mind—I cannot myself contemplate it. If you will moor your ship near the fort, we can begin bringing out the men at once."

"Truly?" Alice said. "They will not raise a fuss about flying?"

"Senora, many of them are in no condition to fuss—in fact, there may be angels waiting to bear them even higher into the heavens while you fly. But we will accept your generous offer in hopes that one or two angels will be disappointed."

With a salute, he wheeled his horse about and the company followed, cantering back in the direction they had come. As the dust blew gently southward on the breeze, Ian said, "There goes a man of true leadership. I can only hope that he never finds out what we have done."

"Is that likely?" Evan asked. "Were you able to make it look like an accident?"

"Stuffing an iron boiler full of explosives in the flow regulator?" Jake said. "If any bits survived, anyone might see it was deliberate."

"We ought to check for debris soon, before they recover enough to conduct an investigation," Captain Fremont suggested. "We might use the pretext of searching for survivors from the guard towers."

"There were some from the south tower," Alice said. "They ran onto the mesa. And there were a few scouts up on the north cliff who saw us underwater, because they shot at us."

"So you can be identified?" Captain Fremont asked, a worried frown creasing his brow.

"The submersible could," Alice allowed. "If pieces of it survive. But they wouldn't have seen Ian and me personally. They might suspect sabotage, but there is nothing to connect the pilots of the *Chaloupe* with the captain of *Swan* rendering aid, that I can think of."

"Let's hope not," Ian said grimly. "We shall have to live with the consequences of what we have done in any case. Let us set to work, then, and expiate our sins as best we can."

"Shall I tow you over to the fort?" Evan said with an attempt at lightening their spirits. "I don't imagine I'll ever get the chance again to fly such a kite."

"Only if you let me up into that monster so I can see how it works," Alice said.

"Certainly. Jake? Benny? What about you?"

But her crewmen were already backing away. "I'll stay with the ship, Captain," Jake told her. "Mechanical horses were enough for me."

Under more cheerful circumstances, Alice would have been agog at the inner workings of the behemoth, and at

Evan's and Captain Fremont's skill as they worked together with seamless ease, one on the legs and one on the gripping arm. She hung out the door to watch her ship floating serenely behind, Ian visible at the helm through the viewing port. Already her mind was buzzing with the possibilities of building their own behemoth, not for war, but for useful tasks about the estate. Even something as simple as pollarding the trees along the avenue could be done by a machine such as this, rather than the groundskeeper's risking life and limb with ladders and saws and shears.

She'd risk life and limb if only she could see the place once again, and grow old there with Ian. How much she'd changed since they'd embarked on a life together!

At the fort, the boys leaped down and secured *Swan* to the flagpole in the middle of the parade ground, and tied her lines to the support posts of the colonnade. Men began to trickle out of the buildings, their mouths agape, and others brought out their companions on stretchers.

Before he had lifted to shadow Alice and Ian's journey down the river, Jake had reported, they and the witches had unloaded nearly all the mechanicals from the hold. Only a single horse remained—the one Jake had ridden back in Resolution in what seemed another life. Alice didn't know why they hadn't taken it out, too, but there was no time to wonder now. She and Ian and the witches had a debt to pay, and she would pay it pronto, before another sunset.

In less than an hour, the injured were laid out on the floor of the hold, with Benny and a couple of de Sola's soldiers to watch over them and bring refreshment if they were able to take it. The commander himself snapped a salute to Alice and Ian as the last of the soldiers disembarked. "With your permission, I should like to go with you. We have sent a message to the mission at Reno, but we will likely arrive first, if what you say is true. It is my responsibility to see my men to safety."

"We would be honored," Alice said solemnly. "You and your men will be the first to fly in the entire country."

He did not seem as pleased about this as one might expect. "I confess it makes me very uneasy—as though I am putting myself on a level with angels."

"We could capture you and take you against your will, if that would help," Evan suggested.

De Sola laughed. "No, if I am to mount up with wings as eagles, I will take responsibility for it. Think of the story I will have to tell my children when we return. Senor Douglas, are you coming, too?"

Evan shook his head. "I hear there are survivors from the south tower who may be stranded on the mesa. Captain Fremont and I will go to retrieve them as soon as you are safely away."

De Sola grasped his arm. "You are as loyal a man as any in my own company. *Gracias, senor.*"

Evan blushed and managed to shake the man's hand before he got himself away. Alice watched him and Captain Fremont climb the behemoth's leg and scramble into the pilot's chamber, then turned to find the man Dutch standing in the gangway as though he wanted something.

"Commander de Sola," he said stiffly, "I request permission to come with you."

The commander seemed taken aback. "Your reason, sir?"

"I am a free man, am I not, by your own prince's command?"

"You are."

"Then I must take my opportunities as I find them. I was told I was brought here from Reno. If I may find any clues as to my identity or the whereabouts of my wife and daughters, it will be there."

"Senor Douglas and the captain will miss your companionship."

"And I theirs. But I must go." When he received the commander's permission, the man called Dutch seemed to stand straighter, and went to the hold to render what assistance he could to the injured.

There was no more time to waste. "Captain Hollys, would you give the order, please?" she asked her husband as Commander de Sola made his way over to the viewing port and looked about for something to hang on to.

Ian leaned into the speaking horn. "Cast off, gentlemen."

When Benny and Jake had done so and boarded, Alice called, "Up ship!" and they fell into the sky.

With a gasp, de Sola clutched a bit of pipe and watched the ground drop away beneath their feet. He clapped a hand to his mouth and for a dreadful moment Alice thought he was going to lose the contents of his stomach. With heroic control, though, he mastered himself, which made Benny, who would have had to swab the deck, visibly relax.

When he could speak, the commander breathed, "I can see nearly all the way to the sea." Indeed, the horizon lay blue and misty in the far distance, and who was to say whether it was stained by sea or sky?

When they gained enough altitude, they crossed the mountains on a northeasterly course, leaving the river to the south, their shadow rippling across the vast expanses of desert land on the eastern slopes. When a smudge appeared at last on the horizon, de Sola pointed. "Those long lines—they are the railroad tracks?"

"They are. The paler ones are roads," Ian told him.

"Landfall at Reno in twenty minutes, Captain," Jake said from the navigation table.

"So small and fragile our effect on the vast earth," de Sola murmured, his fascinated gaze never leaving the sere landscape far below. "I shall never feel proud of man's accomplishments again."

"Pride is a bit dangerous," Alice agreed. "Nothing wrong with gratitude, though. I've been grateful to *Swan* many a time when she's saved my skin."

"I am grateful now," he said, "to both crew and ship. I will not forget this. Never."

"Perhaps your children will take flight for granted one day," Ian said.

But de Sola was already shaking his head. "I will not let them. Not when I have seen myself as God sees me. Such a lesson may change a man's life."

When they moored at the Reno airfield—the only one in the Royal Kingdom, and that only because it was on the major train route into the country and beyond the pale of the mountains, de Sola and his soldiers disembarked. In what passed for dizzying bureaucratic speed in this country, they returned with permission in hand for a special landing in the mission's orchard. By sunset, the last of the injured had been borne away and the doors closed behind them.

Alice leaned against Ian in sheer exhaustion—they had been up more than twenty-four hours. "I want to be carried away on one of those canvas stretchers myself ... though I don't deserve it, since it was my actions that put those poor men there."

"If the old Viceroy had not begun the dam, they would not have been working on it, and we would not have had to act." He kissed the top of her head. "We have done what we could to pay our debt. Now let us pull up ropes and decide what to do next."

Dutch came down the gangway in what appeared to be one of the wool greatcoats *Swan's* original crew had left behind when they had been captured in Venice, before Alice had liberated the empty ship. "I am told by your navigator that I am to take this garment and stop arguing," he said unhappily to Alice. "But I do not feel it is right."

"It's too big for any of us," she pointed out. "Take it and welcome. The nights are cold here, and you may be glad of it. Are you really leaving us?"

"I must," he said simply. "I have nothing to my name but the coins Commander de Sola has given me, and this coat ... and yet this is more than I began with when I met your friend Evan these many months ago. I will begin here in this hospital." He bowed in his oddly formal way, as though there were an entire court behind him and a king standing in front of him. "I thank you for conveying me here ... and for sharing with me the gift of your friendship."

"Please—" Ian ran up the gangway and returned in a moment with one of their calling cards. "If you are in England, or ever need help, I hope you will contact us."

Dutch looked down at the engraved bit of stock, creamy against his deeply tanned and dirty fingers. "Sir Ian and Lady Hollys?" His brows raised, he gazed at them. "Is it so?"

Alice lifted a shoulder with a smile. "We try to keep a low profile. I hope we meet again, Dutch."

"I hope so, too." With a touch of the card to his temple, smiling as if at a good joke, he made his way into the dusk, the rabbit brush whispering against the hems of his coat.

"I don't think I can fly tonight, Ian," Alice said quietly, as the evening closed around them. "Do you suppose they'll let us stay in this field until morning?"

"I don't see why not. I shall find de Sola and inform him we shall return him and his men after sunrise."

Alice staggered a little as she climbed the gangway and made her way back to the captain's cabin. Never had she been so grateful for her bunk, though it smelled stale and dusty from disuse. She would just put her head on the pillow while she was waiting for Ian ... not even take her boots off ...

She woke with a start at the sound of shouting. It was fully dark, and outside the porthole there was far too much movement and flickering light for an orchard. Her mouth was dry and her head ached, but she forced herself up and out of the cabin. Where was Ian? How long had she been asleep? What was happening?

Jake met her in the corridor outside the navigation gondola. "Captain, did you hear?"

"I just woke up. What is happening? Where is Ian?"

"I am here, Alice." Ian ushered Commander de Sola up the gangway, the latter as pale as a man so tanned could be in the light of the lamps. "It seems that while we were providing an ambulance to the men, news arrived."

His voice heavy with dread, Commander de Sola said, "Ambassador de Aragon and his troops have seized the capital of San Francisco de Asis and he has declared himself Regent.

Any man who supports the mad Viceroy is now declared traitor to the Crown."

"Seized?" Alice said with a gasp. "But Gloria—the Viceroy —are they all right?"

"I do not know," de Sola told her. "I must return to my post at once."

"We will prepare to cast off," Ian said immediately.

"No." The commander stopped Ian in mid-turn. "I will go by train. I am very sorry to inform you—that is to say, we are so grateful for your help but I must—"

"Commander, what is it?" Alice had not known him above a day, but he did not strike her as a man prone to stammering and indecision.

"The borders are closed." His fine brown eyes were miserable as they met hers. "By rights I should impound your ship and crew and hold you here."

Alice felt herself sway with exhaustion and shock. This was just like Venice. Would they impose a tariff on her that she couldn't pay this time, too?

"Should?" Ian inquired of de Sola as he passed a supportive arm about her waist, his mind obviously moving faster than hers. "Is that what you are going to do?"

"The missions will declare for the royalist or the regent's cause in the morning," de Sola said wearily. "In the confusion, no one will notice if your ship should disappear. I suggest you move quickly."

"Which side will you choose?" Ian asked.

"The side of right. I fight for my Viceroy, and so will the remaining troops in the south. San Luis Obispo de Tolosa will also, and San Carlos Borromeo de Carmelo. Nuestra Senora de los Angeles, as the religious capital, can do nothing but fight for God's anointed representative. Sandwiched between those centers of power, the smaller southern landholders will see their duty and declare for Felipe as well."

"This is no way for friends to say good-bye," Alice protested.

"You are right. It is not." De Sola offered his hand, and she took it. "Go at once. I will look after your friends Evan and the captain as you have looked after mine. And may God protect us until we meet again."

CHAPTER 19

"*C*ivil war?" Gloria sank to the sofa, one hand going almost of its own volition to her still flat belly. Cold fear cascaded into her stomach like a poison rain that couldn't possibly be good for the baby.

Ignatio de la Carrera had turned nearly as white as the broad expanse of his spotless shirt front, and the bishop of San Luis Obispo de Tolosa was wringing his hands, waiting for his Viceroy's reaction to the dreadful news. Honoria remained upright on her feet, though Gloria could hardly see how. "The south declares for me, as well as Santa Cruz and Santa Clara?"

"Not Santa Clara, sir," the bishop said with regret. "They briefly attempted a neutral stance and were overrun by the Regent's troops before Vespers."

"Do not call him that," Gloria snapped, recovering herself at this insult. "He is not even His Excellency the Ambassador any longer. He is de Aragon of San Gregorio, the traitor."

"Yes, madam," the bishop said mildly. "Your Serene Highness, our first priority must be your safety. The archbishop bids you come to Nuestra Senora de los Angeles for sanctuary immediately, before the railroads close to anything but military traffic."

"Sanctuary?" Honoria folded her arms. "He means me to hide behind his adobe walls while my people fight and die for me?"

"The people need a living ruler for whom to fight," the bishop pointed out. "The walls of our mother house have never been breached."

"Then the archbishop may certainly continue to reside there in safety, and pray for us. I will join my troops in the south, and draw the traitor out. It is a harsh landscape that we know better than he, a man used to green hills and easy provisioning."

"Sir, I beg you—"

"If he wants my crown, he may come and take it from me," Honoria said grimly. "I will meet him on the field above the water meadows."

"But the dam—sire, you are vulnerable in that quarter now that the river is once again open to any criminal who cares to travel it. What if the witches hear that you are there in person and cast a spell? What if they spill through the gap and attack?"

Honoria grinned, feral as a panther. "I should welcome it. Bishop, let the missions—all of them—know my plans. I expect the south to muster and while they do, I will take *Silver Wind* to the water meadows to inspect them as they arrive."

"*Silver Wind?*" de la Carrera repeated. "But that is the—er, well, I suppose it is no longer the traitor's train."

"It is my train," Honoria said in a tone just this side of

dangerous. "Have it waiting at the siding here by sunset, and we will leave in the morning."

For of course, in making his slippery escape, the traitor had not been able to use the beautiful locomotive he considered his own. It was far too visible, and his lines of escape were too cleverly drawn in invisible ink. He had surfaced in San Francisco de Asis and declared himself Regent the evening before last, to save the country from a prince who was not anointed of God in holy visions at all, but mad and under the influence of a witch.

Gloria's wearing of the rose had not gone unnoticed by everyone but the women, it seemed. The traitor knew perfectly well what the symbol meant, and he had been swift to use it against her. The missions of the north had been loud in their outrage, and had positioned their rebellion as a religious war against the powers of witchcraft. Gloria felt ill at the thought of it—that in her loyalty to the women who had saved her life, she might inadvertently have put Honoria's life and the success of their plan at risk.

The bishop and the grandee bowed themselves out, leaving Gloria and the Viceroy with the remains of their breakfast. Gloria could not even look at the table, and focused instead out the window, on the sunlight dancing on the water.

"Gloria, don't let your courage fail you now."

She turned to Honoria, her face crumpling in distress. "But this is all my fault. Everything we've done—all we've both sacrificed—and we are going to war anyway."

"But it is on our terms."

"How can you say that? Having the north declare for a Regent is hardly what we were expecting. When you finally switch places, Felipe is going to have us both executed—and speaking of that, I am not altogether sure I like you in such danger while he is comfortably behind the mountains in complete safety."

"That was the plan, you goose."

"Yes, but at the time you weren't riding to inspect troops. We were supposed to go on progress, and attend balls and fiestas, until he was well enough."

"Are you going to have hysterics, or are you going to listen to me?" If not for her smile and the knowledge that Honoria could be depended on to the very last, Gloria might have lost her nerve and burst into tears.

She gulped her runaway emotions back. "I am listening."

"It is true that we did not expect open, armed rebellion. But we know something the Ambassador does not—that there has been a secret rebellion building up in this country for years, engineered by women like me—spies and travelers. It has come to a head, Gloria, and you will be the one to fan the embers into flame."

Gloria remembered the dream Evan had told her of, back in the little room at the inn that had held her one perfect night of happiness. In the fort commander's dream, she had turned into an iron dragon and burned up her persecutor.

The commander had dreamed true, Evan had said. She needed to hold fast to that.

"What do I need to do?"

"The word must go out. It is time for the women to rise and fight."

Gloria stared. "In this country? Impossible. What can women do when they can hardly step out of doors safely?"

Honoria gazed at her, humor playing at the corners of her mouth. "What have you seen the women doing?"

Since the question appeared serious, Gloria calmed her gabbling fear and set her mind to answer with equal deliberation. "I have seen them sewing, and going to market, and talking, and caring for children."

"And what else?"

She thought back over the days of her stay here. "I have seen them in groups in the marketplace, exchanging news. And riding in carts together from rancho to rancho, with bags of seed for planting season. I have seen them in the trees, picking oranges and lemons with their sons and daughters while the men have been off building the dam."

"Exactly. Everywhere we look, women are exchanging news—of family, of farms, of politics and war. We have merely to set the word in motion, and it will travel the length and breadth of the kingdom."

"But wars cannot be won by marketplace talk."

"Governments have been brought down by that very thing. So we are going to bring down a rebellion. At least in part. You must call the women of the household together and tell them what has happened, if they do not already know of it. And then you must tell them it is time to fight, using any means they have. We women will be the stone in the soldier's boot, the laundry grit in the trousers that causes him to itch, the wheel that comes off and puts the wagon in the ditch. We will be the voice on the Santa Ana wind sowing doubt and irritation, the illness that prevents a man from getting out of bed to muster, the hole in his sock that makes his march a misery."

Gloria touched her lips, as though she had never thought such power might be found there.

"The women of this country are tired of being silent,"

Honoria said. "Granted, there will be those who work against us, who are loyal to the old Viceroy and to the way things have always been. But there are many more who are not. And it is those women who will fight with us by any means they have to hand. The tinder is waiting. It only needs a match."

"And I will be that match." Gloria's mouth tipped in a smile every bit as dangerous as Honoria's had been. She touched the roses in her hair. "I am the iron dragon."

Then she straightened her spine, gripped Honoria's hand for a moment for luck, and went to find Isabela to gather the women of San Luis Obispo de Tolosa for war.

IN THE TWO days it took them to reach the fort at the water meadows, Honoria commanded that *Silver Wind* stop at every rancho station, every town, every siding, so that she might address the people. And while she did that, Gloria tucked a rose into her belt and moved among the women, smiling and encouraging and saying the words that they had been waiting to hear, some for more than a generation. In one place, suspected to favor the Regent's cause, someone threw a rotten orange at her. But even as she deflected it with her parasol, the crowd turned on whoever it was, and by the time Gloria had reached the station platform again, the market was bustling and she heard cheers from under the canvas awnings.

At the branch line that would take them across the desert to the fort, they found the military train sidetracked so that *Silver Wind* might go through. But Honoria recognized the insignia on the flag on the locomotive and asked the engineer to stop the train.

Commander de Sola leaped to his feet when the person he and his men believed to be their sovereign boarded the car, Gloria right behind. "Your Serene Highness!" he exclaimed. "Miss Meriwether-Astor! You ought to have sent a message, and I and my officers would have waited upon you at once."

"I am afraid my impatience for news has swept away the need for protocol. But—why are you on a southbound train, sir? I thought you to be at the fort overseeing the muster."

De Sola shook his head in the wondering manner of someone who has seen things that may not be described. "It is a tale so fantastic you have every right not to believe me. Your Serene Highness—I and these men have flown in an airship."

"An airship!" Gloria repeated. "Whose? The Texican Rangers? For my ships cannot be here so soon."

"It is *Swan*, the ship of one Captain Chalmers and her husband, Captain Hollys, senorita."

"Good heavens." Gloria clutched Honoria's arm. "Alice Chalmers is alive and still in the Wild West!"

"You know the woman, senorita?"

"I certainly do," Gloria said. "Before I fell into the hands of the Ambassador in Resolution, I had taken passage aboard *Swan*. Oh, I am glad!"

Alice and Ian were alive, and close by! But why? What on earth would have kept them here?

"But how did you come to fly aboard such a ship?" Honoria wanted to know. "The law has only just been repealed, and one does not leap aboard the first ship to cross the border, just to see what it is like."

"They sailed over the mountains the morning the dam failed, and to my astonishment, they knew your friend Evan Douglas, senorita. When they saw the destruction, they offered to take the most injured of the men to the mission hospital at Reno." His gaze fell. "But when we heard of the traitor in the north, we immediately closed the borders to foreigners, and were forced to return by train. It was not nearly so rapid a journey."

"But where is *Swan* and her crew now?" Gloria asked. "Are they grounded?" Surely not. Surely an ally like Alice could not be trapped on the far edges of the kingdom with an airship that could turn the tide of their cause. Oh, wouldn't that just be her luck!

De Sola shook his head. "It seems they took to the air before anyone in authority could inform them they were grounded. I am sorry to report that I do not know their whereabouts now."

Blast and bebother it! She would give nearly anything to be able to contact Alice and ask for her help. It was all Gloria could do not to scream with frustration, to instead button her lips and allow the commander to give his sovereign his report.

"You will find able-bodied troops aboard this train from three eastern ranchos, as well as Carmel. We count five hundred men aboard, with more coming on the next train from Santa Cruz, San Miguel Arcangel, and San Antonio de Padua."

"Excellent," Honoria said. "And what of events in the north?"

A pleat formed in the commander's noble brow. "They have begun to muster on the plains near Santa Clara, and our spies report that we must expect six units of cavalry as well as over a thousand troops from San Francisco de Asis alone."

Gloria glanced at Honoria anxiously. This did not sound promising.

"However, there is some difficulty with the cavalry. We have reports of bloat among the horses that is preventing their being loaded into the rail cars. If they must travel over-land, they will naturally be delayed by some days."

"I see." Honoria's face was solemn. "I suppose we can be grateful, and feel for the beasts."

"We have also heard that the train bringing troops from San Rafael Arcangel and San Juan Bautista has unfortunately derailed, and it will be some time before the tracks can be cleared."

"Good heavens," Gloria said. "How did it derail?"

"There was talk of a cow, but our spies have not been able to confirm that, senorita."

Gloria bit her lips together and took a moment to feel sorry for the cow, who had given her life for the royalist cause.

"Have such disasters befallen the ranchos and missions who support me, Commander?"

"We have had no such reports, sir, but if we should receive them, you will be the first to know."

"*Gracias, senor.* And now, if you will instruct your engineer to lay on steam, you may escort us to the fort, if you will."

Commander de Sola bowed, then turned to Gloria. "If I may be so bold, senorita, Senor Douglas will be happy to see you safe once more, though a military encampment is no place for a lady."

Gloria took Honoria's arm. "My place is with the Viceroy. My surroundings are immaterial." She smiled at the commander in a way that told him she was sure he felt the same.

"And Captain Fremont, he is with us, too. He has been

incredibly useful in the rescue effort, contriving ways to save men from the waters with such bravery that he might be one of us."

Gloria's smile cooled with the shock of unexpectedly hearing that name. "Captain ... Fremont? But I understood he had returned to his riverboats and was out of the country." Her fingers gripped Honoria's sleeve hard enough to crumple the wool. How could Stanford be here? Why was he not with the Viceroy and the witches? Why was he deliberately putting himself in danger? And if he was here, was the Viceroy here, too, masquerading as Joe?

De Sola glanced between Gloria and Honoria as if he had belatedly remembered that Gloria had been married to the man under discussion, and his prince might not take kindly to having the subject brought up.

"He returned with Senor Douglas," was all he said before he bowed again, the medallions on the sides of his trousers jingling. "I will have the whistle blown at once, Your Serene Highness. It will hearten the troops to have you among us."

Honoria dipped her chin in acknowledgement and they made their way back to *Silver Wind*. When they were under way once more and the steward had bowed himself out of the luxurious saloon, Gloria's knees gave out.

"Captain Fremont is here," she breathed. "Oh, Honoria, how shall I bear it?"

"I am not going to be required to play the jealous fiancé, am I?" Honoria looked pained. "Of all the disguises I have had to wear, that would be the worst."

"Of course not. I will give you no reason to. We cannot put the plan in jeopardy at this late date."

"I am glad to hear it. Try to rest a little. You will need all your resources in the coming days."

Honoria was speaking of the war. But Gloria knew in her bones that pretending not to care about the man she loved when he was within calling distance was going to tax all the resources she possessed.

Her hand passed over her stomach, and rested upon the secret he did not yet know.

CHAPTER 20

aturally, the man Gloria most wanted to see was nowhere in evidence when the two trains pulled into the station at the fort. If he was working with Evan in the behemoth, one would think it would be fairly easy to spot him, but no massive walking ironwork was in sight. Instead, she must put on a smile, take Honoria's arm, and listen with a semblance of appreciation to the sprightly brass band playing the national anthem as they disembarked from *Silver Wind*. As Honoria gave a rousing speech in the Californio tongue, Gloria spoke to one or two of the officers' wives in her halting version of that language. Fortunately, she had had quite a lot of practice lately, and where words failed her, Ella took up the slack.

They were offered the quarters of the commander himself, but Honoria shook her head. "I thank you, sir, but my fiancée tells me *Silver Wind* was designed as a moving command post, and of all vehicles here save perhaps your behemoth, she is the safest."

The commander conceded, but insisted that a guard of honor be posted on both sides of the sleek locomotive at all times. The royal standard went up the flagpole to indicate the Viceroy was in residence, and a horse was saddled so that Honoria might inspect the troops without delay.

It did not occur to anyone that Gloria might be able to ride, let alone be interested in the troops. As the mounted cohort cantered off, trumpets blowing, Ella took her arm. "To work."

It was not the army that made the fort run with efficiency and precision. It was the women—the cooks, the laundresses, the seamstresses, the leather workers. Even the barmaids and harlots beyond the palisade had their part to play, and Gloria left no one out. She devoted the late afternoon to the women no one saw, encouraging, suggesting, rousing them to the task that lay before them. When the sun set and wagons bearing sacks of uniforms, shirts, and socks formed a train down the dusty road, the reins were shaken with determination and the word began to spread, even here in the heart of loyalist country. Every household must be mustered to the unseen battle.

Gloria sat down to dinner and afterward listened to a concert from the military band with the sense that she had done what she could. Now it was up to those legions of the uncounted, the invisible, the disregarded to take the tiny flames that she had lit and turn them into a conflagration that would burn from one end of the country to the other.

She came back to herself at the end of the dessert course with the certainty she was being watched. A slow perusal of the dining hall revealed the source—Evan Douglas and Captain Stan sitting with the soldiers at the second table from the door. Her gaze locked with that of her husband—he was her husband, and no wretched document denying that fact would make her think any differently—and she blushed under the intensity of his regard.

Evan nudged him, and their connection broke as he turned his head to see what his friend wanted, no doubt to receive a warning about the dangers of showing too much emotion toward the Viceroy's intended bride. Honoria had not missed the tension, or Gloria's indrawn breath. She leaned toward the commander, who was seated at her right hand.

"I should like to speak with the friends of my bride-to-be, as would she. Could you ask Senor Douglas and Captain Fremont to attend us privately aboard *Silver Wind* in a quarter of an hour?"

"Of course, Your Serene Highness. Did you enjoy the performance?"

"Very much." Honoria smiled and saluted the orchestra. "I favor the old composers. They have done well."

Her escape could not be fast enough, yet a quarter of an hour was not nearly enough to calm Gloria's jumping nerves. When the steward ushered Evan and Stanford into the saloon of *Silver Wind*, it was all she could do not to rush to her husband and fling herself into his arms. Instead, she endured the touch of his lips upon the back of her hand with only a shiver that might have betrayed her feelings had anyone but he been close enough to sense it.

She might have pretended to be an automaton for the rest of the evening had not the steward poured the wine and bowed himself out, at which point Stanford whirled about and snatched her up in his arms. "My God, Gloria, are you all right?"

She clutched him close, pressing her face into his neck as

though they might become one flesh immediately. She wanted to speak, to reassure him she was perfectly well. Instead, she began to cry into his shirt—with joy, with relief, with fear for them both—snuffling like a small child who has been hurt.

"Gloria?" he murmured into her hair, kissing her face, her temples, her eyelids—anything he could reach. "Darling, what is it? I'm perfectly well, and so happy to see you again I am close to tears myself."

"What are you doing here?" she wailed, muffled in his shoulder. "You're supposed to be on the river, safe and sound."

"Goosey," he said lovingly, squeezing her hard. "I could not reach you if you needed me were I on the river. So Evan and I are helping out where we are needed. Alice, you will have observed, has been successful."

"I know," she sobbed. "But you are going to be in a war. You could be killed. How am I supposed to tell our child that you are dead?"

He went absolutely still. "Let us not borrow trouble, darling."

"Trouble!" She drew back, searching his face for signs that he might mean it. "Our baby isn't trouble!"

"Wait." He took her shoulders in both hands. "What is this? Are you speaking theoretically or do you mean it?"

"Of course I mean it." A sob rose up and choked her, and she could barely get out, "Why do you think the Viceroy had to move up the wedding?"

He tilted up her chin and kissed her with such firmness that tears and sobs definitely began to get in the way. "There," he said after a moment. "Now tell me properly."

So she did. About how she thought she was being poisoned, and how Isabela and Ella had educated her. Ella added a few choice tidbits, and Honoria helped out with the choosing of the wedding date.

At this point Evan spoke up. "Gloria, you—you know that the Viceroy—that Joe—that this is Honoria, the prince's half sister? That she is a woman?"

Gloria pulled her handkerchief out of her sleeve and blew her nose. "Of course, silly. She told me practically as soon as you and Stanford took the prince away. Speaking of, is he here?"

"Indeed not." Stanford wiped her wet cheeks with the cuff of his shirt, the handkerchief now being inadequate to the task. "But I have had enough of princes. The world has just tipped off its axis and I am still wobbling. You are truly expecting our child?"

"I am." From within the circle of his arms, she asked timidly, "Are you pleased?"

Now those beloved green eyes did well with tears—his face flushed—a sight she had never expected to see. *"Pleased* doesn't cover it. Nor does *astounded.* Or *delighted. Full of the need to climb on top of this engine and shout it to the whole world* just scratches the surface." He kissed her again, and this time, their friends found it necessary to cross the room to the wine decanter and give them a moment of privacy. "I love you." His hand moved to her belly. "And you too, little boy or girl."

"And we love you," Gloria whispered. "We are your family, no matter what the authorities in this country say about it."

He made a rude noise that indicated his opinion of said authorities. "I suggest we get this war over and done. If I am going to be a father, I don't want to be distracted by the Ambassador's nonsense. And while we're at it, let us get Felipe back in his own saddle and running his own country so that we can go home."

"I second that." Honoria handed them each a tiny glass of ruby liquid. "To Stan and Gloria Fremont, and their firstborn."

With a shy glance at Evan, Gloria was warmed inside to see the sincerity of his smile as he toasted them. The last barrier to her happiness fell as she realized once and for all he no longer cared for her in that way. Isabela held his heart now, and if it was the last thing she did in this strange, hospitable yet hostile country, it would be to help him to the fruition of his dreams. After all, a man who could teach himself to operate a behemoth could do anything. Isabela was a lucky woman.

The behemoth. *Silver Wind.*

"Evan," she said, "the south is mustering men and horses and trains, but whatever happened to my mechanicals? Are they still in Resolution in the wreck of the train?"

He blinked at this sudden return to business in the midst of a celebration. But to Gloria, these things were all of a piece. They must win the war and restore the prince to his throne so that they could return to the lives they had left behind—lives that she now valued more than ever before. Lives that now had a future utterly different than any she had imagined. Lives on which she could not wait to embark.

"Why, no," he said. "Alice loaded all of them on *Swan.* That was why she was shot down—the ship was so heavy with all that iron that she couldn't maneuver as quickly, and the cannon on the watch tower put a hole through the stern of the fuselage."

"Were they destroyed?"

"No. They landed awkwardly and with some damage, but

apparently Jake and Benny unloaded them all and to my knowledge, they're still sitting on top of the mesa above the village."

"Mother Mary's village? Is that where the Viceroy is, too?"

"Yes, according to plan."

Gloria handed her wineglass to her husband, and paced the Turkey carpet once across. "We must send someone with a message. We must get the mechanicals down off the mesa and add them to the army. Men on horseback are no match for those mechanicals—I saw them being built, back in Philadelphia. Evan," she said, "you must teach the most likely men in the commander's troops to ride them."

"Me! I've never even seen one. They were crated."

"If you can learn to operate the behemoth, you can do this. You cannot ride them yourself, of course. The behemoth will go to war along with everyone else. That wretch de Aragon will not know what hit him when he sees my iron army coming."

"Technically I believe it is *my* iron army," Honoria said dryly.

"Technically it is neither of yours," Ella pointed out. "It is Felipe's, and he ought to lead it. The question is, how can we send a message? None of us dare go. Honoria might once have been best qualified to slip past the pickets and go where she was not wanted, but not now."

Gloria caught her husband grinning at Evan. "What are you two smiling about? What state secret are you keeping from us?"

Evan leaned in, as though about to whisper. "Thanks to the brilliant system operating within your fleet, the behemoth has attracted a pigeon," he said. "Let us send it to *Swan* at once."

≈

Alice and Ian, Mother Mary and Sister Clara, Felipe—our best greetings.

With de Aragon's declaration of his Regency and the subsequent division of the country in civil war, it seems that all our efforts to stop it have been for nothing. So, we must now put our efforts into bringing it to a short and successful end. Please find a way to convey the mechanicals to the fort at the water meadows without delay. Gloria believes I can teach the soldiers to operate them, and we will take the field against de Aragon's horses.

I am also bidden to tell you that Gloria and Ella have put Mother Mary's grand plan into motion. H. is safe and well here at the fort, and sends her best love. She takes no chances, however, and prefers to remain aboard Silver Wind when she is not carrying out more public duties. H. wishes nothing more than to see her brother in his rightful place once again. We are all working for a better future for a country that will balance independence and innovation with the joys of family, faith, and tradition.

Come with all haste.

Your friend,

Evan

FELIPE HANDED the letter back to Mother Mary. "What he means to convey is that the kingdom I am to take back is no longer the same as the one I was forced to leave."

"Seems unavoidable." Mother Mary was not about to be drawn into an argument. "The moment anyone declares civil war, you can pretty much guarantee that the country is going to be different when all is said and done."

"And this Honoria—my half sister—she has no designs on the throne herself?"

Tia Clara snorted and held out her mug for Alice to top it up with good, hot coffee. Now that the river was running properly again, such luxuries were available once more. "Felipe, my dear, you can ask her that when you see her, but I'll tell you now, the throne is in no danger. There are many more comfortable places to park one's bones."

The Viceroy did not look very reassured. "And what about my mechanicals? How are we to get them down off the mesa?"

"You leave that to me and May Lin," Alice told him. "With her spider at the bottom of the river and only three working gas bags, we can still do it, but we're going to have to make two trips in *Swan*."

"What does May Lin have to do with that?" the prince asked stiffly. "Is she familiar with airships as well as all manner of gears and levers?"

Alice had noticed that he was as jumpy as a bean on a hot stove around the slender, dark-eyed young engineer. She couldn't decide if it was because he had never been within speaking distance of a person of Canton descent, or if it was simply because May Lin treated him like any other riverman —which was to say, with a respect that might be called casual at best. Alice could see where a person who was used to bowing and scraping would find this irritating—though Ian could be said to command immense respect in his proper sphere, and he got along with May Lin just fine.

Or maybe there were deeper forces at work. Alice smiled to herself behind her mug of coffee, and reflected that being attracted to someone who was not only utterly unsuitable but had no use for anything you represented would certainly make the course of love run any way but smooth.

"May Lin is going to teach the witches to ride the mechanicals," Alice told him. "She'll start as soon as we unload them at Santa Croce."

"What?" Felipe sat up straighter in his chair, if that were possible. "My soldiers are to ride them. *I* am to ride them, if it comes to that, and lead the charge."

"Are you? How are you going to explain the sudden appearance of two Viceroys at the fort?" Mother Mary gazed at him, one dark eyebrow raised. "You can't just ride in and lead the soldiers when Honoria is already doing that."

"Why—why—then why did Evan Douglas suggest it?"

"It probably seemed like a good idea at the time, but it ain't. The mechanicals are spoils of war, and they happen to be in our hands. Not yours. Not de Sola's. And in our hands they're going to stay."

"But they're mine, bought and paid for!"

"And a lot of good they're doing you, up on the mesa," Mother Mary said calmly. "We don't mind you riding with us. We don't even mind you claiming victory when you have it. But when we beat de Aragon's forces and he's in your gaol waiting for the firing squad, we'll be riding off with the tools that helped you win. Seems to me they'll come in pretty handy."

Felipe's mouth worked as he tried to rein in the imperial temper ... which told Alice the boy had some sense, at least. Alice had not known Mother Mary long in person, but she'd known of the mythical leader of *las brujas* for several years. One didn't inspire a reputation as wide as the Wild West by lying down and letting people walk on you.

Felipe nodded once, abruptly, to indicate that he knew when he'd been beaten. There was no throne here, after all, and the chair he sat in had been used by all manner of folks with no consideration for prince or pauper.

Alice put down her mug and stood. Ian rose with her, having finished his breakfast rolled up in its pancake of corn, and was now plainly itching to get to work. "Felipe," she said, "I've suggested to May Lin that she teach you how to ride the largest armored horse, since it looks like it's meant to lead the charge. Once you learn, then you can teach others. It will go faster that way. There have to be a hundred horses and cats up there, and we'll all need to be as expert as we can be before we see the northern forces coming."

"That will be suitable," he said, still a little stiff with affront at not getting his own way.

"Now that it is common knowledge that the Viceroy himself is mustering the troops in the south," Ian added, "de Aragon will be even more determined to take the field with all speed. I am sure he believes that once Honoria is captured, the entire southern part of the country will capitulate."

"That won't happen," Tia Clara said grimly, getting up as well. "My girl has never been beaten in a fight, and I don't see it happening now."

If Felipe had any thoughts about his half-sister's capabilities in comparison with his own, he kept them to himself as he followed Alice and Ian from the sun terrace. Messengers were dispatched to sister villages up and down the river to muster for the fight, and two of the riverboat captains collected their crews for the journey upriver, where they would convey those from farther away down to Santa Croce.

Up on the mesa, Jake found himself in the unenviable position of teaching both an engineer and a prince how to ride the armored horse without first making a complete fool of himself. He had learned his lesson the first time, though, so at least there was no waste of armaments.

"It holds cannon in its chest!" exclaimed Felipe, examining the twin barrels. "Truly, it is a marvel."

"The marvel will be whether or not you can fire it accurately at full gallop," May Lin said. "If you are to lead the charge instead of someone like Alice, or me, then you're going to need some practice."

"I am perfectly capable of firing it!" the prince snapped. "I can hit a target with pistols at forty yards."

"Your target probably isn't moving, and neither are you."

"That is beside the point!"

"That is entirely the point. Get up, then, and see if you remember the ignition sequence."

Fuming, seeing that Jake was already aboard his horse, he climbed into the saddle and fitted his knees and feet into the shields that would protect them. The horses operated using kineticks, so getting them moving was a sequence of smaller movements, one gear fitting into another until the whole was galloping on razor legs that flashed in the light. Alice imagined what the mesa must look like from a distance—like a lightning storm without a single cloud.

Mounted on the smaller mechanicals, the witches formed a wedge. Up and down they galloped, a quarter mile this way and a quarter mile back. Then, upon an arm signal from Felipe, he, May Lin, and Jake released temporary projectiles from their mounts' cannon. Alice had advised them to save the real ones for when it counted. Their target, a boulder lying near the uninhabited edge of the mesa, sustained no damage at all except a glancing blow.

May Lin pulled her mechanical into a walk and shouted at Felipe, "You're going to have to do better than that if you plan to put an end to your enemy."

"I have only just learned to manage this monster this morning!" he shouted back, clearly incensed at her criticism. "You are doing no better."

"Not so—mine was the only cannonball to hit the rock."

"She's right," Jake said, much to Alice's amusement. But it would not do to show so much as a quiver of the lips at such a tense moment. Had the prince ever been allowed to fail at anything, other than being poisoned?

"I'll show you, you painted female," Felipe fumed, and set his beast in motion. All alone, he thundered across the flat top of the mesa and released his cannonball in a puff of smoke.

A chunk of the boulder flew off and tumbled down the cliff.

May Lin hadn't an ungracious bone in her body, though heaven knew she had plenty of stubborn ones. She cheered as the prince rode up, sweating and filthy and triumphant. "Now, back into formation and we'll do it again," she called to the others through her speaking horn.

By dawn the next day, witches in full paint had begun to stream into the village and set up camp on the sun terraces and up on the mesa. Those who had ridden the day before demonstrated the mechanicals to the new arrivals. Instead of taking the day off and resting on his laurels, Felipe went back up the stone chute to the top, limping a little but determined to master the armored horse. Not to be outdone, May Lin and Jake went with him, though the latter assured Alice that it was only in a teaching capacity. "I'm not looking for another job, Captain," he said. "When you're in the air, Benny and I will be, too."

On the morning of the third day after they'd received Evan's pigeon, Alice sent back a reply.

Evan, Gloria, &c,

Drills taking place on the mesa have prepared our forces to ride. With due respect to de Sola and you all, F. will lead the witches himself. Tell no one. In the confusion H. must slip away.

I will watch from the air and alert you to the approach of northern troops. They will not be able to surprise us.

Alice

CHAPTER 21

"Captain," Benny Stringfellow said from his post at the viewing port, "there's an awful lot of dust down there."

They had been circling the water meadows for two days now, allowing the witches to form their phalanxes of mechanicals, to practice riding and shooting, and to eat and rest before the inevitable battle. The soldiers at the fort had eventually stopped ducking and running at the sight of *Swan* making her slightly less than graceful way across the sky, having clearly been briefed by Evan and Commander de Sola. But Alice had not dared to moor at the fort in case someone decided it would be a good idea to impound *Swan* in exchange for the missing mechanicals. She had no idea what story Evan would have told de Sola to explain the change in plans, but in any case, the soldiers had been marching and exercising in the warm sun as though they fully expected to fight this battle on foot.

Alice left the helm in Ian's care and joined her gunner at

the viewing port. Far below, trains chugged southward. Spread across the rolling, dry landscape were the multiple causes of the dust clouds—thousands of men and horses.

"Jake, I need your sharp eyes to estimate numbers," she said over one shoulder. "Ian, be prepared to increase speed for a return to the fort."

Jake joined them at the viewing port, his gaze rapidly assessing as his quick brain made calculations. "Seven thousand foot and horse," he said. "Perhaps another three on the trains, if each carriage holds fifty."

"I think we may assume they do," Alice said, nodding. "All right, then, back to the fort as fast as we can. They're still half a day away, and I doubt they'll attack. They'll need to set up camp and rest the horses."

"If they follow the classic rules," Ian said, spinning the wheel to bring them round, "they'll send Honoria an ultimatum first."

"That will go over well," Alice observed with some pleasure at the thought.

Benny had not left the port. "We could shoot some of them now," he said eagerly. "I bet I could derail a train if we came low enough and I had a clear shot."

Alice grinned and ruffled his hair. "I bet you could, too, but this isn't our war. We'll assist where we're needed, but I'm mainly concerned with protecting our friends, even if that means scooping them up in the basket to get them out of harm's way."

"You mean we're not going to bomb the traitor?" Benny's face fell in disappointment. "We've got all kinds of bombs—it would be silly not to use them."

"If Gloria and Honoria give us the go-ahead, then we will,"

Alice assured him. "But technically, you know, these are not our skies."

"I didn't hear you say that when you were leaving to blow up the dam," Benny grumbled.

"I have enough on my conscience on that score, young man. The witches asked for our help and we gave it to the best of our ability, but what we did is not an easy thing to live with. Besides, if not for you and Jake, what was left of Ian and me would be washing out to sea about now. I want to be able to render our friends the same kind of service you and Jake gave us."

"I suppose," Benny conceded, unwillingly. "But you'll need a gunner in any case, won't you?"

"I certainly will," she said. "Even using the basket could be a dicey business if Gloria's pa happened to have sold them a crate of those nasty propelled bullets we saw in the Canadas. I'll need you then for true."

Evan had sent the pigeon back with an encouraging note from Gloria and Honoria, so Alice scribbled a message, enclosed it in the little device's brass body, and sent it on its way to the behemoth.

Northern forces half a day off, with two trains closing fast. Jake estimates 7000 foot and horse, and 3000 aboard the trains. Ian thinks they'll issue an ultimatum, but I don't trust de Aragon to abide by the rules of war. Keep your eyes open. We'll moor at Santa Croce and be in the sky tomorrow by dawn.

Alice

∿

THE SENTRY POSTED in the fort's watchtower blew his horn, and in moments the southern escort rode out to close around the envoy from the northern forces camped upon the ridge. Only one, however, wearing the white sash of truce, was allowed into Honoria's and Gloria's presence in the saloon of *Silver Wind*, and only then under close guard.

The envoy did not bow. "I bring you greetings and a message from His Serene Highness the Regent of the Royal Kingdom of Spain and the Californias."

Honoria folded her arms. "This is a sad beginning, to be flinging an illegal title in my face without so much as a by your leave."

The envoy swallowed and said nothing. He must be a very brave man, to come in the traitor's place knowing he could be shot and sent back over an unsaddled horse, his feet and hands tied together.

Honoria waved a hand. "Very well, say what you have come to say."

The envoy inclined his head. "I speak for the Regent, who advises you to surrender before any blood of your countrymen is spilled. You will be treated fairly, for your father's sake, and your madness treated as well as may be in the mission hospital at San Francisco de Asis, where you may dwell in peace for the rest of your days."

"And if I do not accept these generous terms?"

"Then upon my return to His Serene Highness, war will be declared and we will meet you forthwith upon the field of battle."

Honoria gazed at him for some moments, during which the envoy shifted his weight from foot to foot. "Have you had any difficulty in your journey south?"

"Difficulty, sir?"

Gloria did not miss the honorific, and neither did anyone else in the saloon.

"Yes. Provisioning, perhaps, or ill health among horses and men?"

The man's brow puckered. "How would you know this, unless you had spies among us? Which is impossible, considering the speed at which we came."

"How, indeed. Are you quite sure you are fighting on the winning side, sir? I will hold nothing against you if you decide you are not."

Now both the man's brows rose in disbelief. "Sir, with all due respect, the Regent's is the winning side. We have ten thousand men against half that number here."

"Are you sure?"

"You are not the only ones with intelligence men."

"Quite so. You insist upon returning, then?"

"I am duty bound to carry your answer to my commander."

"Ah, my answer. I had almost forgotten. You may tell de Aragon that the sooner he returns to San Gregorio to await my pleasure—I have not yet decided between death or banishment—the less blood of his countrymen will be spilled. Once he does that, I will pardon those misguided men who have believed his lies, and they may return to farms and families without let or hindrance."

The envoy stared. What did he expect? Gloria wondered. Abject surrender to a madman?

Then he bowed. "As you wish, sir."

"I thank you for your bravery. It is not easy to stand in for a coward who could not face me himself."

"Yes, sir. That is to say, no, sir."

"Commander de Sola, see that this man and his party are conveyed to a neutral place where stray bullets from either side may not find a target."

"At once, Your Serene Highness."

At the portal, the envoy turned back. "Sir, they say you are mad and in the control of a witch."

"Yes, I know. Do I strike you as mad?"

The man seemed to struggle between forces of equal strength—duty and belief. "I cannot say, sir. You seem very civil and honorable, for which I am grateful."

"Does my fiancée strike you as being a witch?"

Gloria gave him her best smile, softened by sympathy.

"That is even more difficult to say. I have—I have heard—excuse me, senorita—"

"Do go on," Gloria said with gentle encouragement.

"I have heard you called the iron dragon. But if I may say so, you do not appear to be such a thing, either." He bowed from the waist this time, and was ushered out.

Gloria and Honoria exchanged an astonished glance. "Ten to one that name has been whispered to de Aragon, too," Honoria said. "On the lips of his own men, no doubt, coming full circle in the nick of time. That is good news." She shrugged out of her short formal jacket, and lifted the scarlet sash over her head. "Come, let us find Mr. Douglas and the captain, call the troops to arms, and give that slippery rascal the surprise of his life."

It was only appropriate that Gloria should prepare to meet her Maker in the clothes that Commander de Sola had seen in his dream. When he saw the ruffled cream petticoats, drawn up to expose her boots for ease of movement, the man's waistcoat with its brass buttons, and her husband's bowler hat set upon her braided hair, a red rose tucked into its band, he turned pale.

"It is true, then," he said to her. "This war turns upon you fighting on the Viceroy's side."

"So it would seem." She touched his arm, and felt it jerk under her fingers, though—brave man that he was—he did not step away. "No matter what happens—no matter the strange things you see—know that I am as loyal to the Viceroy as you are. Do not doubt me or my friends, I beg you."

"There is no room for doubt today, senorita," he said, his eyes grave. "I have seen signs and wonders since you came here that I would never have believed. Even if you were to paint your face like the witch the northerners believe you are, I will hear no ill of you."

Gloria could not help it. She leaned in and kissed him on the cheek. "You may see signs and wonders yet," she said. "Keep the faith. And watch for the rose. You will find friends and allies wearing it who are not to be underestimated."

His gaze lifted to her hat. "It is the symbol of Santa Maria de Guadalupe, our patron saint," he said. "I will do so. And now, let us prepare ourselves for battle. You and His Serene Highness will remain here, aboard the train?"

"Certainly not," Honoria said. "We will be in an even safer place. We will be at the head of my loyal forces, striding to battle in the behemoth."

CHAPTER 22

*H*ad the poor pigeon ever worked so hard in all its mechanical life? Evan wondered. Yes, they were designed for long distances between non-fixed addresses—airships—but as it buzzed between the behemoth and *Swan,* carrying messages of strategy and plans, it was certainly proving its value in the sprint in addition to the distance race.

The southern forces fell in behind the behemoth and Evan set it in motion. Excitement and nerves battled in his stomach. Could he ever have dreamed of this—leading a prince's forces into battle, his friends close at hand? For besides himself, Captain Fremont and Gloria, and Honoria and Ella occupied the chambers of *el Gigante.*

Ella clung to her security line at the side of the viewing port next to him, breathless with awe. "Oh, if only Isabela could see you now—so magnificent!"

Hot blood flooded his cheeks and longing filled his heart. "I possess no magnificence at all, Ella—but the behemoth is certainly awe-inspiring."

"You are not seeing what I see," she told him with certainty.

He blushed all over again, concentrating fiercely on the behemoth's stride so that he would not put it into an arroyo, trip, and send them all flat on their faces. "You must watch for the troops from San Luis Obispo de Tolosa," he suggested. "I have no say in these matters, but if we can protect Isabela's father and her friends from harm, I would be happy."

Honoria joined them at the viewing port, passing an arm around Ella's waist and squeezing her tight. "And as long as we are together, come what may, then I am happy."

"I could have been spying for you," Ella said reproachfully. "And here I am being completely useless, reduced to watching the spectacle from a safe height, like a princess."

"You are far from useless," Honoria told her. "Who was it told me not an hour ago of the dysentery that seems to be plaguing the northern troops?"

"A gift from heaven," Captain Fremont called from his post above them, where he worked the behemoth's arms. "I can see from here that there are fewer on the field than the ten thousand that Alice reported. Unless they have men in reserve behind a hill somewhere, they seem to have lost two thousand or more."

Gloria and Ella grinned at each other, then turned to the viewing port as though their very concentration could help their side to victory.

No matter how many might have awakened this morning unable to fight, thanks to the loyal women preparing their food, there were a frightening number on the field before them. At the sight of the behemoth, a trumpet sounded the charge, and the opposing cavalry thundered down the gentle slope toward them.

"Captain!" Evan called.

"I have it." The behemoth's arms swung up, and clutched in its pincer was a long tree trunk that might once have been a support beam salvaged from the dam. "Brace!"

Evan brought the behemoth to a halt and bent its knees, and Captain Fremont swung the beam as though he were sweeping the northern force from the very floor of the desert. Horses and men went down screaming and the charge broke to either side of them, leaderless, its wedge formation destroyed.

The southern cavalry plunged into the disarray of the northern side, and the fighting with sword and pistol became savage.

"Evan, the cannon!" Gloria said suddenly. "Behind the charge, on limbers!"

"I see them—a dozen. They must be half a century old! Where did they find them? A museum?"

Smiling, he straightened and set the machine in motion once more. The cannon masters saw him coming, of course, cutting a swath through the cavalry with the beam. As the behemoth strode nearer they chivvied their six-horse teams into motion and wheeled the guns around into an arc, each carriage about ten yards from its neighbor. Working feverishly, they began to unlimber them.

In the distance, two carriages lay abandoned on the plain. A broken wheel had done for one, and a retreating cloud of dust revealed galloping horses somehow broken free of their traces. "It appears the cooks have been using their knives and saws for more than preparing game for the northern army,"

Gloria observed with some satisfaction. "They began with fourteen."

In his civilian service in building the dam, Evan had never shown the Californios what *el Gigante's* arms had actually been designed to do. "Throw the beam!" he commanded, and the right arm swung forward, releasing it straight toward the centermost gun. Wood splintered and men and horses went flying, but not nearly enough. Eleven cannon remained.

"Looks like they weren't expecting us this soon," Honoria said, watching intently. "Those guns may be old, but they can still hurt us if they can get them loaded in time."

"Fire!" Evan shouted to Captain Fremont. "Before they can load the remaining guns!"

Captain Fremont straightened the behemoth's left arm, which contained the Meriwether-Astor Manufacturing Works' much more modern cannon, and took aim at the nearest gun. The shell was more powerful than the balls the old-fashioned cannon could fire, and its range was greater, too. Their shell exploded in one gun. Shrapnel blasted into the limber box behind it, and the powder and shot it contained exploded. The men at the adjacent cannon were just close enough that the explosion set their own limber afire, with the result a deafening and demoralizing second explosion.

"That's three!" Evan cried. "Fire!"

A second shell was all the behemoth had until they could stop and reload—hence the need for the Gatling arm that had not operated since the battle of Resolution—but there was something to be said for brute force. Captain Fremont aimed the second shell at the fourth limber box with equally gratifying results. In the melee, Evan waded in to deal with the eight cannon remaining.

Men leaped, panicked, from them as Evan and Captain Fremont picked up a gun carriage here, kicked a wheel off there, and smashed a limber box next in line. The last crew, bravely manning their gun despite the oncoming threat, attempted to fire, but luckily for the behemoth, terror made their aim faulty. The cannonball clanged on the outside edge of the behemoth's ironclad shoulder, sending Evan spinning off balance. He kept his head and moved one mighty foot back, bending the iron knees until the rocking stopped.

Ella, white-faced, swung from her safety line like a pendulum until Honoria caught her and set her on her feet. "That was close. They and their museum pieces nearly had the last laugh."

Evan smashed a carriage wheel with more force than was strictly necessary. Behind them, the rearing horses' lines snapped like embroidery thread and they galloped back toward the camp. Then he straightened and made a gradual turn toward the battle.

"We are behind them now," Honoria said with satisfaction. "Can you pick up a cannon and simply throw it into their midst?"

"We can try," came the cheerful voice from above.

The gun carriages might weigh half a ton, but the barrels were easier to manage. The behemoth lifted one and, like a Greek athlete doing the shot-put, heaved the bronze cannon into the fray.

But it was not enough.

"Toss the remaining carriages, burn the limber boxes, and we will cut our losses," Honoria said. "This beast can do the same damage simply by taking a stroll through their forces."

And so it proved to be. Throwing as many of the carriages

as remained intact was the work of a few minutes each, throwing a limber box or two on the already burning fires produced satisfying and demoralizing explosions, and then they waded into the fray, swinging and stomping with abandon.

But it was *still* not enough. One massive machine, no matter how powerful, and five thousand southern troops were still outnumbered by the northern forces. As the sun reached its meridian, Evan began to tire. "I must rest," he said, gasping for oxygen to fuel his exhausted limbs.

"You cannot," Honoria told him grimly. "If we come to a stop, even to reload, they will swarm us. I do not think we can hold them off if they make us fall. You must keep moving."

"Head for our side," Gloria told him. "Behind our lines at least we can load two more shells and do as much damage as we can while you rest for a few minutes."

But their side—so far away—Evan's head swam and he felt he would give his very soul for a sip of water. He was hot and exhausted and his energy was running out of him like an outgoing tide.

"Why did I not teach a replacement?" he groaned. "I do not think I can make it down this slope without picking up so much speed the legs will get away on me. Then we will fall and then—"

"Let us help," Gloria said. "Honoria, to his other side. Mimic the motions he is making."

"But there is not room," he protested.

Honoria's foot slid into the truss next to his left, Gloria's to his right, while their arms locked behind him. His own feet were moving, slower and slower, but with the additional weight on the trusses, perhaps it would not be so difficult.

The behemoth responded, and he remembered just in time to make the knees bend as they stumped down the hill and crashed into a troop of horse just wheeling around to re-form.

"Onward!" Honoria cried, and the behemoth obeyed her. But even with the added strength, they still had three hundred yards of enemy forces to negotiate. "Do not give up!"

"Look out—they are coming at us with ropes!" Ella shouted from the viewing port. "They plan to trip us!"

So simple, and yet so deadly. They were going to die, flat on their faces after all, marooned in the midst of the northern troops while their own fought savagely toward them.

And then—and then—

"What is that?" Ella pointed into the distance. "That glittering—is it *Silver Wind?*"

"It is far bigger than *Silver Wind,*" Gloria said, staring. "And it is moving fast. Evan, we cannot stop now. What if it is some northern auxiliary force and they have us surrounded?"

Flashing, undulating across the arroyos and hillocks of the plain, the extraordinary vision came closer. Evan dashed sweat out of his eyes and strained to identify what in the name of heaven this new threat could be.

And then in the distant skies, sailing behind the flashing silver array, came *Swan.*

"Alice!" Evan exclaimed as a rush of relief and joy flooded him. "Finally! Where have they been all this time?"

"Mother Mary!" shrieked Gloria in the next moment. "Evan, take heart—it is the witches, riding my mechanical horses!"

With an indrawn breath that was half gasp, half prayer, Evan got his legs moving in the trusses again. By now, the men on the edges of the northern force were looking over their shoulders, less able to identify the new threat than Evan and his friends had been. For who in this country had ever seen such a sight as this?

With a speed that he could not have believed possible, the silvery, deadly herd covered the distance remaining. Now he could see them clearly, and the sight nearly took his breath away. An enormous armored horse led the charge, its rider waving a pistol and urging on an unstoppable river of death that flowed behind him. The legs of the horses churned the dirt, scything it up and flinging dust into the sky. On the outer edges ran metallic feline shapes, stretching and compressing in a ground-eating gallop that soon brought them within reach of the northern horsemen on either flank, who were now screaming and wheeling to meet them.

With a crash that the occupants of the behemoth could hear even at such a distance, the metal troops ripped into the hem of the enemy, the very legs of the horses cutting man and beast to ribbons. The Viceroy's forces rallied, with captains galloping up and down, trumpets blowing and ordering both foot and horse into their divisions once again. They flowed into the gap behind the mechanical horde, cutting down the survivors on the ground and those mounted who, by some miracle, had survived the charge.

"Evan!" Honoria shouted. "The traitor—we must go after him before he slips away from the battle like the coward he is."

As she spoke, the armored horse in the lead released both its shells, and in the resulting explosion the tide of the battle turned. Now, rather than plowing from the rear through an impenetrable wall of mounted soldiers, the behemoth waded through a tide of fleeing men and horses who had had no training whatever in fighting the mechanicals that their late Viceroy had bought and never received.

New hope and determination seemed to fuel Evan's exhausted limbs, and he turned the behemoth about, stamping and injuring as many around him as he could. And there, watching from the ridge with his councilors, safely out of harm's way, was the traitor de Aragon with a small armed guard.

"There you are, you devil," Evan said with grim intent. "The time has come for an accounting. Captain!" he called to the man above him in the gunner's chair.

"Aye!"

"We have one mission, and one only," he said, moving with determination across the plain, faster than the fleeing foot soldiers and gaining momentum with each step. "We will snatch de Aragon off his horse and hold him high. He will not escape."

"Yes indeed," came the captain's merry voice. "This is one juicy apple I shall be happy to pick. Will he bruise easily, do you think?"

"You may squeeze him in half until his blood runs red in the dirt, as far as I am concerned," Gloria said savagely.

Captain Fremont laughed. "I love you when your blood is up, my darling," he said. "Heads up, everyone, our friends approach!"

A shadow eased over them, and the troops that had managed to take a stand and wait for them below their commander's vantage point lost control of their horses. Panicked beasts dodged and galloped as the airship settled into a holding pattern above their heads. The temperature inside the pilot's chamber seemed to drop a couple of degrees in the welcome shade.

Evan focused all his energies on his objective. Up—up the hill—one more stride and heave over the rocky crest—

And the commander's party seemed to understand that they, not their troops, were the behemoth's target. Screaming orders right and left, de Aragon whipped his horse and he and two of his councilors took off in a mad dash down the reverse side of the slope, toward the relative safety of the trains waiting at the siding.

Except ... the trains seemed to be waiting because a huge bonfire made of tents and wagons and barrels burned out of control upon the tracks, cutting off their means of departure. "Oh, well done," Ella cried. "But he will find another way if we do not stop him now."

"No, he won't, the wretch," Evan muttered. "Arm ready!"

"Ready!" the captain called, and the pincer arm rose into the air.

Evan caught up in two ten-foot strides. "Now!"

The Ambassador's horse screamed in terror and juked to the side away from the massive metal arm descending upon it. De Aragon lost his seat just in time for the pincer to snatch him up and hoist him into the air, probably higher than he had ever been unless he had ever desecrated the sanctity of a church by climbing the tower to ring its bells.

Shrieking in fear and pain, the man who had done his best to bring down a prince and take his kingdom by force wriggled like a caterpillar between a child's fingers.

"Got you!" the captain said from above with no little satisfaction. "Broke a rib or two, though, I'll wager."

Honoria snatched up the speaking horn and, with two

fingers in her mouth, whistled an ear-splitting amplified blast that cut across the sound of the fleeing troops. "In the name of the Viceroy of the Royal Kingdom of Spain and the Californias, I command you to surrender! We have you surrounded and de Aragon is our prisoner. Lay down your arms at once and you will be spared a traitor's death."

Evan noted that she did not identify herself as the Viceroy. It was well done—especially since here came what had to be the real Viceroy, thundering through the disarray of the usurper's troops with his metal army at his back. Mounted on the horses and felines was a truly terrifying sight—hundreds of witches painted for war like the skulls of the dead, red roses upon their brows and black mouths grinning with triumph.

This was the last straw for the northern forces. All the brave words they had been spouting about the Viceroy's being under the control of a witch seemed to be forgotten in the horror of actually seeing so many of the legendary *brujas* face to face. Swords and pistols clanged and crashed as men flung them to the ground. The witches rode in a triumphant circle around them, in the center the terrified knot of men who had been foolish enough to side with de Aragon against their rightful prince.

At last the rider mounted on the armored horse brought it to a canter and then to a walk. Finally, it came to a stop. Beyond them, the airship settled close to the ground, and two lithe figures leaped out to secure its lines to two of the rocks on the ridge. Alice and Ian ran down the gangway. The rider, instead of dismounting his deadly mechanical, climbed into the saddle and stood tall upon the silvery form.

"Men of the kingdom!" he shouted. "You have fought for

what you believed in, but believe this now—I, Carlos Felipe, Viceroy of the Royal Kingdom of Spain and the Californias, Defender of the True Faith, and General of the Armies of Heaven, am your true ruler. Will you follow me henceforth, and not this usurper whose greed has put all of your lives in mortal peril?"

Behind him, the witches shrieked with a cheer, and after a single frozen moment, the men on the ridge, who had thrown down their arms, raised their voices in an answering roar of assent. Beyond the ridge, thousands of southern voices rose in a cheer that seemed to echo across the fields turning gold in the low afternoon light.

The Viceroy raised both arms in triumph and the sun, glowing red through the dust in the air, outlined his form. The sky, the earth, the sun—symbolized in flag and crown—welcomed the prince back to his kingdom.

CHAPTER 23

"*C*ome on," Honoria said abruptly. "Time to end this charade for good. Gloria, Ella, give me one of your petticoats each, quick!"

"What—"

"If we are to carry this off, there cannot be two Viceroys. Hurry!"

Without another word, both women unhooked one of their petticoats and tossed it to Honoria, who had already toed off her boots and kicked off her wool trousers. The medallions on the sides jingled as they hit the metal floor of the pilot's chamber. She flung the short jacket at Evan, who was in his shirtsleeves, yanked the petticoats up, and pulled her boots back on.

And there stood a woman—tall, rangy, and as slender and dangerous as a whip. Gloria had just seen her transformation, and yet she still could hardly believe that this proud woman had once been Joe—gaol companion of Evan—spy—prince—

who at every step had been instrumental in saving all their lives.

Ella took one of the red silk roses from her braids and stuck it into the thick curls over Honoria's ear. *"Now* you are dressed," she said, her chin tilted with pride.

"What shall I do with de Aragon?" Stanford called from the gunner's chamber.

"Put him on the ground, but don't let go of him," Honoria replied. "I'm sure Felipe will have a thing or two to say to him, if the man is capable of listening."

Evan stopped gaping at Honoria and recalled himself to business. Carefully, he bent the behemoth so that Captain Fremont could lower his screeching prisoner, clamped firmly between the two arcs of its iron pincer. As the Viceroy addressed the army from the saddle of his massive horse, the occupants of the behemoth climbed down the ladder built into the iron leg. Even as he spoke, Gloria could feel the moment when the Viceroy's gaze took her in, as her husband lifted her from the last rung and swung her to the ground— and into his arms.

Gloria could have clung and wept and kissed every inch of Stanford's face for eternity ... except that there were a thousand men staring at them, and thousands more on the slope below. And their work was not yet finished.

The Viceroy's gaze swung to the right—he started—stared —and Honoria stared back. Challenging. Daring. Welcoming. The rose over her ear seemed to burn in the reddish afternoon light, the same light that had illuminated his moment of triumph before his people.

With a final flourish, he finished speaking, and an answering cheer rose that sounded less hysterical and more sincere. Felipe slid down from his metal mount and approached Honoria. He held out a hand, and her strong brown fingers gripped his. "Come, sister. Let me introduce you."

Instead of the horse, Felipe climbed up on the nearest rock, and pulled Honoria up beside him. From where she stood, Gloria heard someone in the crowd gasp—perhaps at the uncanny resemblance of these two children of the same father.

"This day holds many victories. Allow me to introduce my half-sister Honoria, daughter of my late father and Senora Clara de San Gregorio. Honoria has put her own life in danger in my service for many years."

A howl of rage issued from between the pincers of the behemoth, and iron clanged as de Aragon beat upon it helplessly with his fists.

"I hereby elevate her to the *gente de razón* and proclaim her the Lady Honoria. I grant her the rancho of San Gregorio in its entirety, with hacienda, fields, and cattle, to belong to her and her descendants from this day forward."

Screams of rage from the pincer were drowned out by the witches' cheers, and Gloria heard a thump as one of the witches—that glossy blue-black hair and the crescent moons painted on her temples identified her at once as May Lin—rode up beside the pincer and clocked the ambassador in the back of the head with a rifle butt.

It was dreadfully uncharitable, but Gloria could not help a glow of satisfaction.

The Viceroy then turned to Gloria and her captain, and motioned them forward. Gloria saw her own fear reflected in Stanford's eyes—the prince was so unpredictable, and so much had happened since they had parted. What did he mean to say? She was half tempted to swing up on the armored horse and ride away as fast as it would carry them.

"It was my dearest wish that Miss Meriwether-Astor should be my wife, but her heart has always been true to the man who was her husband." Felipe's gaze held hers from his lofty position on the rock. "My dear friend, I release you from our engagement and wish you every happiness in the years ahead. You have helped to give me back my kingdom, and I will always be grateful."

With relief and joy cascading through her like a waterfall after a long drought, Gloria smiled and mouthed *thank you*. She nestled into the circle of her former and future husband's arms, now tight about her as though he would never again let her go.

The Viceroy's shoulders lifted and fell for a brief moment, before he turned to the captive now practically weeping with rage and pain in his iron prison. Tears had made tracks through the dust on de Aragon's lean cheeks, and a dribble of saliva was making its way down his chin.

"Augusto de Aragon, you have declared yourself Regent when you had no right to do so. You have taken the field against me. You have lost the gamble you were foolish enough to make. I declare you traitor, and sentence you to death."

De Aragon screamed a name, and from someone in the crowd who had just been cheering the Viceroy, a dark shape cartwheeled over their heads. De Aragon snatched the rifle from the air, flipped it over to rest against his shoulder, and aimed it at the Viceroy's heart. "Release me, give me safe passage past our borders, and you will not die," he rasped.

The men around them froze. Aside from the traitor's traitor, none of those formerly loyal to him were within reach of their weapons, which lay on the ground, and the Viceroy and Honoria stood exposed upon the rock. One bullet would end the kingdom's future, and de Aragon could take the Regency once again by force.

A curious humming noise, like a very small hive of bees, seemed to be approaching. Frozen with fear, Gloria slowly turned her head as something cool was slipped into her hand from behind. Her fingers closed around the grip of a lightning pistol as if it were the most natural thing in the world.

"You seem to have lost yours," Alice Chalmers breathed in her ear. "Claire would be so annoyed."

Gloria's lungs contracted for just a moment as she realized what she must do. What she had been fated and feared to do from the very beginning. Then her forefinger curled around the trigger and she dredged up the courage from somewhere deep within.

She stepped forward. "De Aragon!" she shouted. "I am the iron dragon, and I forbid you to do any more harm!"

Even as de Aragon swung to his left to take aim at her, she pulled the trigger. A bolt of blue-white light sizzled from the flared barrel and arced across the space between them. It caught de Aragon in the chest, under his raised arms and over the iron prison. The shock of it made him drop the rifle. As it clattered off the pincer and onto the ground, tendrils of light crawled all over his body, curving lovingly around his neck, illuminating his hawklike nose, and finally, as he screamed in despair, sizzling his eyes into vapor and claiming his brain ... and at last, stopping his heart.

CHAPTER 24

*M*other Mary smiled at the bishop, her lips painted in lines of black to indicate skeletal teeth, which made her look rather eerily as though she had two sets. The poor man lost his place and the wedding ceremony came to a halt.

Ella, who was holding the bride's bouquet of roses of all colors, picked from the gardens at San Luis Obispo de Tolosa just an hour ago, leaned toward him. "It's all right," she whispered. "That's my mother. She won't do anything unexpected as long as I'm standing between you."

This did not seem to comfort him at all. With an effort of will, the bishop found his place. "By the power vested in me by God and His holy kingdom of Spain and the Californias, I now pronounce you husband and wife together. You may kiss your bride."

For the second time, Gloria tilted up her face in obedience to the request of a man of God—only what a difference in her feelings at this wedding! This kiss was a celebration, a smile of joy, a commitment that no man could put asunder this time. As he wrapped his arms about her, her husband repeated in a low voice in her ear, "For as long as we both shall live."

When they entered their names in the parish register, and then signed the wedding document, the bishop added his signature and wax seal, as did the Viceroy. "Now you will not have to travel to Nuestra Senora de los Angeles. This document is legal from this moment. Not everyone may stand at the altar with the Viceroy of the Royal Kingdom of Spain and the Californias as his supporter."

With that, Stanford shook the Viceroy's hand and tucked the precious document into his inside vest pocket, where it would not go astray. Then all four came out to greet the people filling the first few pews of the mission chapel, who left their seats and crowded round them to offer their congratulations.

The Viceroy kissed Gloria's cheek. "I hope you will stay a few days so that we may honor you with fiesta?"

She squeezed his hand. "I am afraid not, Felipe. We have been gone too long, and all of us are anxious to return home."

He gazed at her, then lifted her left hand, on which Stanford's gold ring once more reposed. "I shall miss you. Your counsel. Your courage. Your beauty."

"You have the first, at least, in the lively correspondence I promise you will have to endure. I shall dispatch a complement of pigeons the moment I reach home, so that we may correspond as frequently as we like."

"You will come back?" he asked anxiously. "I should not like to think I will never see you again."

"Of course. You have made me a grant of land in San Francisco de Asis, have you not? I intend to found a school there for girls—the Gloria and Stanford Fremont Preparatory Academy. There they will be educated in all branches of knowledge, and will be the first generation to fully take their places in the new society that will grow up around their forward-thinking prince."

"You have a great deal of faith in me, Gloria."

"I am rather good at reading character," she told him with affection. "I know you can do it."

"With Evan's help."

"With his, and mine, and that of your loyal friends. Even May Lin has agreed to establish the Viceregal Society of Engineers, much as she deplores such a title. You may call upon her, you know, at any time."

But the Viceroy only flushed and turned to answer a question of Ella's.

Alice came up and kissed her, and gave Stanford a hug of congratulations. "We are ready to lift when you are. We shall have to put down in Denver, though, for proper repairs to poor *Swan*. She will not make it all the way to Philadelphia to your orchard, never mind to Somerset and *our* orchard, without them."

"The sooner, the better, to my mind," Stanford said.

"In a hurry to leave us?" Mother Mary gave the bishop another smile as she joined them. Gloria had the sense that, despite her brave show, this kind of church made her uncomfortable and that she hankered for her own canyons and caverns fashioned by God himself. Sister Clara stuck close by her side, as though she expected to be tossed out at any moment for attending the wedding wearing paint. But all the witches were ... the Viceroy had insisted upon it. Despite his nerves, the bishop had been a practical man. For when the

Viceroy had welcomed and embraced the women who had saved his life and helped to save his country, the bishop could not very well forbid them entry to his church.

"Not in a hurry to leave you," Stanford responded with a hearty smack on the cheek, lifting the older woman off her feet.

"Now, now, none of that. What will the younger ones think?"

"That you are lucky to have a kiss from such a handsome devil," Gloria teased.

Mother Mary's face softened as she gazed at the twice-over bride. "We are lucky to have friends like you, sister. You have saved us—though how long this truce with the Viceroy will last, I cannot say."

Gloria leaned in to whisper, since Felipe stood not far away talking with Captain Hollys. "I believe he is rather sweet on May Lin. You may find the truce lasting longer than you think."

Mother Mary's eyes widened. "Impossible. A prince—and a witch?"

"Is it any more impossible than a dragon and a riverman?"

Mother Mary made a *pfft!* of derision. "I could see that coming a mile away, the first time he laid eyes on you."

"Mark my words," Gloria said wisely. "Stranger things have happened in this country—and will continue to."

"For true, sister. Clara and Honoria and Ella and I will slip away now that we have seen the ring safely back on your finger. You must write to the padre at Santa Croce and tell me if it is a boy or a girl."

"I will," Gloria promised. "If a girl, we have decided to call her Honor Isabella Claire—Isabella with two *L*s for the two girls who helped us—and whom we love."

Mother Mary's face flushed with pleasure. "And if a boy?"

"Why, Stanford Philip Evan sounds rather dignified, does it not?"

Sister Clara nodded in her brisk way. "Felipe will be pleased to be remembered, and so will Honoria. Good-bye, sister. A safe journey and a happy homecoming to you."

Tears welled in Gloria's eyes as one by one, her sisters under the rose embraced her, whispered words of congratulation and encouragement, and slipped out the church door into the garden. Ella was the last to go.

"I cannot leave you," she said in despair. "Who will paint your face and do your hair properly?"

"Who will listen to my worries and give me sensible advice?" Gloria's voice cracked. "I will return, never you fear, if only to hear your laughter again."

"Do you promise?" Ella's face turned fierce around the misery in her eyes.

"With all my heart."

Ella kissed her. "Then I will wait for that day, and in the meantime be happier than I have ever been."

Gloria's tears spilled over as Ella joined Honoria at the door and they stepped out into the sunlight to where their family and sisters were waiting. When Gloria looked back, Evan stood beside her.

"Senora Fremont."

"Senor Douglas." She smiled through her tears. "Congratulations on the post the Viceroy has offered you. Shall you take it, or come home with us?"

Evan's face turned a little bleak. "I cannot tell you yes or no until I ask a certain party a certain question."

"And when shall you ask it? If it were me, I should take the party concerned out into the gardens and have it out with him forthwith."

"Do you think so?" Evan's gaze found Ignatio de la Carrera y Borreaga, who was laughing with the Viceroy and the bishop. "Should I not wait for a more appropriate time?"

"What better time than at a wedding? Seize your chance, Evan, and take the helm of your own ship. Your days of drifting in the shadows of others ended in Resolution, the moment you climbed into the behemoth to do what you thought was right."

He straightened his shoulders under the short black wool jacket that Gloria privately thought became him better than any tweedy English garment. "You are right, as always." He bent to kiss her on the cheek. "I shall go at once. Wish me luck."

"That—and every happiness afterward."

~

EVAN STEPPED up to Senor Ignatio, acutely aware of Isabela's gaze as she talked and laughed with Alice and May Lin and tried not to look at him. "Senor, might I have a word with you outside?"

Senor Ignatio's brows rose, but since he was not at present conversing with the Viceroy, whom one did not leave unless granted permission, there was no reason for him to refuse. Evan had chosen his moment carefully. "Certainly. Let us see if the roses have bloomed yet. The bishop insists on planting them on the east side of the refectory and not the south side of the church, despite all my advice."

They strolled outside, where Senor Ignatio seemed to be doing his best not to stare at the sight of witches within the very walls of the mission. The roses were indeed blooming, so he bent to breathe in their sweet scent. "So, will you go with your friends back over the sea? I understand they prepare to leave immediately in that airship that came to fight with us."

"That depends on you, Senor. For I must ask you a question."

He straightened to give Evan his full attention. "A gentleman need not ask." Understanding and sympathy glinted in his eyes. "If you are out of pocket after such brave acts, a friend can only ask if he might be of assistance. Do not fear—my pockets are deep enough to fund a ticket on the train and perhaps even a steamship over the sea."

Evan blushed at the vast chasm of misunderstanding this represented. He and Isabela had hidden their feelings from her family very well indeed. "That is very kind of you, sir. But I am in no need of that sort of assistance. You see, I do not intend to return to England. The Viceroy has offered me a post on his privy council—as minister of what he calls *magnificent devices*."

Had de la Carrera been wearing the spectacles his wife urged him to use, they would have fallen from his nose, so slack with astonishment did his face become. "Is it true?"

"It is, sir. Which brings me to my question."

"To be sure, whatever it is, one does not refuse a privy councilor. Such a man holds more authority even than a cabinet minister."

Evan's heart felt as though it might beat right out of his

chest, and go flying up over the bell tower. "Then it is simply this—I wish to court your daughter. Will you allow me to do so?"

A full ten seconds of silence ticked by as Senor Ignatio stared. "My daughter? You wish to court Beatriz?"

Now it was Evan's turn to stare. "No indeed. I am in love with Isabela, and I would like your approval before I attempt to win her heart."

"Isabela? *La mariposa*, who probably never had a single rational thought of you or any other man in the whole of her life?"

Evan thought of the kiss under the olive tree, and of her flashing dark eyes as she stole a horse and cart and did what she could to save her prince's life. He thought of the women like her, strong and brave and utterly magnificent, banding together under the rose to do what must be done so that a tyrant and a usurper should not take the place that was not his.

"Yes," he said with a smile that he could no longer hold back, so much did the thought of her delight him. "Isabela. She is the most precious thing in my life, and I should like the chance to see if she feels the same way."

"Why—*Madre de Dios*—upon my soul," her father sputtered. "Who would have thought of such a thing? With San Gregorio's boy out of the picture, I suppose one must begin from the beginning. But ... a privy councilor, of all things."

"Does that mean you approve, Senor?" Evan persisted. He was of a logical and practical turn of mind, and liked the answer to a question to be clear—particularly when the rest of his life depended on it.

"Why, yes. I can think of nothing I would like more." De la

Carrera took his hand and shook it rather violently. "Isabela. Her mother will be delighted. Yes, indeed, Senor Douglas. You are welcome to your chance."

"Thank you, sir." Smiling, Evan freed his hand, bowed, and went to find Gloria to give her the answer he owed her.

Once that was done, he would end Isabela's suspense, and take the helm of his life once and for all. Or perhaps it would be better said that they would steer their ship together. At the thought of Isabela's bravery and good sense, and of the Viceroy's trust in him, Evan walked a little faster.

He could see joy and clear sailing ahead—and could not wait to begin.

~

AT THE HELM of her ship, Alice, Lady Hollys, gave the last commands to the automaton intelligence system in preparation for lift. Ian turned from the viewing port, where Captain and Mrs. Fremont were standing together, their arms about each other, and joined her.

"Is he really not coming?" Ian indicated Evan Douglas below, whose smile seemed to engulf his thin face, his arm around the dark-eyed beauty with whom he now had an understanding. The two of them stood at the forefront of the waving, chattering crowd.

"His life is here now," Alice said. "Isabela seems to be the one for him, and with his new post and his friendships in high places, I can see him being a gentle but driving force behind change and progress in this country. He will be happy here in a way he never seemed to be in England, from all accounts."

"Then I wish him the best. For I am ready to go home with

you, and look about us, and perhaps plant a few crops before we decide to go adventuring again."

Alice felt her throat close, and she swallowed back the ache of happiness. "I have never been so thankful for anything as I have that we have been together. Can you imagine one of us sitting in England while the other endured what we have endured?"

He kissed her hair and slipped an arm around her. "I cannot. Let us promise each other—even if it is only to fly a cargo to Bristol, we will not be separated."

"You may get tired of that."

"Of flying with you?" Ian smiled. "Never."

"Shall I give the order, then?"

"You are the captain, my darling."

Alice grinned and kissed him.

Then—

"Up ship!" she called.

Evan and the witches on the ground released the ropes, Jake and Benny reeled them in ...

... and *Swan* fell joyously into a sky so bright and clear they could almost see forever.

EPILOGUE

JULY 12, 1895

Lt. Robert van Ness
Commander, Texican Rangers
Santa Fe, Texican Territory

*D*ear Sir,

I am writing to request your renewed assistance in the matter of a missing person. Over a year ago, my father, Dr. Rudolf Linden, RSE, vanished under mysterious circumstances, and has never been found, alive or dead. As you may recall, we were traveling as a family to Victoria in the Canadas so that he might take up a post at the new university there. My mother searched for weeks with the Rangers' assistance, and finally returned to England, where she succumbed to influenza and grief.

Now that I have reached my majority and am independent, I am renewing the search. I have taken passage aboard the packet to Paris, where I will board Persephone to New York, departing on Tuesday next. I will take the transcontinental airship from New

York to Denver, and thence to Santa Fe. I shall present myself in your office at the barracks shortly thereafter.

Would you be so kind as to renew inquiries for me into whether anyone, in the airfield and railyards, or in the town, remembers a man of Prussian descent, five feet ten inches tall and of a substantial build? He was a professor of engineering at the University of Edinburgh, and speaks with a Prussian accent. He was last seen wearing a Homburg hat, tweed trousers, and a tweed hunting jacket with patches of loden green at the elbows. Loden green, as you may be aware, is a very particular and distinctive color, not to be confused with hunter green. I say this to reduce confusion and to provide a detail that may assist in our further inquiries.

I look forward to meeting with you and renewing our necessary acquaintance.

I remain, sir, sincerely,
Margrethe (Daisy) Linden
Bath, England

THE END

AFTERWORD

Dear reader,

All good things must come to an end ... or must they?

For we seem to have a loose end, and for Daisy Linden and I, such a thing is maddening. Daisy is a young lady of intelligence that only the adventures of life may transform into courage and good sense. She is also a watercolor painter of some skill, which means she is possessed of powers of observation that many a Texican Ranger or frontier-town sheriff might envy. When a maddening loose end is nothing less than her missing papa, then clearly something must be done—and she is determined to do it.

I hope you will enjoy Daisy's adventures in my new series set in the Magnificent Devices world. The first in the Mysterious Devices series is *The Bride Wore Constant White*. I envision each title as the name of a watercolor pigment that would have been found in a lady's paintbox at the end of the 19th century ... and, sadly, a hint as to the unfortunate circumstances in which Daisy becomes embroiled through—it must be confessed—her stubborn but affectionate nature and an unflinching sense of justice.

You may find a number of familiar friends coming to her assistance ... to say nothing of a number of villains determined to prevent her from succeeding, including a snake-oil salesman who is certainly not what he is allowing Daisy to believe ...

I hope you enjoy reading the adventures of Gloria, Lady Claire, and the gang in the Magnificent Devices world as much as I love writing them. It is your support and enthusiasm that is like the steam in an airship's boiler, keeping the entire enterprise afloat and ready for the next adventure.

You might leave a review on your favorite retailer's site to tell others about the books. And you can find print and electronic editions of the entire series online, as well as audiobooks and translations into German and French. Do visit my website, www.shelleyadina.com, where you can sign up for my newsletter and be the first to know of new releases and special promotions.

And now, I invite you to turn the page for an excerpt from *The Bride Wore Constant White* ...

Fair winds!
Shelley

THE BRIDE WORE CONSTANT WHITE

Chapter One

July 1895
Bath, England

*I*t is a truth universally acknowledged that a young woman of average looks, some talent, and no fortune must be in want of a husband, the latter to be foisted upon her at the earliest opportunity lest she become an embarrassment to her family. This had been depressingly borne in upon Miss Margrethe Amelia Linden, known to her family and her limited number of intimate friends as Daisy, well before the occasion of her twenty-first birthday.

"Certainly you cannot go to a ball, escorted or not," said her Aunt Jane. "You are not out of mourning for your dear mother. It would not be suitable. I am surprised that you have even brought it up, Daisy."

Daisy took a breath in order to defend herself, but her aunt forestalled her with a raised salad fork.

"No, I will invite a very few to lunch—including one or two suitable young men. Now that you have come into my sister's little bit of money, you will be slightly more attractive to a discerning person than, perhaps, you might have been before. Mr. Fetherstonehaugh, now. He still cherishes hopes of you, despite your appalling treatment of him. I insist on your considering him seriously. His father owns a manufactory of steambuses in Yorkshire, and he is the only boy in a family of five."

"I do not wish to be attractive to any of the gentlemen of our acquaintance, Aunt." *Particularly not to him.* "They lack gumption. To say nothing of chins."

This had earned her an expression meant to be crushing, but which only succeeded in making Aunt Jane look as though her lunch had not agreed with her.

"Your uncle and I wish to see you safely settled, dear," she said with admirable restraint.

Aunt Jane prided herself on her restraint under provocation. She had become rather more proud of it in the nearly two years since her sister had brought her two daughters to live under her roof, and then passed on to her heavenly reward herself. When one's sister's husband was known to have gone missing in foreign parts, one was also subject to impertinent remarks. Therefore, her restraint had reached heroic proportions.

"When you have been married fifty years, like our beloved Queen, you will know that a chin or lack thereof is hardly a consideration in a good husband—while a successful manufactory certainly is."

Daisy was not sure if Aunt Jane had meant to insult the prince, who from all accounts was still quite an attractive man. It was true that she could no more imagine Her Majesty without her beloved Albert than the sun without a moon. They had a scandalous number of children—nine!—and still the newspapers had reported that they had danced until dawn at Lord and Lady Dunsmuir's ball in London earlier in the week. Her Majesty was said to be prodigiously fond of dancing—between that and childbirth, she must be quite the athlete.

Daisy had never danced until dawn in her life, and doing so seemed as unlikely as having children.

Especially now.

For as of ten days ago, she was no longer a genteel spinster of Margaret's Buildings, Bath, but a woman of twenty-one years and independent means, having procured not only a letter of credit from her bank, but a ticket from Bath to London, and subsequently, passage aboard the packet to Paris, where she had boarded the transatlantic airship *Persephone* bound for New York.

"My goodness, you're so brave," breathed Emma Make-peace, her breakfast companion in the grand airship's dining saloon this morning, the third of their crossing. She had been listening with rapt attention, her spoonful of coddled egg halting in its fatal journey. "But at what point did you realize you were not alone?"

Daisy glanced at her younger sister, Frederica, who wisely did not lift her own attention from her plate, but continued to shovel in poached eggs, potatoes, and sliced ham glazed in orange sauce as though this were her last meal.

"As we were sailing over the Channel. At that point, my

sister deemed it safe to reveal herself, since there would be no danger of my sending her back to our aunt and uncle." She gave a sigh. "We are committed to this adventure together, I am afraid."

"I certainly am," Freddie ventured. "I used all my savings for the tickets, including what I could beg from Maggie Polgarth."

"Who is that?" Miss Makepeace asked, resuming her own breakfast with a delicate appetite. "One of your school friends?"

Freddie nodded. "Maggie and her cousin Elizabeth Seacombe are the wards of Lady Claire Malvern, of Carrick House in Belgravia."

"Oh, I have met Lady Claire. Isn't she lovely? What an unexpected pleasure it is to meet people acquainted with her."

While Daisy recovered from her own surprise at a reliable third party knowing people she had half believed to be imaginary, Freddie went on.

"With Lady Claire's encouragement, both Maggie and Lizzie own shares in the railroads *and* the Zeppelin Airship Works, though they are only eighteen—my own age. But that is beside the point." Another glance at Daisy, who had been caught by the deep golden color of the marmalade in her spoon.

If she were to paint a still life at this very moment, she would use lemon yellow, with a bit of burnt umber, and some scarlet lake—just a little—for the bits of orange peel embedded deep within.

"The point?" Miss Makepeace inquired, and Daisy came back to herself under their joint regard. It was up to her to redirect the course of the conversation.

"The point is that, having had some number of astonishing adventures—I have my doubts about the veracity of some of them—Miss Polgarth was all too forthcoming in her encouragement of my sister's desertion of her responsibilities to school and family."

"You deserted yours, too," Freddie pointed out. "Poor Mr. Fetherstonehaugh. He is not likely to recover his heart very soon."

"Oh dear." Miss Makepeace was one of those fortunate individuals who would never have to settle for the chinless and suitable of this world. For she was a young woman of considerable looks and some means, despite the absence of anyone resembling a chaperone or a lady's maid. Perhaps that individual kept herself to her cabin. Her clothes were not showy, but so beautiful they made Daisy ache inside—the pleats perfection, the colors becoming, the lace handmade. Clearly her time in Paris before boarding *Persephone* had been well spent in purchasing these delights.

Miss Makepeace had been blessed with hair the shade of melted caramel and what people called an "English skin." Daisy, being as English as anyone, had one too by default, but hers didn't have the perfect shades of a rose petal. Nor did her own blue eyes possess that deep tint verging on violet. At least Daisy's hair could be depended on—reddish-brown in some lights and with enough wave in it to make it easy to put up— unlike poor Freddie, who had inherited Mama's lawless dark curls. No one would be clamoring at the door to paint Daisy, but Miss Makepeace—oh, she was a horse of a different color.

She absolutely must persuade her to sit for a portrait in watercolors.

But talk of poor Mr. Fetherstonehaugh had brought the

ghost of a smile to their companion's face, so Daisy thought it prudent not to abandon the subject of gentlemen just yet, despite its uncomfortable nature. They had been in the air for three days, and after the second day, had found one another convivial enough company that they had begun looking for each other at meals, and spending the afternoons together embroidering or (in Daisy's case) sketching. The lavish interiors of *Persephone* fairly begged to be painted in her travel journal. In all that time Daisy had not seen Miss Makepeace smile. Not a real one. But now, one had nearly trembled into life, and she would use Mr. Fetherstonehaugh ruthlessly if it meant coaxing it into full bloom.

"Have you ever been to Bath, Miss Makepeace?" she asked, spreading marmalade on the toast.

"Only once, when I was a girl," she said. "Papa's business keeps him in London and New York nearly exclusively, and after Mama passed away, I did not have a companion with whom to go to such places. I remember it being very beautiful," she said wistfully. "And at the bottom of the Royal Crescent is a gravel walk. I wondered if it could be the very one where Captain Wentworth and Anne Elliot walked after all was made plain between them."

Frederica, being of a literal turn of mind, blinked at her. "They were not real, Miss Makepeace."

The English skin colored a little. "I know. But it was a pretty fancy, for the time it took me to walk down the hill to the gate."

"Poor Mr. Fetherstonehaugh," Daisy said on a sigh. "He attempted to quote Jane Austen to me while we were dancing in the parlor of one of my aunt's acquaintance three weeks ago."

"That sounds most promising in a man," Miss Makepeace said.

"But it was the first sentences of *Pride and Prejudice,* Miss Makepeace." She leaned in. "And they were said in reference *to himself.*"

To her delight, the smile she had been angling for blossomed into life. "Dear me. Miss Austen would be appalled."

"My sentiments exactly. And when he turned up on my aunt's doorstep the next morning proposing himself as the companion of my future life, I took my example from Elizabeth Bennet on the occasion of *her* first proposal. I fear the allusion was lost on him, however." She frowned. "He called me a heartless flirt."

Miss Makepeace covered her mouth with her napkin and Daisy could swear it was to muffle a giggle. "You are no such thing," she said when she could speak again. "I should say it was a near escape."

"Our aunt would not agree," Freddie put in. "She and my uncle have very strong feelings about indigent relations and their burden upon the pocketbook."

"Granted, it is not their fault their pocketbook is slender," Daisy conceded. "But that is no reason to push us on every gentleman who stops to smell the roses nodding over the wall."

"How do you come to be aboard *Persephone?*" Freddie asked their companion shyly.

She was not yet out, so had not had many opportunities to go about in company. Add to this a nearly paralyzing shyness —for reasons both sisters kept secret, and despite the misleading behavior of her hair—and it still astonished Daisy that she had had the gumption to follow her all the way to

London with nothing but her second-best hat and a valise containing three changes of clothes, her diary, and a canvas driving coat against bad weather.

Now it was Miss Makepeace who leaned in, the lace covering her fine bosom barely missing the marmalade on her own toast. "Can you keep a secret?"

"Oh, yes," Freddie said eagerly.

Which was quite true. Among other things, she had concealed from everyone—except perhaps that deplorable Maggie Polgarth—her plans to run away and accompany Daisy on her mission.

"I am what is known as a mail-order bride." Miss Makepeace sat back to enjoy the effect of this confidence on her companions.

"A what?" Freddie said after a moment, when no clarification seemed to be forthcoming.

"There is no such thing," Daisy said a little flatly. Well, it was better than sitting and gaping like a flounder.

"There I must contradict you." Miss Makepeace aligned her knife and fork in the middle of her plate, and the waiter, seeing this signal, whisked it away. "In the guise of a literary club, I have been meeting these last six months in London with a group of young ladies determined to make their own fortunes. An agency assisted us in finding the best matches of ability and temperament in places as far-flung as the Canadas and the Louisiana Territory."

"There are agencies for this sort of thing?" Daisy managed under the shock of this fresh information. It was lucky that Aunt Jane was as ignorant of these facts as Daisy herself had been until this moment, or heaven knew where Daisy might have been shipped off to by now.

And what was a young woman like Miss Makepeace, with every blessing of breeding and beauty, doing applying as a mail-order bride? It defied understanding.

Miss Makepeace nodded. "I have been writing to Mr. Bjorn Hansen, of Georgetown, for some months, and am convinced that he will make me a good husband." She touched the exceedingly modest diamond upon the fourth finger of her left hand. "He sent this in his last letter, and I sent my acceptance by return airship."

"My goodness," Freddie breathed. "I have never met a mail-order bride. I thought they only existed in the flickers— you know, like *Posted to Paradise*." She and Daisy had stood in the queue outside the nickelodeon on Milsom Street for half an hour to see that one, much to their aunt's disgust. But it had been so romantic!

"We are quite real, I assure you." Two dimples dented Miss Makepeace's cheeks. "My suit and veil are in my trunk. I will meet Mr. Hansen in person for the first time when I alight in Georgetown, and we will be married two days later in the First Presbyterian Church on Taos Street. It is all arranged."

"Where is Georgetown, exactly?" Daisy asked.

Not that it mattered—she and Frederica were bound for Santa Fe, on a quest that could not be postponed. Their father, Dr. Rudolph Linden, had been missing for nearly two years. Influenza had taken their mother last winter—hastened, Daisy was certain, by the anxiety and depression she had suffered after his mysterious disappearance. Now that she had reached her majority, Daisy was determined to take up the search where her mother had left off. And this time, if love and determination meant anything, she and Freddie would find him.

"It is in the northern reaches of the Texican Territories, in the mountains," Miss Makepeace explained in answer to her question. "From Denver, it is merely an hour west by train. It is said to be one of the loveliest towns in the territory—and certainly one of the richest. Silver, you know. It is surrounded by mines on every side, and has a bustling economy, I am told."

A young man who had been passing on the way to his table now hesitated next to theirs. "I do beg your pardon. Forgive me for intruding, but are you speaking of Georgetown?"

If Aunt Jane had been sitting opposite, Daisy had no doubt there would have been either the cut direct—or an invitation to breakfast if she thought the young man might be good husband material. But they were en route for a continent where one might stop and strike up a conversation without having to be formally introduced by a mutual acquaintance— or to give one's family antecedents back four generations.

"We are, sir. Do you know it?"

His square, honest face broke into a smile, and Daisy noted with interest the quality of the velvet lapels on his coat, and the fashionable leaf-brown color of his trousers—not the dull brown of earth, but the warmer tones of the forest in autumn.

"I am bound there as well. Please allow me to introduce myself. My name is Hugh Meriwether-Astor, originally from Philadelphia. I have recently bought a share in the Pelican mine."

"And are you going out to inspect your investment, or have you been there before?" Miss Makepeace asked.

"This is my first visit. I'm afraid I have an ulterior motive —that of escaping the bad temper of my older brother, who is not quite so conservative in his business dealings. I should like to get my hands dirty, and do a little excavating myself if I can, before I go back to law school. And you?"

As the eldest, and practically a married woman, Miss Makepeace made the introductions. Daisy noted that she did not vouchsafe any personal details of their voyage, she supposed because she had no personal observations of her future home to offer him. They parted with promises of seeing one another at the card tables after dinner, and the young man continued to his table by the viewing port.

"What a nice person," Frederica ventured. "He does not seem much older than you, Daisy, and yet he owns part of a mine. His family must be rather well off."

"If my facts are in order, he is closely connected to the Meriwether-Astor Manufacturing Works in Philadelphia," Miss Makepeace said in a low tone. Heaven forbid the young man should know they were discussing him. "Surely even in Bath you will have read in the papers about his cousin, Gloria Meriwether-Astor, who owns the company."

"It's a difficult name to miss," Daisy said. "Wasn't she the one who singlehandedly stopped a war in the Wild West and returned home in triumph with none other than a railroad baron's long-lost heir for a husband?"

Honestly, while it might have been quite true, it did sound like one of the sensational plots beloved of the flickers.

"I am sure it wasn't singlehandedly," Miss Makepeace said. "But I will say that the union of two such industrial fortunes made headlines in the Fifteen Colonies, and London and Zurich as well. It was all any of my father's cronies talked of at dinner for weeks."

"My friend Maggie knows her," Freddie said most unexpectedly. "Gloria, I mean. Mrs. Stanford Fremont."

"Nonsense," Daisy said. Honestly, she was becoming very tired of these references. "Another of that girl's absurd fabrications."

"It isn't!" Freddie drew back, affronted, and refused to speak for the rest of their meal.

There were some misfortunes for which one could only be thankful.

~

FOR MORE, *find* The Bride Wore Constant White *at your favorite online retailer!*

ALSO BY SHELLEY ADINA

STEAMPUNK

The Magnificent Devices series

Lady of Devices

Her Own Devices

Magnificent Devices

Brilliant Devices

Magnificent Devices: Books 1–4 Quartet

A Lady of Resources

A Lady of Spirit

Magnificent Devices: Books 5–6 Twin Set

A Lady of Integrity

A Gentleman of Means

Magnificent Devices: Books 7–8

Devices Brightly Shining (Christmas novella)

Fields of Air

Fields of Iron

Fields of Gold

The Mysterious Devices series

The Bride Wore Constant White

The Dancer Wore Opera Rose

The Lady Wore Venetian Red

The Governess Wore Payne's Gray

The Judge Wore Lamp Black

The Soldier Wore Prussian Blue

ROMANCE

Moonshell Bay: The Men of CLEU

Call For Me

Dream of Me

Reach For Me

Also in the Moonshell Bay series

Caught You Looking

Caught You Listening

Caught You Hiding

The Wedding Scandal (a Four Weddings and a Fiasco novella)

PARANORMAL

Immortal Faith

ABOUT THE AUTHOR

Shelley Adina is the author of 24 novels published by Harlequin, Warner, and Hachette, and more than a dozen more published by Moonshell Books, Inc., her own independent press. She writes steampunk and contemporary romance as Shelley Adina, and as Adina Senft, writes Amish women's fiction. She holds an MFA in Writing Popular Fiction from Seton Hill University in Pennsylvania, where she teaches as adjunct faculty. She is currently working on her PhD in Creative Writing at Lancaster University in the UK. She won RWA's RITA Award® in 2005, and was a finalist in 2006. When she's not writing, Shelley is usually quilting, sewing historical costumes, or hanging out in the garden with her flock of rescued chickens.

Subscribe to her newsletter here!

Shelley loves to talk with readers about books, chickens, and other interesting things!
www.shelleyadina.com
shelley@shelleyadina.com

CPSIA information can be obtained
at www.ICGtesting.com
Printed in the USA
LVHW04s2340191018
594246LV00001B/94/P